A gorgeous Frenchman?

A mattress deliveryman?

A Victorian hostess?

Be careful what you wish for!

Three delightful brand-new stories by

**Anne Stuart
Vicki Lewis Thompson
and
Marisa Carroll**

Anne Stuart has written over sixty novels in her twenty-five-plus years as a romance novelist. She's won every major award in the business, including three RITA Awards from Romance Writers of America, as well as their Lifetime Achievement Award, has appeared on various bestseller lists, been quoted in *People, USA Today* and *Vogue,* has appeared on "Entertainment Tonight," and, according to her, done her best to cause trouble! When she's not writing or traveling around the country speaking to various writers' groups, she can be found at home in northern Vermont, with her husband, two children, a dog and three cats. Her free time is spent listening to music, watching old movies on television and "enjoying the incredible power of turning fifty."

Vicki Lewis Thompson has loved writing since she was a child. After beginning her career as sports reporter for a local paper in high school, she became a journalist, and her adventures ran the gamut from interviewing sky divers and witches to photographing a man who milked rattlesnakes! But Vicki sold her first book to Harlequin Temptation in June of 1983, and found her niche. Readers must agree, as she is a six-time RITA Award finalist, and winner of awards from *Romantic Times* and *Affaire de Coeur.* She has now written extensively for Temptation, Superromance, Love & Laughter, and a number of special continuity and anthology projects, bringing her total of books up to forty-three. Six more are in the works for this prolific wife and mother of two, who makes her home in New Mexico.

Marisa Carroll is the pen name of the award-winning writing team of sisters Carol Wagner and Marian Scharf. They have published more than twenty-eight novels in their sixteen-year writing career, and have been the recipients of a Career Achievement Award from *Romantic Times* for their acclaimed Saigon Legacy series in Superromance. They have participated in a number of special continuity projects, including Tyler and Hometown Reunion, and enjoy the challenge of writing interrelated stories in a series format. They have set "Special Deliveries" in their home state of Ohio, where they proudly reside with their families.

My Secret Admirer

ANNE STUART
VICKI LEWIS THOMPSON
MARISA CARROLL

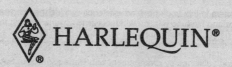

HARLEQUIN®

TORONTO • NEW YORK • LONDON
AMSTERDAM • PARIS • SYDNEY • HAMBURG
STOCKHOLM • ATHENS • TOKYO • MILAN • MADRID
PRAGUE • WARSAW • BUDAPEST • AUCKLAND

ISBN 0-373-83398-9

MY SECRET ADMIRER

The publisher acknowledges the copyright holders of the individual works as follows:

DANGEROUS LOVER
Copyright © 1999 by Anne Kristine Stuart Ohlrogge

ONCE UPON A MATTRESS
Copyright © 1999 by Vicki Lewis Thompson

SPECIAL DELIVERIES
Copyright © 1999 by Carol Wagner and Marian Scharf

Printed in U.S.A.

Table of Contents

Table of Contents

Dangerous Lover
Anne Stuart

Dear Reader,

I'm a sucker when it comes to holidays. I celebrate every one I can. Being a romance writer, I consider Valentine's Day to be my national holiday, but I have to admit that my mind tends to work in quirky ways. In the past I've written about squabbling gods and saints and time-traveling survivors of gangland massacres. This time I thought it might be fun to throw two completely unsuited people together and make it work.

Think of this as "Ally McBeal" meets *La Femme Nikita.*

Happy Valentine's Day!

Anne Stuart

Chapter One

"VALENTINE'S DAY has got to be the most depressing holiday on the face of the earth," Emma O'Bannion muttered, staring at the rows and rows of pink and red greeting cards that lined the wall of the immense bookstore.

"Are you nuts?" her friend Marnie demanded. "You don't have just one boyfriend, you have two, and they're both handsome, charming, eligible and crazy about you. You'll be getting double flowers, double cards, double candy, and they don't even mind that there are two of them."

"No, they don't, do they?" Emma said. "They're both completely reasonable. Annoyingly reasonable. Why don't I give one to you?"

Marnie laughed. "I don't think it's that easy. Which one can I have?"

"It doesn't matter."

"Emma, Emma," she admonished her. "Don't you feel your biological clock ticking?

Aren't you ready to fall in love? What in heaven's name is your problem?''

Emma looked at her friend and sighed. ''You're right, I'm nuts. Either Philip or James would make a wonderful husband, a perfect father, any woman's dream come true. I don't know what's wrong with me.''

''You're turning thirty this year, that's what's wrong with you. It's one of those difficult times in a woman's life. But that doesn't mean you should throw away two perfectly good prospects, just because you're going through an early midlife crisis.''

''I'm not throwing anyone away,'' Emma said. ''I'm just…restless. I want adventure, I want passion, I want pirates and gangsters and James Bond. I don't want a stockbroker in a three-piece suit.''

''The romance section is upstairs, Emma. You can find all that in books.''

Emma sighed. ''I'm tired of finding adventure in books. I'm tired of being a good girl. I'm tired of being just what Philip and James expect me to be.''

''So? What's the alternative?''

''Luc Dubois.''

''Say what?''

"He lives in my building. I don't know when he moved in—he just appeared one day—and the superintendent, Mr. Hassan, says he's very mysterious. He doesn't even have his name on the mailbox, but Mr. Hassan told me what it was. You should see him, Marnie. He's utterly gorgeous, in a ruthless, French sort of way. He always dresses in black, he has long, dark hair and bedroom eyes and the sexiest mouth you've ever seen. I've decided he's either a drug dealer or a retired secret agent."

"Yuck," said Marnie. "Does he smell like garlic?"

Emma sighed soulfully. "He smells of coffee. I rode in the elevator with him once, and I almost fainted. He ignored me, of course."

"So why bother? He's probably gay. Half the men in this city are. Especially if he's gorgeous and dresses well."

"French men are allowed to be gorgeous and dress well without being gay. No, I think he has a broken heart."

"And you want to mend it? Get a life, Emma."

Emma laughed. "I don't seriously want him, Marnie. I'm not that crazy. I'm just enjoying myself, lusting after the unattainable. I think he's avoiding me—probably because I made a fool of myself staring at him when I first saw him. You've never seen such a sexy mouth in your life.''

''And I don't want to. I think you've flipped…''

Emma reached for one of the cards in front of her. The picture on the front was a reproduction of a Pre-Raphaelite painting, two lovers entwined beneath a wisteria branch. Inside, in gold letters, it said simply, ''I want you.''

''This is perfect,'' Emma said smugly.

''Don't you need two of them?''

''It's not for Philip or James. It's for my neighbor. From a secret admirer.''

Marnie read the card, letting out a low whistle. ''This isn't really your style, Emma. In all the years I've known you you've never been particularly lustful. This card is erotic—there's no other word for it. Why would you want to send it to a stranger?''

''That's exactly who I'd send it to. So there aren't any unpleasant repercussions. It's safe.''

''Unpleasant repercussions like sex?''

Emma ignored the comment. ''I told you, I don't really want him. It's just a harmless fantasy. A card, an impassioned love note, maybe some flowers, all from some mystery woman, ought to make his day. He'll never know they came from me.''

''Do you want him to?''

''Absolutely not!'' Emma said, and she meant it. ''Do you think I'd be seriously interested in someone who looks like a French gangster? Even a gorgeous one? I don't think so. If he found out and decided to reciprocate I'd be horrified.''

''Would you?''

''You know me. I'm a sane, sensible woman with my life planned out ahead of me. I'm a junior partner at Kelton and Kelton, and if I'm lucky I might make full partner before I'm thirty-five. I'm a damned good lawyer. I need a man who understands my career and my needs. I suspect a Frenchman would expect his wife to stay at home, barefoot and pregnant.''

''If he's that good-looking it might be worth it,'' Marnie suggested.

''Not for me.'' She quickly pulled another couple of Valentine's Day cards from the rack. ''These will do for Philip and James.''

''And while you're playing with fire, when are you going to decide which one of your devoted boyfriends deserves you?''

Emma shrugged. "I guess I should decide soon. Maybe I'll see which one of them comes up with the most romantic Valentine's Day idea, although—as sweet as they are—sometimes I feel like neither of them has much imagination."

"Three days, Emma. I'll be waiting to hear which one you picked. And ready to console the poor loser."

"And what about my sexy neighbor?"

"I don't want him. And if you have any sense you'll leave him strictly alone as well. He sounds dangerous."

Emma laughed. "I don't think so. Luc Dubois is probably nothing more than an out-of-work actor who's enjoying being dramatic. And I'm enjoying myself as well. It's a harmless pastime."

"Maybe," Marnie said doubtfully. "But if I were you I'd make certain he can't trace that card back to you."

"Don't worry, I know how to keep myself safe in the city. Besides, I told you, he's harmless."

He didn't look harmless, Emma thought an hour later as she unlocked her apartment door. Her building was an old one in the east thirties, with a creaky elevator that only Mr. Hassan seemed capable of running properly. Luc Dubois lived alone on the top floor, and since that one time she rode the elevator with him, he'd always taken the stairs.

But Mr. Hassan wasn't anywhere to be seen that February afternoon, and the sign on the elevator proclaimed it to be out of order for the third time that month. Emma prepared to climb five flights of stairs to her apartment.

She met him between the third and fourth floors. He was coming down, she was going up, and as usual he ignored her. As he hurried past her, his remarkably sexy gray eyes slid over her as if she were a piece of architectural detail.

He was dressed in black, as always. Black jeans, black T-shirt, black bomber jacket, even his long hair was pulled back with a black leather thong. He was probably in his late thirties, almost ten years older than she was, and his black boots were oddly soundless as he hurried down the flights of stairs.

She started to say something, but he ignored her, and a moment later he was gone, disappearing around the turn in the staircase. Emma muttered something beneath her breath. He was the epitome of her dream Frenchman—gorgeous, arrogant, sexy and rude.

She could just imagine his reaction when he got that beautiful bouquet she'd ordered on her way home from work. She'd gone a bit overboard, choosing lush white roses just faintly touched with pink, but Mr. Hassan had mentioned that he thought white roses with a touch of pink at the heart were the most romantic flowers he'd ever seen. Emma didn't find them romantic, she found them frankly sexual. They were almost as erotic as the card she'd already put in the mail.

She certainly hoped he never guessed she was the one who sent them to him. He didn't look as if he had much of a sense of humor. That gorgeous mouth of his probably never smiled. However, it could probably do all sorts of other remarkable things.

She laughed to herself as she began unlocking her myriad of locks guaranteed to keep her safe in the heart of Manhattan. For the first time in what seemed like months she was enjoying herself immensely. Maybe tomorrow she'd send him some chocolates.

LUC SLID INTO THE SEAT in the darkened theater, sinking down low and stretching his long legs out in front of him. The couple on the screen in front of him were in the midst of badly simulated sex, but he hadn't come into this seedy movie house for the feature film. He waited, patient, watchful, until he heard Maurey come up behind him.

He didn't bother to turn and look—he didn't need to. His instincts were razor-sharp—he would know Maurey anywhere. If it had been someone else he would have instantly known his or her gender, age, nationality and sexual orientation, all without turning around. He was that good.

"Tell me," he said in French.

"Someone doesn't want you to retire, my friend," Maurey replied in the same language. "I've had word that someone is looking for you."

"Who?"

"That I'm not sure of. It might be anyone. Gallais thinks it's a young woman but you know he has a romantic soul. I'm guessing it's one of our old friends from Algeria. Someone who holds a grudge. Of course that doesn't narrow it down much—almost anyone we've met in our line of business holds a grudge."

Luc stared up at the writhing figures on the screen. "What makes you think they know where I am?"

"We still have some of the best informants, including some recruited by you. We don't know much, but what we do know is certain. They know you're in the States and they're coming after you. If I were you I'd come back to France and let us take care of the problem."

"I don't need you looking after me, Maurey. After fifteen years in the Department I can take care of myself. Better than you ever could, old friend."

Luc sensed Maurey's shrug. When he was out in public he kept such gestures to a minimum, but in the darkened movie theatre he could give in to his natural tendencies. "I still think you should come back in. There's no telling who might be after you, and there's no way we can protect you over here."

"I'm not going back. I told you, I'll never go back. There's no way I can find any kind of peace over there. This is a new place, a new start for me, and it's been good."

"I don't know if people in our line of work can ever retire. I warned you of that when you left last year."

Luc stared up at the screen, unseeing. "I intend to make it happen. Tell Gallais not to worry about me. I can handle this. But I thank you for the warning. Have a safe journey back."

"I'll tell him," Maurey said. "But I'm not sure if I'm heading back right away. I've got some free time coming to me..."

"I don't need you shadowing me."

"Don't worry, I'll keep my distance. You're right, you were one of the best. If anyone can handle this situation you can. But I'll be available for backup, just in case."

Luc sighed. It would be a waste of time trying to dissuade Maurey. After thirty years in the covert Department he was immovable and unstoppable once he got something in his mind. He would also be discreet. He would keep his distance, and only someone with training and talents as sophisticated as Luc's would realize he was anywhere around.

The action on the screen reached a simulated crescendo, complete with noisy groans and thumping music, and Luc sensed Maurey was already disappearing up the aisle of the ancient theater. He settled back, closing his eyes. Maurey's warning came as no surprise—he'd never made the mistake of thinking he could leave the Department without complications. But he was a master at dealing with such things. He'd handled more than his share in the past decade and longer. He could handle this.

He walked the twenty blocks back to the apartment building in the dark, pulling his jacket up around his ears. He thought he'd covered his tracks well—he'd bought the building on East Thirty-seventh Street ten years ago, planning his escape that far back. The people who managed the property had no idea who owned it, no idea that the owner himself had taken over the top floor a couple of years ago, and he preferred it that way. They hired the superintendent, collected the rents, and all the money was deposited into his Swiss bank account. And he lived in peace.

He'd fiddled with the elevator so it wouldn't go any higher than the fifth floor, and he had tiny surveillance cameras set up all over the place to monitor who came and went from the building. After a year of keeping his guard up he'd thought he could begin to relax, but Maurey had proved him wrong.

Most of the people in his building were harmless. He had a total of twenty-three tenants, most of them partnered, some gay, some straight, some old, some young, from various ethnic groups. He'd done thorough background checks on all of them, and they were as innocent as only naive Americans could be.

The only one who troubled him was the woman who lived below him. Emma. The facts were ordinary enough—she came from a small town in Maryland, had two married sisters and both her parents were still living. She was thirty years old, pretty in an ingenuous sort of way, with soft brown hair and a vulnerable mouth. He didn't like her clothes—the colors didn't suit her subtle coloring, and they did little to complement her small, feminine shape. She was an unremarkable young woman, a lawyer working in a firm that dealt with tax issues. Nothing shady in her past at all.

But she had no lovers, and it bothered him. She was too pretty not to have a lover. She had two perfectly respectable men she dated—he'd checked them out as well to be on the safe side, but as far as he could tell she didn't sleep with them, nor with anyone else. And that made no sense.

It couldn't be religious convictions that kept her celibate—she never went to church. The books and magazines in her apartment were to be expected—fashion magazines and newsmagazines, books on law and biographies, mysteries and romances.

No spy novels, which was an interesting omission, but he couldn't be sure whether that meant anything.

She did, however, have the most erotic underwear he'd ever seen. Beneath her demure suits she wore peach and teal, ripe plum and fuchsia silk. She either had a charge account at Victoria's Secret or a lover he hadn't discovered.

But if he couldn't discover something about her, then he was in trouble.

She hadn't been in the apartment long. She moved in just nine months ago, and had immediately struck up a friendship with Hassan. That in itself was also interesting—most tenants didn't get chatty with the super.

His instincts had kept him alive in the most dangerous business in the world, and his instincts about Emma O'Bannion had always been on alert. There was something going on with her. Something about the way she pretended to ignore him, all the while acutely aware of his every move.

If someone was a threat to him right now, she was the logical choice.

Mr. Hassan was in the vestibule, fiddling with something. He'd been a good choice for a superintendent—a widower, friendly, competent, always on the premises. The managers of the buildings had forwarded him a background check on the old man as well, one that Luc had rechecked thoroughly. For a while he'd even considered enlisting Hassan in his security efforts, but at the last minute he'd decided not to. Hassan didn't need to know the truth about him. No one did.

"Good evening, Mr. Dubois," Hassan greeted him. "There's a package for you."

Luc froze. No one sent him packages. He was half tempted to throw himself back out the front door before a bomb could detonate, but he didn't move. He'd spent too long looking out for himself and no one else. He couldn't walk away with so many innocent people in the building. His building.

"Where?"

"In the mail room. I'll get them for you."

"Them?"

Hassan looked like a mischievous elf. He disappeared into the alcove that held the mailboxes, then came back holding a huge bouquet of roses. Lush, pale roses, just faintly touched with pink.

Nicole's favorite flower.

His blood froze. He took them from the old man, automatically tipping him, secure in the knowledge that his horrified reaction wouldn't show. It was the first overt warning. Someone knew him. Someone was after him.

"Who are they from?" His voice was faintly harsh, but Hassan just shook his head.

"I don't know. Maybe there's a card."

Luc didn't believe for one moment that the old man hadn't checked for a card. People were insatiably curious, and men didn't usually receive such romantic bouquets.

"I want you," the card read. He stared at it, his face carefully blank. He looked up at Hassan and gave him a cool smile.

"Apparently I have a secret admirer," he murmured.

"And it's almost Valentine's Day. How romantic," Hassan said. "I hope you find out who she is."

"I will," Luc said grimly. "Trust me, I will."

Chapter Two

THE NEXT DAY DAWNED COLD and clear, and Emma walked home from work in the brisk weather, bubbling over with high spirits. It was too close to Valentine's Day to risk the United States Postal Service, affectionately known as snail mail, so she had had the mail room arrange for a courier. There'd be no way it could be traced without a great deal of difficulty, and she could just imagine her grumpy, gorgeous neighbor's reaction when he got it. Had he liked the flowers? Had he called all his girlfriends to find out who sent them?

But she didn't think he had any girlfriends. She never heard anything from the floor above—for all she knew he could have been living there for years instead of the month or so she'd been acutely, erotically aware of him.

Mr. Hassan swung the door open for her when he saw her coming, a smile wreathing his elderly face. "There you are, young miss," he greeted her. "It's too cold a day to be walking these streets. You should take better care of yourself.''

''I was bundled up.'' She took the pile of mail he handed her. He was the sweetest old man in the world, she thought fondly. The previous super had simply lurked in his basement apartment, coming out when a tenant had an emergency. Mr. Hassan was always around with a friendly smile on his face, opening the door when he saw her coming so she didn't have to bother with her keys, getting her mail for her, telling her all about his day. He reminded her of her grandfather Louie, and it had been both simple and irresistible to confide her silly crush. The old man had been charmed.

''Your friend has gone out,'' he said in a conspiratorial voice. ''I thought you might want to send him this.'' He unearthed a box of Godiva chocolates from a pile of newspapers on the hall table.

''Oh, be still my heart,'' murmured Emma, a serious chocolate addict. ''Where did they come from?''

''They were sent to a tenant who already moved out. She moved to California—there'd be no way to get them to her by Valentine's

Day. Why don't you take them and send them to your friend upstairs?''

"Mr. Hassan, you are an incorrigible romantic," she teased him.

"I like strong young women who aren't afraid to turn the tables on us poor men," he said with a twinkle in his eye. "Mr. Dubois takes himself too seriously. He needs a good woman like you."

"He's not going to get a good woman like me," she said with mock severity. "It's just a harmless game."

Mr. Hassan smiled knowingly. "If you say so, young miss. Do you want me to deliver those for you?"

She looked down at the box of chocolates longingly. What was more important, her childish little game, or a box of Godiva chocolates all for herself? James and Philip wouldn't do much better than Whitman's.

"Maybe I'll have them myself," she said.

Mr Hassan shrugged. "Surely a pretty girl like you will get chocolates from her admirers?"

"Not these chocolates." She took the gold box from him and gave it a fond pat.

"Whatever brings you the most pleasure,

Miss O'Bannion. I'm at your service if you want me to deliver them.''

''You're very sweet, Mr. Hassan,'' she said with a soulful sigh, gripping the chocolates tightly. Godiva chocolates were far better than sex, but she was a sensible girl. She didn't intend to indulge in either.

It was clear Mr. Hassan wanted her to keep up her little game—it must enliven his otherwise dull job to play Cupid. ''Take them up to Mr. Dubois, and tell him they're from his secret admirer.'' She released the box reluctantly. If she took it upstairs and opened it she'd end up eating at least half the box and making herself sick. If she could send anonymous gifts to a sexy stranger she could certainly buy herself a tiny box of Godiva chocolates.

It could also be her acid test. James and Philip both sent her flowers and chocolate last year, and they'd both become more determined in their attentions. If one of them actually had sprung for Godiva then maybe she'd be convinced to make a commitment.

She kicked off her shoes the moment she stepped inside her tiny apartment, flicking on the light switch. Outside a light snow had begun to fall, the white flakes drifting softly down, and she dumped her coat over a chair, dropped her mail on the coffee table and moved straight to her favorite spot, the window seat. She loved curling up there, looking out over the city, feeling safe and cozy inside. She loved the city, the noise and bustle, the excitement, the thousands of people moving through her life. It was stimulating, wonderful, food for the mind, energy for the spirit.

But it was absolute hell on the soul.

She could see Luc's dark figure moving down the sidewalk five stories below. She didn't know how she could be certain it was him—something about his walk stuck with her. It was both sexy and stealthy at the same time, like a cat sneaking through an alleyway. The snow drifted down, landing on his dark head and then melting. She leaned back and sighed.

She was half tempted to put on the Edith Piaf CD she'd bought on a lark, but just because she couldn't hear him above her didn't mean he couldn't hear her below him. She didn't dare do anything to give herself away.

Valentine's Day was the day after tomorrow. Her foolish, fun little game would be over. Marnie thought she was nuts, Mr. Hassan thought she was charming, Luc Dubois was presumably mystified and intrigued. He would have to stay that way. Her Valentine's Day was well booked—she was having lunch with James and dinner with Philip, and they'd both sounded unexpectedly serious when they called her. Her fantasy fling with her neighbor would be over, and it would be time to face reality and the two good, unexciting men who cared about her. She could make a decent, happy life with either of them, she knew it. She just had to be practical and lower her expectations.

She leaned back and closed her eyes, wishing she hadn't given up those chocolates. For some reason she was in dire need of them. Maybe she could race back down the stairs and stop Mr. Hassan before he delivered them.

No, it was too late—she'd already seen Luc just outside the apartment. By now he would have already ripped open the wrap and been eating the best ones. Mandarin orange truffles. Chocolate mousse. She could have wept.

The foolishness of her actions suddenly hit home. She could have had great chocolate, instead of the empty pleasure of harmless, anonymous flirtation. Marnie was right—she was seriously nuts.

HE DUMPED THE CHOCOLATES in the trash. For a moment he considered giving them to Maurey to get them analyzed, then changed his mind. He had no doubt they were poisoned, or at least drugged. Finding out what they'd used might point to a possible suspect, but he already knew who was after him. He just didn't know why.

It had to have something to do with Nicole, of course. It had been on Valentine's Day, five years ago, that she had tried to kill him. His darling wife, beloved partner, duplicitous counter-agent had almost managed to gut him with that razor-sharp knife she always carried, except that he'd never been able to bring himself to trust her.

She was dead now, though not by his hands, thank God. And he'd managed to put her and her treachery firmly in the past, until the white roses, the ones she'd always adored, showed up at his doorstep. A warning he couldn't ignore.

The chocolates were overkill. Though there was a good chance that was exactly what they were, laced with cyanide or something far more sophisticated. Something that would kill him instantly and yet leave no trace.

But the agent who was after him had underestimated him. He had no weaknesses. Not for flowers, which had gone down the incinerator, not for chocolates, not for women and not for old memories. He would find out why she was stalking him and he would turn her over to Maurey. And it would be up to Maurey and the Department to deal with her.

He pulled the card from his leather jacket and stared down at it. He got no mail, but Mr. Hassan had informed him with his usual cheer that this had been brought by special courier. There was no trace of which service had been used, but he already had enough information.

He ripped it open, staring down at it. Pretty, foolishly pretty, but he wasn't fooled. Whoever sent him the card wasn't the romantic she appeared to be. He flipped it open. *I want you.*

He heard her moving around beneath him, and he stood very still, listening. She wanted him all right. Wanted him dead. He had no idea whether she was on assignment or if her grudge was more personal. As far as he knew Nicole had had no family, but that didn't mean she didn't have people who might seek revenge, even after five years.

It had been child's play to trace the flowers. She was either very bad at what she did, or she wanted him to find out. Maybe she was setting a trap in that pretty little apartment of hers. He lived in sterile, Zen-like isolation, she lived in a charming welter of antiques and clutter. Her apartment was a carefully crafted front, one he saw through but couldn't keep from responding to. It reminded him of his grandmother's house in Provence, full of small touches of beauty amidst the jumble.

Was she planning to kill him on Valentine's Day, as Nicole had tried to do? It seemed a reasonable symmetry, and even the most ruthless female liked a certain amount of melodrama in her skills. He could sit around and wait, watch as she escalated the tension.

But he wasn't a man who sat around. The flowers had been ordered by a pretty young woman, paid for in cash. But the flower shop was only one block away from the apartment building, and the romantic young clerk already knew where she lived, knew she was having those flowers delivered to the same address. It had been that simple.

He glanced out his window into the dark city night. He would need to make a few arrangements, but he had time. He wouldn't tell Maurey just yet. Maurey might react a little too quickly, and Luc wasn't certain he was ready to hand her over so fast. Not until he found out exactly who and what she was.

And why she wanted to kill him.

FRIDAY, February thirteenth had not been a good day, Emma thought as she climbed the long flights to her apartment. The elevator was broken again, and there was no sign of friendly Mr. Hassan. The mail had contained nothing but bills, work had been the pits, her feet hurt and her soul craved fine chocolate. Two boxes had arrived at work today from her two devoted swains. Drugstore chocolates. She'd left them in the mail room.

The game with her mysterious neighbor had lost its ability to entertain her. The idea of choosing either James or Philip horrified her. The notion of one more day of work made her want to scream.

She unlocked the three locks on her door, stepped inside and kicked off her shoes, reaching for the light switch.

She never connected. Someone came up behind her out of the darkness, a huge, dark body trapping her inside a prison of iron-hard arms. A leather-gloved hand covered her mouth, silencing her scream as the door was kicked shut, plunging them into the inky blackness.

She fought her instinctive hysteria. She'd taken a few self-defense classes taught specifically for city women, and she knew she needed to be calm. She'd never been terribly good at it, but it had given her at least a measure of confidence out on the dark streets of Manhattan. But did she step back with her right foot and pull toward the left, or was it the other way around?

She couldn't remember. The other rule was not to provoke an attack, not to start the violence. All her intruder had done was entrap her—he hadn't actually hurt her yet.

"If you scream," he whispered in her ear, "I will break your neck."

So much for not hurting her. She knew the voice, of course, though those weren't exactly the words she'd imagined in his sexy French accent.

"Are you going to scream?" he demanded in a barely audible voice.

She shook her head, as much as his imprisoning grip would let her. He was bigger than she realized, his lean, wiry body pressed up against her own. She'd always thought Frenchmen were supposed to be short. Luc Dubois towered over her, enveloping her smaller frame.

He slowly removed his hand from her mouth, just barely, and she had no doubt he would be able to shut her up before she let one scream out. Besides, there was no one around to hear her. Mrs. Madigan across the hall was down in Florida for the winter, and the Andrewses were on a cruise. There was no one who would help her.

"What do you want?" There was no way to disguise the tremor in her voice, the fear in her body. He would feel her trembling.

"I want to know who you're working for."

Emma blinked, confused. Why would it matter what her job was? "I work for a law firm. I'm a junior partner."

"Don't play games with me." His voice was cold and deadly. Strange how the faint French accent could make him sound even more dangerous. "I know what's going on, I know what you're trying to do. I just want to know who's behind it."

Oh, crap, Emma thought, totally and deeply humiliated. He'd figured it out and he had no sense of humor whatsoever. "Look," she said. "It was just a little joke. Harmless, really. I was bored, it was getting close to Valentine's Day and I thought…''

The faint tightening of his grip wasn't actually painful. It was more a hint of what he was capable of doing. ''Don't,'' he said. ''It won't do you any good to lie.''

''I'm not lying,'' she said desperately, for some reason whispering as he was whispering, clamped against him in the darkness. ''I was just flirting. I thought the French understood flirting…''

''The French understand treachery,'' he said.

No sense of humor at all, she thought dismally. ''If you just let me go and turn on the light I can explain it all to you. You probably don't have stuff like this in France…''

''You're very interested in France, aren't you?'' His voice was silky soft with danger.

''Well…er…I guess so. I mean, it's a very pretty country,'' she stammered.

''We have women like you in France,'' he said. ''I was married to one, but then, you know that. That's why you're here.''

He'd flipped. It served her right for doing such a stupid thing. New Yorkers were a notoriously crazed lot—the most normal-looking human face could hide a dangerous psychotic.

She'd somehow picked a paranoid loony for her secret crush.

"I don't know your wife," she said patiently, realizing it was better not to excite maniacs. "And I live here, I've lived here longer than you have."

"You moved in on August fifth of last year. I've been here for two years. You've come after me."

Emma mentally counted to five. "Listen, I haven't come after you, I'm not interested in you, I'm no threat to you whatsoever. It was a joke, you understand? A practical joke. If you'll just turn on the light…"

She felt his grip loosen for a tiny moment, and she opened her mouth to scream for help.

She felt a momentary stinging sensation in the side of her neck, and she wondered whether he'd actually snapped her neck.

And then everything went black.

SHE DIDN'T weigh very much, even as a deadweight. For some reason he didn't drop her on the floor, but set her down gently, carefully, stepping over her unconscious body as he switched on the light.

Her color was pale, but that was due to the

drug he'd injected into her neck. It should keep her out for a solid six hours, maybe more, given how slender she was. He knew a moment's qualm. If he'd calculated incorrectly she might be in serious danger. It shouldn't bother him— he knew how dispensable life could be.

But he'd lived without death and betrayal for too long. He could no longer be quite so cold-blooded about it. No matter how ruthless a killer this seemingly fragile young woman really was, he couldn't stand by and do nothing if he'd accidentally given her an overdose.

Maybe Maurey was right. He'd been out of the game too long—he needed help.

He put his hand inside her blouse, against her chest. Her heartbeat was slow and steady, her breathing even. She was just knocked out for a good long time, not in any particular danger. And he allowed himself an uncharacteristic sigh of relief.

She was wearing a thin silky wisp of a bra, one that just contained her small, round breasts. Ever since he'd searched her apartment and found her racy underwear he'd found himself wondering how it would cling to her body.

It clung quite nicely.

He got his mind back on business, searching

her limp body with professional thoroughness. She carried no weapons, which surprised him. Most operatives were well armed, and if they weren't equipped with hardware they were adept at hand-to-hand combat. Emma O'Bannion, which of course couldn't be her real name, had shown absolutely no talent for self-defense. But that could have been part of a ruse.

He left her on the floor, searching the apartment once more for anything that might have turned up since his last visit. She was excellent at cover-up—anyone would think it was simply the slightly cluttered apartment of a normal young woman in New York City. Anyone who didn't know better.

Snow was falling again, more heavily than the light flurry that drifted down the night before. He had no idea whether any real accumulation was expected, and he didn't care. He could drive his battered pickup truck through any kind of weather.

For some reason he pulled her coat back around her. When he ended up handing her over to Maurey she wouldn't be needing a coat, but for right now he had a strange urge to keep her warm.

She was too pretty. Too soft and vulnerable-looking for his peace of mind. But he had learned five years ago that pretty, vulnerable-looking women could prove deadly. And it was almost Valentine's Day.

Chapter Three

HE'D ORIGINALLY INTENDED to stuff her in the back of the truck, wrapped in a couple of old blankets and hidden by the cap. He changed his mind. The night was colder than he'd expected, the snow coming down heavily. And there was always the chance that exhaust might leak into the back, asphyxiating her. It wasn't weakness on his part, to tuck her into the front seat with a blanket wrapped securely around her. After all, he needed her alive to answer some questions, didn't he?

He had his own entry and exit in the old building, a metal ladder down a laundry chute left over from the days when it had been a private residence. He had simply tucked Emma's body over his shoulder and descended, heading out into the icy weather with no witnesses.

He drove fast and well, despite the weather, down the New Jersey turnpike to Pennsylvania, then out into the countryside, the roads getting progressively narrower, progressively emptier, as the snow piled up around him. Emma slept beside him, a deep, drugged slumber, and she kept drifting, sliding over sideways. Finally he gave up and let her lie on the seat beside him, her head almost in his lap. Her long, silky hair flowed across his leg. It disturbed him.

By the time he reached the old farmhouse it was getting close to dawn, and even his expert driving couldn't make much headway against the thick blanket of snow. The old property had a long, winding driveway leading up to it, and the truck gave up halfway there, clogged with snow. The woman beside him was still unconscious, though her color was better.

He got out, switching off the headlights, and unfastened Emma's seat belt. He was tired after the long drive, but she still didn't feel that heavy as he trudged through the deep snow, cradling her in his arms.

The farmhouse was unlivable—he hadn't even begun to make repairs, but the old stables had been easier to fix up. He pushed the door open and moved inside, setting her down on the bed. The room was icy cold, but it wouldn't take long before the small furnace brought it up to decent temperatures. In the meantime he found a duvet and covered her with that as well, then he began to wander around the room, reacquainting himself with his surroundings.

He'd bought the farm and one hundred acres in Bucks County a long time ago, even before he'd bought the apartment building, and he'd spent weeks there when he was hiding out, or recuperating, or just needing a rest. Since he'd left the Department he hadn't been out more than a handful of times, but it had seemed the perfect place to conduct a discreet interrogation. She had to be working on this with someone. Someone who'd realize that things had gone wrong. Someone who'd be desperate to find them.

Or at least to find Luc, and finish the job Emma had started.

He could have used handcuffs, or rope, to tie her to the bed. For some reason he chose to use some of the silk ties that he'd left behind, part of his array of proper disguises when he'd needed to appear as a normal French businessman. Silk was soft but infinitely strong, and if she struggled it would only tighten the knots. There was no question of it being a lenient choice.

The bed was big, even with her spread-eagled and bound on the mattress, and he was tired. It was dawn, and he knew with complete certainty that no one had followed him. He could allow himself a few minutes of rest.

The room was getting warm. He took off his leather jacket, slipped out of his boots. And he lay down on the bed beside the enemy, falling into an immediate, peaceful sleep.

EVERYTHING HURT. Her shoulders, her wrists, her knees and her ankles were screaming in agony. Most of all, her head hurt—pounding, stabbing, throbbing pain. She tried to put her hand against her forehead, but her arm wouldn't move, caught by something, entrapped.

She wasn't at home. The room smelled different. There was no scent of potpourri, no soft comforting smell of clean linen. Instead she smelled leather. And coffee.

Her eyes shot open in the shadowy room, but it was too dark to tell anything about her surroundings. Only that she was lying tied to a bed, helpless, vulnerable. And someone was lying beside her.

Coffee and leather. She tried to remember what had happened the night before. She'd come home late, tired, letting herself into the apartment, when…

She turned her head. Luc Dubois lay sleeping beside her, his long dark lashes fanned out against his tanned skin.

For a moment she just looked at him. The drug was wearing off swiftly now, but she still felt in an odd, detached state. Except detached wasn't exactly the proper word for it, considering she was lashed to the bedposts.

He needed a shave, she noted. His lashes were very long, very black, resting against his skin. He had an angular face, with high cheekbones, and at some point someone had broken his impressive French nose. Even with his bedroom eyes closed, he still had the sexiest mouth she had ever seen in her life.

He was also out of his mind. She opened her mouth to scream for help.

His eyes opened. "Don't bother," he murmured. "There's no one around for miles. They won't hear you, and it will just annoy me. You wouldn't want to annoy me, would you, chérie?"

"Chérie?" she echoed, snarling. "What the hell is going on?" She yanked at her arms and legs, but it was useless, she was still trapped on the bed. Next to him. He turned on his side, watching her with wary curiosity. "What kind of maniac are you to kidnap me? Where have you taken me? People are going to wonder where I am, and they'll find me, sooner or later, and they'll throw your French ass in jail so fast you won't have time to say, 'Bon voyage'!''

"No one will find you," he said simply.

"You can't just kidnap a woman and think you can get away with it."

"I can," Luc said. "I have experience. Stop struggling. You'll only make the bonds tighter."

Those weren't the most comforting words she'd ever heard. She held still, meeting his gaze.

He didn't look insane. There was no maniacal glee in his dark gray eyes, no glint of madness. He simply looked calm, decided, implacable. But what had he decided?

She took a deep breath, determined to try again. "Where are we?"

"At my place in the country. In an area called Bucks County, in Pennsylvania..."

"I know where Bucks County is," she snapped. "Why am I here?"

He sat up, swiveling around on the side of the bed to look down at her. She felt miserably vulnerable, even though she was covered with layers of blankets and an enveloping duvet. Her short skirt had ridden up to her hips beneath the covering, and she could feel her silk blouse gaping open. And there was nothing she could do about it.

"You're here because I brought you here. Because I want answers, and it would have been much too noisy to try to extract those answers in the city."

Even less comforting, she thought, staring up at him. "I'll tell you anything you want to know," she said. "Just don't hurt me. I…don't like pain."

His expression was odd. "Don't you?"

She felt like an idiot. "Do you know anybody who does?" she snapped.

"A few."

It silenced her, though only for a moment. "Is there any chance you could unfasten these…these ropes? My hands are killing me, and besides, I have to…"

"Have to what?"

She glared at him. Kidnapping was a capital offense. If they sent him to the electric chair she'd be ready to throw the switch herself. "I have to use the bathroom."

"Certainly," he said with surprising ease. "I'll get you a bedpan."

"No!"

"No?" he echoed.

Funny, he didn't look like a sadist. Then again, he didn't look like a brutal, drug-dealing kidnapper either. "Please," she said in a calmer voice. "I really need to go to the bathroom. I promise if you release me I won't try to run."

He waited agonizing minutes, considering. And then he reached up and unfastened the knots at her wrist with insulting ease. She sat up swiftly, her muscles screaming in pain, and began untying her ankles with a great deal more difficulty than he had had. "I don't know what kind of danger you think I am," she muttered, struggling with the ropes, which turned out to be muted silk ties. "You strike me as someone more than adept in these situations, and I'm afraid my experiences have not included escaping from kidnappers." She slid her feet around, onto the floor, stifling a little yelp of pain. "Where's the bathroom?"

He nodded toward the far corner. Now that she was sitting up she could see she was in a small room, sparsely furnished, with several doors off one end. She stood up and immediately collapsed on the floor in a heap.

Luc stayed where he was on the bed, watching her. "The drug takes a while to wear off," he murmured.

"Why did you do it?"

"I thought it would be obvious—to keep you from fighting and making noise. So I could bring you up here without attracting any attention."

She should have been able to find a perverse kind of excitement in the situation. After all, she'd been stupidly lusting after this gorgeous creature for more than a month now, and the notion of being abducted fit in with both her erotic fantasies and the romances she'd been reading. Except that she liked the fantasy, not the reality of passion.

He didn't seem to be overcome with lust, which was a mixed blessing. While she had no desire to be raped, even by the object of her recent fascination, she still wished she had even the faintest idea what he wanted with her. Desire might at least have been an answer.

But she knew perfectly well he didn't desire her. He'd ignored her, avoided her, practically run from her presence whenever their paths happened to cross in the apartment building.

First things first, though. She scrambled back onto her stockinged feet without any help from him, pulling herself up by the bed, and made her wobbly way to the door in the back. The bathroom was small, utilitarian and fully functional, and she slammed the door and locked it with a sigh of relief.

It was early morning, with just the first promise of dawn spreading out across the snow-covered landscape. It was still snowing heavily, blanketing everything, and he'd taken her shoes. Even if she dared dive through the locked window she wouldn't get far.

He was standing by a chair watching her when she came back, and he gestured to it with the nasty little knife he was holding. She didn't move, eyeing both it and him with caution.

"I can tie you to the bed again," he offered mildly, "but I think you'd prefer the chair." He was holding those silk ties in his other hand.

"Do you have to tie me up at all?" she asked. "If I try to run you'll be able to catch me, considering my shoes have disappeared somewhere." She felt a breeze against her skin, and she suddenly realized her blouse was unbuttoned down to her waist. She immediately yanked the two sides together, covering herself. Why in heaven's name had she decided to wear the teal lace bra?

She was fumbling with the buttons, trying not to look at him, when he spoke. "Don't waste your time, Emma. I'll just unfasten it again."

She ignored him, fiddling with the tiny pearl buttons with feverish determination.

"Sit!" he thundered suddenly.

She sat. Her blouse was now buttoned to her neck, higher than she'd known she had buttons, and even though her skirt was halfway up her thighs she was still wearing pantyhose. Ripped, laddered pantyhose, she noticed in the growing light, but at least they were something. She stared up at him defiantly.

"Put your hands behind your back."

"Why?"

"I'm the one asking questions, remember? I'm the one who kidnapped you."

"I'm not likely to forget it," she muttered.

"Then if I were you I'd put my hands behind my back. Do it now, before I lose my temper."

"I don't want…"

"If your hands are tied you're less likely to

flinch. I wouldn't want to inflict any damage by accident.''

The ''by accident'' phrase was even more ominous. She put her hands behind the chair, biting her lips.

He wrapped one of the ties around her wrists with cool efficiency, not too tight, and yet there was no way she could slide her hands free. He stepped back for a moment, surveying her like an artist surveying his subject. His eyes were smoky gray, bedroom eyes, unreadable in the early light.

''Who are you working for?'' he asked softly.

''I told you, I don't work for anyone but a small law firm. We specialize in income tax cases and…'' Her voice trailed off in a nervous little gulp as he moved closer. The knife came up under her chin, and she heard a pearl button go skittering across the floor.

''Don't lie,'' he said calmly. ''Who sent you after me?''

''No one.''

The knife moved downward and another button went flying. ''You sent me flowers. White roses with a blush center. Why?''

''It was a joke.''

"I didn't find it amusing."

She closed her eyes for a moment, shielding her annoyance at his literal response. "It's almost Valentine's Day," she said. "I just thought it might be fun to be your secret admirer. Haven't you ever heard of such a thing? Someone who sends anonymous gifts and love letters?"

"I didn't receive a love letter."

"A card. It was just a harmless prank. I stupidly thought you were..." She couldn't say it, not with him looming over her, that small knife in his large, well-shaped hand.

"Thought I was what?" Another button went flying, this one between her breasts, and the silk blouse fell open.

"I'm beginning to lose my temper," she snapped.

"I've already lost mine. Answer the question. You thought I was...what?"

"I thought you were attractive. Romantic. Mysterious. I thought it would be entertaining to send you a few anonymous gifts. After all, you'd never know they came from me, and you'd wonder. You'd be intrigued."

"You're a very poor liar," he murmured. The next button popped off. She could barely feel the pressure of the knife, which oddly enough was even more unnerving. "Why the poisoned chocolates then? Were you feeling rejected?"

"They weren't poisoned!" she protested.

"No?"

"What makes you think they were? Obviously you didn't eat one, because if they were poisoned you'd be dead and I'd be a lot happier."

"You admit you want me dead."

"Right now I certainly do," she said grimly.

The last button went, and her silk blouse hung open, exposing her indecent little wisp of a bra. "And what made you choose my apartment building? What made you decide to move in beneath me, and watch me every time you could catch a glimpse of me?"

"I didn't even know you were there," she said wearily. "I told you, I didn't think anyone lived upstairs until a couple of months ago. And it's not your apartment building, buster, it belongs to the owners and it's run by Mr. Hassan and I have just as much right as you have…"

"It *is* my building. I own it."

She could feel the tip of the knife against her bare skin, a strange, painless caress. A shiver of pure fear ran across her skin. She looked up at him, into his opaque, unreadable eyes, and she held her breath.

And then he slid the knife between the bra and her skin, cutting it open.

With her hands tied behind her she couldn't pull her tattered clothing around her, but the ruined bra still clung to her breasts. She looked down at the shredded remnants of her best bra, and then lifted her head.

"That's it!" she said in a dangerous tone of voice. "Do you realize how much that bra cost me? You complete and utter jerk! It's a good thing I'm tied up or I swear I'd deck you."

She'd finally managed to startle him out of his cool complacency. He looked at her as if she was demented. "You've been kidnapped, held at knifepoint, and threatened, and you're worried about your damned bra?" he said in amazement.

"It's a very good bra!" she snapped.

Big mistake, she realized a second later. Those bedroom eyes of his drifted slowly down her body, lingering over the ruined bra as it cupped her small, rounded breasts. And then he shrugged. "You don't need one."

"I'm going to kill you," she said calmly.

"Now we're getting somewhere. Why?"

He was not only a maniac, he was stubbornly, obtusely male. She sighed. "I'm going to kill you because you kidnapped me and held me at knifepoint and ruined my favorite bra, and then to top it all off you insulted my body."

"I didn't insult your body," he said slowly. "You have beautiful breasts. You just don't need a bra."

Her skin prickled with awareness. "Look," she said, "let's not discuss my breasts, since you have no interest in them or me. What do I have to do to convince you I'm harmless?"

"I thought you wanted to kill me."

"I want to kill a lot of people who annoy me. I never do anything about it, though. I'm essentially a devout coward."

"A coward," he echoed, skeptical. "So you say this is all a game? A stupid practical joke? You took one look and fell madly in love with me…?"

"No! God, you're obtuse. I thought you were attractive. Gorgeous, not to put too fine a word on it. The stuff erotic fantasies are made of."

"Prove it."

She stared up at him. "What do you mean?"

"If I'm the stuff of erotic fantasies for shy little lawyers, let's see how you react to this."

She saw it coming, and panicked. She tried to jerk her head away, but he simply put both hands on her face, holding her still, the knife between his hand and her cheek, and he kissed her.

There was a reason they called it French-kissing, she thought, not moving. He kissed her with clinical finesse, a deep, open-mouthed kiss that he controlled completely.

And then he stepped back, looking down at her. "I don't see you overcome with desire," he said coolly.

Men, she thought wearily. "I thought we'd been through this. Being kidnapped does not put me in a romantic mood. My hands are tied, and that simulated sex you just did with your mouth may work on some women but it doesn't work on me."

He stared at her for a long, contemplative moment. And then he reached behind her, unfastening the knots at her wrists, and her arms fell free. She immediately started to pull the blouse back around her, but he caught her arms, pulling her upright, inches away from him.

"All right," he said. "We'll try it this way."

Chapter Four

SHE WAS GOOD, he had to admit it. Very good indeed. She stood paralyzed in his arms, staring up at him with a mixture of panic and defiance, the shy little lawyer with her blouse coming off. He might almost believe she was absolutely innocent, that that completely ridiculous story was so absurd it had to be the truth.

He hadn't been that gullible in years, and he knew just how convincing a beautiful woman could be.

He pulled her arms up around his neck, tossing the knife onto the bed. He didn't need a weapon to keep her in line. If he couldn't beat her in hand-to-hand combat he deserved to die. He put one arm around her waist, bringing her body up close to his, and he caught her chin with his other hand, tilting her face up.

He used the merest brush of his lips against hers, a soft, feathering motion, back and forth, while she stared at him, wide-eyed, wary. He moved in closer, pressing his hips up against her, knowing he was getting hard, knowing she could feel it. It didn't matter. Having an erection wouldn't interfere with his ability to defend himself. He'd been in love with Nicole, and while her betrayal had torn him apart, he had never hesitated once he knew the depth of her treachery. He hadn't killed her, thank God. He wasn't even sure he could have. But he couldn't have let her go.

Her own people killed her, a reminder of how unforgiving certain terrorist factions could be when it came to incompetence. He hadn't even mourned her, though he mourned the stupid faith he'd once had.

The woman standing in his arms was even better than Nicole at lying, at pretending outraged innocence. She was frozen, her lips soft and passive as he brushed his mouth against hers. He wondered how far he could go before she would realize she had to simulate some sort of passionate response. He wondered how far she would go to convince him.

And he wondered how far he'd be willing to take her.

He kissed her beneath her ear, using his tongue, and he felt a shiver run through her body. He put his mouth against the side of her neck, tasting her pulse, letting his teeth glance against her skin, and she shuddered, a frisson of response.

Yes, she was good. He could feel her pulse, racing beneath his hungry mouth, he could feel the ripple of reaction shimmer across her flesh. The very best, most talented operatives could summon forth the required physical responses; they could even slow their hearts to an imperceptible stillness to feign death. It was a simple enough matter for a talented operative to train her body to supply the necessary physical proof of passion.

He moved his mouth to the base of her throat, allowing himself a tiny little nip, and she jerked in his arms, her formerly passive fingers digging into his shoulders.

He slid one hand through her hair and kissed her on the mouth again, taking his time, no need for hurry, no need for force. He was willing to wait, to see how long it would take her to respond.

Her mouth opened beneath his slow, deliberate kisses, reaching for breath, reaching for words, reaching for his mouth, letting him, asking him, her lips clinging for a shy second and then falling back, then kissing him again, and this time when he used his tongue it truly was like sex, entering her, pushing inside the dark wetness of her mouth, and she let him, taking him, a hot damp clinging of mouth to mouth.

He slid his hand down over her buttocks, pushing her against him, sliding her short skirt up higher. He wanted to feel her against him, he wanted the silky smoothness of her legs, he wanted her wrapped around his hips, taking him deep inside.

He lifted his mouth, looking down into her face, her half-closed eyes, the dreamy, erotic expression on her face. She murmured something, a small, sexual sound, and reached up for his mouth again, seeking him like a nursling seeking its mother, and how could he deny her hunger?

He cupped her hips, lifting her, wrapping her legs around him, and moved her back to the bed. Her open blouse was an exquisite torment, and he wanted to touch her, everywhere. He laid her down on the bed, not quite ready to follow her, wanting to look at her, judge her reactions. Her skin was flushed, her nipples were hard and peaked in the warm room with her blouse and ruined bra half off her, and her short skirt had ridden up to her hips. She was wearing ripped pantyhose, an affront, and he reached down and pulled them off her, leaving the skimpy teal silk panties in place, their presence an erotic challenge.

She looked up at him, a dazed, dreamy smile on her face, and he almost came, looking at her. He knelt on the bed, straddling her body, reaching down for the waistband of her skirt, when her arm came up, the knife clutched in her fist, stopping at the base of his throat.

He didn't move. The dazed, erotic expression on her face was almost gone, though there were still remnants in her eyes, and her small, round breasts rose and fell with her rapid breathing. "Get off me," she said in a hoarse, strained voice, "or I'll kill you."

He made no effort to move, keeping his expression, his amazement carefully blank. Her hands were trembling slightly, and the sharp knife nicked his skin. He knew the dampness that began to slide slowly down his skin wasn't sweat, wasn't water, and he wondered what her reaction would be if she realized she'd cut him.

Probably panic. He still didn't know who or what she was, but one thing was suddenly certain. She had absolutely no experience and no skills in his own particular trade. She couldn't hurt a fly.

It would have taken a flick of the wrist to disarm her, but instead he climbed off her, moving away into the shadows before she could realize she'd cut him. The black T-shirt would soak up the blood, and it was nothing more than a scratch. He wasn't ready to panic her—he'd use it when he needed to.

She sat up, yanking her skirt down around her surprisingly long legs, and with faint disappointment he watched the triangle of teal silk disappear. He was still hard. Still very hard.

She was having a difficult time tying the tails of her shirt together while clinging to the knife, and he thought of offering to hold it for her, but decided she wouldn't appreciate his kindness. She managed to tie a knot in her shirt, over her midriff, leaving a delicious amount of skin showing, and then she glared at him.

''Where's the telephone?'' She was trying very hard to sound dangerous, implacable, but her voice trembled slightly. He must have terrified her.

''Who do you want to call?''

''The police, of course. Though I think a

mental hospital would be better. You're absolutely crazy!''

''There is no phone.'' He had an untraceable cell phone in the truck, but he wasn't about to tell her that.

She glared at him, biting her lip. Obviously she knew her choices were limited—she couldn't both hold a knife on him and get away at the same time. Of course she didn't realize the only reason she was still holding the knife and he was keeping his distance was because he chose to have it that way. He could disarm her with relentless ease. But it was too informative, letting her think she had the upper hand.

''Where are my shoes?''

''In the truck. Do you want me to get them for you?''

''Don't move,'' she snapped. She glanced over her shoulder, out the window into the eerie morning light as it illuminated the heavy snow. Another major mistake—no trained person would dare allow his or her attention to wander for even a moment. He could have disarmed the best of them in that split second. With Emma he didn't even bother to try.

''If you want to use my boots you could go out to the truck yourself,'' he suggested mildly.

"Sure. And then you'll get away when I'm not looking," she said.

"Would you mind?"

The question startled her. "No, I suppose not. I just want you to keep away from me. If you'll do that I won't press charges."

She was such an innocent it almost broke his heart. How could someone like her live in the huge, dangerous city and still survive? "Anything you say," he murmured, trying to look harmless.

She went for his boots lying by the side of the bed, putting her small feet into one and then stopping. "What's this?" she demanded, reaching inside the boot. Pulling out the long thin stiletto he kept tucked there.

"A knife," he said.

She picked up the other boot, and pulled out the thin cord in it, looking up at him in horror.

"What's this?"

"A garrote. It's only for emergencies." As an excuse it sounded a little lame, and she clearly wasn't appeased.

"What kind of monster are you? Are you a hired killer? An assassin?"

"Not exactly."

"What exactly are you?"

"I'm retired."

"Retired from what?"

"A small, covert department of the French government. The name would mean nothing to you. The name means nothing to most people in France."

"You're a *spy?*"

He shrugged. "I told you, I'm retired."

She looked at the various weapons she'd dropped from his boots. "Sit down," she said sternly.

"Why?"

"I'm the one with the knife, remember? I want to see if you're carrying any other weapons."

Maybe she'd survive after all, he thought, taking the straight-back chair where he'd tied her. "You might want to secure my hands," he suggested calmly.

"I don't need your help!" she snapped. She picked up one of the silk ties from the floor. "I'd already thought of that."

He put his arms behind the chair, blandly obedient, and she tied his wrists together with the most pitiful excuse for a knot he'd ever felt. He didn't bother to offer suggestions—she wouldn't have taken kindly to them.

She came around in front, and he immediately slipped his hands out of the noose, keeping them clasped together as he looked up.

"I suggest you start at the bottom and work your way up," he said softly.

She glared at him. "Good idea." Unfortunately it gave her no choice but to kneel at his feet. He rather liked her that way. She set her stolen knife down beside the other weapons, and gingerly touched one leg.

She found the ankle holster with the tiny, flat gun, a prototype he'd taken with him when he'd left France. She found the knife on the other ankle, a twin to the stiletto in his boot. He leaned back in the chair slightly, prepared to enjoy himself as she reached his knees.

Her hands slid up the outside of his jeans, ostensibly searching for anything out of the ordinary. He was getting hard again—in fact, he was still hard from that kiss. And he was still reeling from the fact that she was exactly who she said she was. There was no longer any reason for her to lie—if she were here to kill him she would have done so, either with cold efficiency or with sloppy passion. Or at least she could have tried.

But she was clearly terrified of him. Furious.

And yet there was something more. Something between them. Something stronger than fear and anger.

She rose on her knees, reaching for his torso, when she made the mistake of looking at him. She was kneeling between his long legs, completely vulnerable, and she'd finally begun to realize it. The pile of discarded weapons was growing on the floor beside her, but it would have been a simple matter to just lock his legs around her.

God, he wanted her. He wanted her sexually, every way he could think of. But he wanted her to look at him with those sweet, smart, bewildered eyes as well. He wanted her body, but for some strange reason he wanted her heart as well.

Maybe it was the months that had gone by, listening to her move around on the floor beneath him, the way she sang old rock and roll and operas, sweet and breathy and slightly off-key. He liked the scent of the foods she cooked as they drifted upward; he liked the faint aura of her perfume in the hall. He'd dreamed of her during the long nights, annoyed with himself for doing so. She wasn't what he wanted, what he usually slept with. He liked his women sleek, sophisticated, in control of their emotions and their hormones and their lives.

Emma O'Bannion was a smart, foolish woman. And if someone didn't look out for her she was going to end up dead.

Her hands slid up his T-shirt, then stopped as she reached the dampness of the blood. "What's this?"

He smiled at her. "Blood."

She tried to back away but he tightened his knees around her, just slightly, holding her there. "You haven't finished searching me. I'm like a children's puzzle. Find the hidden picture. There are at least three weapons you haven't found yet."

She stiffened, clearly challenged. "Kind of you to inform me," she muttered.

He leaned back again, giving her access to his body. He wondered whether she noticed how hard he was. Kneeling between his legs, she would have a hard time avoiding his condition, but she was doing her best to keep away from his hips. Major mistake, of course. He had another gun tucked just inside his waistband by the row of metal buttons that fastened his black jeans. She was going to have to be very brave indeed to find that one.

"So tell me, Emma..." he murmured, "if I may call you 'Emma'."

"Feel free," she muttered, pulling up his T-shirt to expose the small knife that lay strapped against his side.

"Why are you sending gifts and anonymous love notes to a stranger when you have two lovers of your own?"

She spared him an annoyed glance. "What do you know of my life?"

"Possibly more than you do. I know how to get information. You're seeing two men, and have been for more than a year. You're thinking of marrying one of them, but you can't decide which, but you're not sleeping with either of them."

"How do you know that?"

"I live above you, remember? I have very acute hearing."

"The floors and ceilings are soundproof. I never hear you at all."

"I'm very quiet. I know you sing opera sometimes, when you're cleaning. Very badly, I'm afraid."

She glared at him. "It's not for an audience."

"Clearly."

"And I'm going to be married."

"To one of those men? No, you're not."

By this time she had found the vial. "What's this?"

"Be careful with it. That might be the most dangerous weapon I carry. Don't open it."

She might have been contrary enough to do so, but clearly Emma O'Bannion had sense, even when she was frightened and furious. "Are you going to tell me what it does?"

"I'm not quite sure. All I know is that it's new, experimental and very deadly."

She set it down with exquisite care. "What makes you think I won't marry one of them?"

"Because you're not sleeping with them. And neither of them care enough about you not to mind that they share you. You don't need that kind of lukewarm affection. You need someone who can't keep his hands off you. You need someone who makes you tremble."

He watched as the tremor rippled over her skin again, and he tightened his legs just slightly around her body, enough so that he could feel her against the inside of his thighs, not enough so that she would realize she was being trapped.

He didn't understand his response to her, but he was past the point of caring. For some reason she had the ability to move him in ways he'd forgotten, or maybe he'd never felt that way at all, even in his idealistic youth. It didn't matter. All that mattered was now. The rise and fall of her chest beneath the clumsily knotted blouse, the parted lips, the knitted brow.

She sat back on her heels and suddenly realized she was trapped. She looked up at him, not ready to admit her vulnerability. "Is that all?"

"All what?"

"All the weapons?"

"No," he said, bringing his unbound hands around. He pulled his shirt up and reached inside his jeans, pulling out the tiny, flat gun. She held out her hand for it, dazed, and he placed it in her open palm.

She flinched. "It's warm."

"Yes," he said. "It was against my skin."

Her hand closed around the gun, and she pulled away from him, stumbling backward. He let her go—she had nowhere to run to.

He rose, slowly, and reached for the bottom of his T-shirt. She hadn't moved from her spot on the floor, her skirt had ridden up over her long, bare legs, her eyes were dark and confused, and she simply waited.

"What are you doing?" Emma was still naive enough to ask.

"Taking off my shirt." He pulled it over his head. The blood had trickled halfway down his chest, and the wound was still dripping slightly. He mopped it up with his crumpled T-shirt.

He had been half afraid she'd faint. She was tougher than that. She looked white, but she shook back her long hair. "I didn't mean to stab you."

"Obviously. Otherwise you would have done a better job of it." He reached down a hand for her, but she made no effort to take it, momentarily determined to keep her distance, even if it meant sitting on the floor.

"I don't make a habit of stabbing people, even people who deserve it."

"I don't deserve it," he said. "And I need you to make it better."

"It's your hideout, you must know whether you have a first-aid kit or not."

He reached down and caught her wrist, pulling her up whether she wanted to come or not. "I'm not talking about that kind of help," he said.

Her eyes were huge, wary. She was wise to

be nervous. He could be a very dangerous man. "What do you want from me?" she asked.

"I want you to kiss it and make it better."

She blinked. He put his hands on her and began unfastening the clumsy knot at her breasts, infinitely patient. "Hold still," he admonished her. "You'll make it worse."

"Why are you untying it?"

"I like women to be entirely naked when I make love to them. At least for the first time."

"The first time?"

She was being deliberately obtuse, but he didn't bother arguing with her. The knot came apart, and he put his hands on her shoulders, sliding the shirt and the ruined bra off her until they fell on the floor behind her. "Very good," he whispered. "Very good indeed." And he brought her gently forward, still holding her smooth, soft shoulders, until her breasts rested against his bare, still bloody chest.

Chapter Five

WHAT IN GOD'S NAME was she doing? But she knew the answer to that perfectly well. She was standing with her bare breasts pressed up against the naked, blood-stained chest of the man who'd kidnapped her and terrified her, a man clearly experienced in violence. If she'd ever thought she'd had an advantage over him with the puny defense of that knife, she now knew otherwise. There hadn't been a moment when he wasn't in control. All he'd had to do was remove another of those countless weapons he had hidden around his body. All he had to do was take that gun from the front of his jeans.

God, it had still been warm from his flesh! And her pitiful attempt to tie his hands had been worthless, completely worthless. His strong, elegant hands were clamped on her bare shoulders, holding her against him, and the blood that she'd drawn when she'd accidentally stabbed him was wet on his hot skin.

He had every intention of taking her to bed,

she knew that, was amazed by it. What was even more impossible, unbelievable, was that she was going to let him. It had been so long since she'd had sex that she'd probably forgotten how to do it, and a renegade French spy was probably the dumbest choice she could have made to end her voluntary celibacy.

Except that it wasn't precisely her choice. She could probably stop him. He might take no for an answer, or at least give up in disgust if she lay beneath him like a comatose mannequin, the way she had the very last time she'd had sex with someone. Of course, Larry Talbot had been a horrible choice—the rising prince at Kelton and Kelton before he'd founded his own partnership, he'd gone through every available female junior partner and those unavailable as well. And Emma had been just as gullible as the rest of them.

She'd learned her lesson thoroughly. Just because a man is polished, gorgeous, charming and sexy doesn't mean he could make sex more than a messy endurance contest. It was no wonder she'd kept out of bed with Philip and James. No wonder she'd stuck with men who weren't that interested in sex. She'd learned to accept that she didn't have an erotic bone in her body, and she'd lavished her emotions on the fantasy man who'd lived above her and moved through the apartment building like a shadow.

But things had backfired, and here she was. It almost might be better if he used one of those nasty weapons and killed her.

But he wasn't a killer, she knew that, despite the array of weapons, despite whatever had gone on in his past. But if she went to bed with him the harm might be just as devastating.

"Let go of me," she said in a rough whisper.

He made no move to release her. "Why?"

"I don't want to do this." It was a lie, or half of one. She didn't want to fail again. She didn't want to lie beneath him, cold and embarrassed and pained.

"Why not?" His fingers were slowly kneading the smooth skin of her shoulders, and they were oddly soothing.

"I'm a sensible woman, I have a life, I certainly don't go to bed with crazed ex-spies…"

"That's not it," he said flatly, and she wanted to kick him.

"Don't you think that's a good reason?"

"Very good. But that's not the reason. What are you afraid of, Emma?"

"I don't sleep with strange men, and you're

a very strange man. I want you to drive me home and I'll find a new apartment and we'll forget all about this..."

"You could just move in with your new husband. Assuming you're idiotic enough to marry one of them."

"Why would it be idiotic?" Her lips were quivering. He was too close, too unsettling, and she was beginning to hate him even more than when he had held her at knifepoint. A knife wasn't as frightening as the hard ridge of flesh beneath his jeans, pressing up against her belly.

A strange expression came into his gray eyes, one that was oddly knowing. "You can't be afraid of sex," he said, as if the notion was unbelievable.

"I can be anything I want."

He released her. She told herself she was dizzy with gratitude, that he didn't want a frigid partner, that she wasn't worth the trouble, that the sudden rush of cold air against her skin was a blessed relief. Except that as she stood there in nothing but her too-short skirt, and she turned to search for his shirt, her eyes were blinded by tears of embarrassment and humiliation and the overwhelming onslaught of emotion brought by the unbelievable craziness of the last twelve hours.

He caught her. There was no other word for it—he reached and pulled her against him, her back against his chest, and he looped his arms around her, imprisoning her. "Is that why you don't sleep with them?"

"Look, I'm not very good at this," she said, thanking God that at least she didn't have to look him in the eyes as she made her wretched confession. "Some women are made for sex, some not. I'm much better off with a fantasy life…"

He laughed. A soft chuckle that was both erotic and infuriating. "You haven't met the right man."

"Don't even begin to tell me you're the right man," she snapped, struggling for her earlier outrage to push away her vulnerability.

"How can you deny it? You were the one who chose me, Emma. Some instinct must have told you it was right."

"I lusted after Brad Pitt as well," she said. "I don't think my future lies with him either."

"You lusted after me? How encouraging."

She couldn't very well deny it since she'd been fool enough to say it. She tried another tack. "You'd only be disappointed. I'm not your type, trust me on this. I'm not worth the trouble, I'd just lie there and cry..."

"Don't you realize that no man can resist a challenge?" he murmured in her ear, his hands sliding down over her stomach, splayed across the soft flesh, pressing her back against him. Pushing her back against the hard, wanting part of him.

She shivered, in despair and acceptance, and he put his hand on her face, turning her head to meet his mouth. Wet and hot and seeking, and she turned in his arms, blindly, putting her arms around his neck, kissing him back. Some things were worth the risk.

She heard his murmur of approval, deep in his throat. He pulled her up, wrapping her legs around his lean hips, her skirt up to her waist, and he kissed her.

"Don't think about it," he whispered against her mouth. "Don't think about anything. Just feel."

She wanted to cry. She lost herself in the taste of him, the sweet texture of his mouth and his tongue, the silken heat of his skin beneath her trembling hands. He hadn't touched her breasts, yet they felt exquisitely sensitive, almost burning.

He was rocking her against him, a slow, lascivious rhythm, her wispy silk panties against the buttoned fly on his jeans, and the sensation was a powerful one, making her breath catch in her throat. His eyes were half closed, watching her, and she was shy, edgy, her fingers digging into his smooth shoulders, as her stomach knotted and a jolt of something streaked through her body in anticipation.

His smile was so faint it was almost imperceptible. Satisfaction, perhaps even triumph. She didn't care. She wanted to get closer to him. Closer.

And then he released her. Slid her down his body, so that she stood, just barely, her knees weak, her heart pounding. He waited until she could stand alone, and then he stepped back.

"Take off your skirt," he said. "Then get on the bed."

Her heart stopped. As if he hadn't done enough to her in the last few hours, he was going one step further, one step that might have been too far. He was asking, no, demanding that she trust him. Trust him sexually, which was more terrifying than trusting him with her life.

She didn't move, and he waited, seemingly patient. Content to give her whatever time she needed.

Her skirt had slid around her body, and the zipper was on the side. It took her a moment to find it, and her hands were awkward, fumbling as she unfastened the hook and pulled down the zipper. He made no move to help her, to hurry her along. He just watched her, out of those hooded eyes.

She dropped the skirt and stepped out of it, thankful she didn't trip over it. The panties were nothing more than a scrap of teal silk, and she'd felt sensual and deliciously naughty when she'd bought them, certain no one would ever see them. When she finally chose who she was going to marry she'd be wrapped safely in white cotton.

Luc didn't touch her. He didn't need to. He lifted his heavy eyelids, and his eyes were almost black with heat, scorching her flesh. "Get on the bed," he said again, softly.

She backed up against the bed, moving slowly, feeling strange, almost dreamlike. She sat on the mattress, then slid back, lying across the rumpled bed, her hands by her side, waiting for him.

The room was bathed in a strange blue light, the glow of dawn reflecting off the heavy snow. It seemed like a magic place, and she closed her eyes, pretending it was all a dream, a fantasy she could live out, one that wouldn't hurt her, wouldn't crush her. And then she felt his hands on her ankles, and her eyes shot open.

They slid up her calves, strong, caressing, soothing and arousing, and when he reached her knees his mouth followed, kissing her, tasting her skin. His long hair hung around his face, brushing against her legs, and as he leaned over her in the blue shadows he seemed like some strange, erotic creature, larger than life.

He'd stripped off his jeans, she knew it, even though she didn't want to look, afraid her panic would grow once more. She simply lay back and felt his hands and his mouth moving up her body, his long fingers sliding beneath the strips of lace that comprised her underwear, sliding the panties off, down her legs. All the while he murmured soft, encouraging words in a mishmash of languages that was part French and part words she'd never heard before. She didn't care—all that mattered was the sound of his voice and the feel of his hands.

She felt him move up beside her, his skin hot

and smooth as he lay alongside of her, but she kept her eyes shut, afraid to look at him. He was no longer touching her with his hands, only with the insistent length of his body, and she wondered what he was doing. She opened her eyes a crack, to see him staring down at her, a sleepy, sensual expression on his face.

"That's better," he murmured. "You're not supposed to be pretending I'm anyone else. I'm your fantasy man, remember?"

"Fantasy men know where their place is," she said in a muffled voice.

"I know where my place is." He slid his hand between her legs, startling a little cry out of her. "It's here." He touched her, sliding his long fingers against her, inside her. "And you know it. You're damp for me."

She wanted to deny it. She wanted to hide her face, pretend she was somewhere else, and he laughed, a low, deep sound that was unexpectedly arousing.

"Poor, shy infant," he whispered. "You can hide your head while I take care of things. You need to get over your shyness."

She needed to get over a lot of things, she thought miserably, when he put his hand behind her head and pressed her face against his shoulder, hiding the room, hiding everything from her, so that she was in darkness, safe, protected, and he slowly touched her, his hands clever, stroking, pushing, and she was clutching his arm tighter and tighter, moaning softly as she felt the waves of response begin to build.

She wanted to weep and scream. Somehow the frustration with Luc would be the worst of all—she was cold and useless and nothing would make the difference, not even being desperately, stupidly, blindly in love with a dangerous stranger. She wanted to run away, anywhere, away from him, away from her stubborn, unresponsive body that would bring her so far and no farther.

She didn't know why she was so wet, and she didn't care. He was holding her too tightly for her to pull away, her face was pressed close against his shoulder, and she could feel the thunder of his heart, could feel the tension thrumming through his muscles, and she wanted to lick his skin, she wanted his mouth, she wanted everything, she no longer cared what he wanted to do with her. Nothing mattered but the wet, delicious waves of sensation he was coaxing from her, an almost lazy cycle of response that began to build, sharply, until without warning it exploded, and she screamed against his chest and her body arched off the bed in a spasm of hot, prickling response.

It went on forever, and she was barely aware that he was prolonging it, touching her, pushing her beyond and over until she could do nothing but shake in his arms, her body suffused with the power of her climax.

It didn't matter when he put both hands around her—she still was racked with the remnants of her powerful orgasm. She could feel dampness on his chest, and she didn't know if it was his blood or her tears. She was past the point of caring. Her heart was thundering, she could barely breathe, and if she died right then and there it would have all been worthwhile.

She told him so. He laughed, and kissed her, and she climaxed again, a tiny clenching of response. "We've only just started, Emma," he whispered. "You're just lucky I decided you were too shy for me to use my mouth. We'll have to get you used to these things."

She turned to look at him. In the blue light she could see the rough growth of his beard, the dreamy, sexual light in his eyes. Her face was wet with tears—he'd made her cry after all. "I adapt quite easily," she said, rising up on her

knees. He reached up to cup her breasts, and
the feel of his hands on her tender flesh made
her quiver, but she had something else in mind.
"And I'm braver than you think." And before
she could change her mind or chicken out she
put her mouth on him.

His surprised groan was almost as gratifying
as the unexpected taste of him. He was smooth
and hard and silky in her mouth. She had no
idea what to do now, but he cupped her head
and showed her, letting her take as much as she
wanted and no more, and he trembled beneath
her, his entire body rigid with controlled desire.
To her half-dazed astonishment she felt her own
rich needs begin to spiral once more, and she
began to shake, uncertain what to do, what she
wanted, only knowing that she needed more.

She cried out in protest when he pulled away
from her, barely aware of the dark, shuttered
expression on his face as he tucked her beneath
him, spreading her legs and settling between
them. "I'm only human, Emma," he whispered. "And I want you this way."

She could feel him against her, hard and
sleek, and he slid deep inside her, filling her
until she cried out at the unexpectedness of it.

He froze, every muscle, every nerve in his body tight with the effort.

"Did I hurt you?" he whispered against her skin.

She shook her head, almost past speaking. "I just…wasn't expecting…" She couldn't think, couldn't talk, couldn't do anything but tighten around him, lost in the splendor of his fierce, impaling body.

"Open your eyes, Emma," he whispered in a harsh voice, and there was no ignoring him.

Her eyelids fluttered open, and she stared up at him in dazed confusion. He cupped her buttocks, pulling her up closer against him, but she simply wrapped her legs around him, tight, drawing him in deeper still.

His faint smile was answer enough. "You like it?"

"I like it," she whispered.

"You want more?"

"Yes, please."

He was perfect. A part of her knew she should be distressed that he was so very good at this, so obviously experienced, but she was more interested in the myriad of sensations he was coaxing from her body. He knew when to go fast, he knew when to go slow. He knew how to vary the depths of his thrusts, he knew how to coax her to come along with him down the dark, wicked path of desire. He knew how to touch her at just the right moment when he surged into her, he knew how to hold deep inside her as she shattered around him.

And he knew how to take everything from her, every scrap of response, every defense, every lingering emotion and devour it, and when he came, he returned it to her, tenfold, filling her body with everything he had stolen and more besides. Giving her himself.

When his breathing finally slowed and she thought he might be sleeping, she tried to pull away, but his arms tightened around her, keeping her plastered against him, and there was no escape. She had no choice but to stay nestled against the warm, comforting length of him.

"You're not going anywhere," he murmured sleepily.

She sighed. "I don't want to go anywhere."

"Good." One hand cupped her breast in a casually possessive gesture that had the disturbing side effect of arousing her when she would have thought she was well past the possibility of arousal.

He must have known what he was doing to

her. His mouth had curved in a wicked smile, and his long, elegant fingers were casually kneading her sensitive flesh. ''I'm not finished with you yet. I haven't even tasted these yet.'' Her nipples were hard against his hand, the stimulation reaching down between her legs.

''When will you be finished with me?'' It was one of those questions you weren't supposed to ask. But rules didn't mean much given the past twelve hours.

''Never.''

For a moment she didn't even realise what he'd said. ''Never?'' she echoed.

''Never. You might as well accept it, Emma We belong together. Your body knows it, and your heart knows it. Your brain might be getting in the way, though you haven't been paying much attention to it so far.''

There was a vague insult couched in what came close to a declaration of commitment, but it was only what she deserved. She should have listened to Marnie's warnings, not to Mr. Hassan's encouragement. But then, if she had, she'd be getting ready to marry James or Philip, getting ready to spend the rest of her life with an empty soul.

''Never,'' she echoed in a pleased voice,

wondering whether she had the energy to climb on top of him and take him again. She was too exhausted to move, no matter how effective he was at arousing her. He'd promised they would have a lifetime together, and illogical as it was, she believed him. She could afford to wait till she had a little time to recuperate.

But she could feel her face curve in an idiotic grin even as she fell asleep.

Chapter Six

WHEN SHE AWOKE, hours later, the light in the room was odder still, the peachy pink shades of sunset reflected off the snow. She sat up in the bed, pulling the sheet around her. Luc lay sprawled beside her, sound asleep, his long hair tousled around him. She yawned lazily, watching him at her leisure. He was very strong, deceptively so. He was lean but well-muscled, lying on his stomach. She wanted to sit there forever, watching him, she wanted to lean forward and stroke his sleek flesh, but she didn't want to risk waking him. She'd had an eight-hour, drug-induced nap while he'd been driving. He needed sleep.

And she needed to look at him. To count the scars on his body, the two that were obviously bullet holes, one in his shoulder, the other in his side. There were knife scars as well, and other signs of a hard life. It made his current state of relaxation even more appealing, and she wanted nothing more than to curl up next to him, breathing in the scent of his skin.

Well, almost nothing more. Right then a shower seemed even more inspiring, and she slipped out of bed quietly, careful not to wake him.

She wasn't used to walking around naked, even in the privacy of her apartment, and she was half tempted to grab the sheet and drape it around her. But it was tangled around Luc's sleeping body, and she wasn't going to waken him. And for the first time in her life she wasn't feeling particularly modest, or shy. She was feeling absolutely glorious.

She'd feel even more glorious when she was wet and clean and ready to come back to bed with him. She had every intention of using his toothbrush—there was no limit to the intimacy they were sharing.

She took her time, letting the water sluice over her body, enjoying the tactile sensation surrounding her, reveling in it. She heard a noise from the room beyond, and she was half hoping he'd join her in the shower, but the door remained closed.

She was suddenly in a hurry to finish, to get back to him, to continue exploring the brave new world he'd begun to show her. She dried herself hurriedly, wrapping herself in one of the huge white towels and opening the narrow bathroom door as silently as she could, in case he was still asleep.

He'd changed positions since she'd gotten up, and now he was swathed in the sheet. She could see his long dark hair, the shape of his body beneath the sheet, but little else in the dark room.

She heard the noise, the muffled thump, thump of something as the figure on the bed jerked and then lay ominously still. She was paralyzed, backing away with sudden horror as her brain began to process what she'd just seen. "Luc..." she whispered brokenly.

A tall man appeared out of the shadows, still holding the gun with the silencer. The gun that had fired into Luc's sleeping body. He looked familiar yet strange, and she didn't move, staring at him in numb horror.

"I'm afraid Luc won't be answering you, Miss O'Bannion," the man said smoothly, just the trace of a middle Eastern accent enriching his voice. "I've finally had my revenge."

"Mr. Hassan?" She couldn't believe it. Couldn't believe that the man she'd just spent hours loving was suddenly, instantly dead.

"That's not my real name, of course, but

there's no reason for me to introduce myself. We won't be spending time together.''

The towel was huge, more like a blanket, but her hands were too numb to do more than clutch it to her. ''Are you going to kill me?'' she asked in a choked voice. Not certain that she cared.

''Of course. I am as well trained as Luc was, though trained by a different side, of course. And I have my weaknesses, one of which was my dear wife, Nicole. If it hadn't been for Luc, Nicole would be alive today. I told myself I would hunt him down and make him pay for it if it took me the rest of my life. It's only been five years, and it was well worth it.''

''He killed your wife?'' she asked weakly.

''He married my wife. Unfortunately Nicole underestimated him and overestimated his infatuation for her. Once he discovered she was a double agent he turned on her. He put her in the hands of people who had no mercy.''

''And what about your people? Do you have any mercy?'' she whispered.

Mr. Hassan shrugged. He was ten years younger than he'd appeared, somewhere in his mid-fifties, and his kindly demeanor was still eerily in place. ''Mercy is weakness, and I am not a weak man. As a matter of fact, it was my people who killed her, for failing in her job.''

"Then why kill Luc?" she said, in a choked voice.

"Because he had her. She'd grown quite fond of him, I think. As you have. He must have been very good indeed, but then, I shouldn't be surprised. The French are reputed to be powerful lovers. You should be grateful to me.''

"Grateful?''

"If I hadn't steered you in his direction you might not have had a chance to enjoy a lover of his repute. Of course, you're going to die, but I'd decided that the moment I killed the real Mr. Hassan and took over his job and apartment. You were the obvious key to Luc Dubois, though I wasn't sure at first how I'd use you. I'd thought to frame him for your murder, but then I realized you had that schoolgirl infatuation for the man. It was simple enough to encourage you.''

"And I'm supposed to thank you?" Her tone was cold.

"Look at it this way, Miss O'Bannion. You got to enjoy what would probably be the supreme sexual experience of your life, and then die before anyone could taint it. There's something to be said about dying at a high point.''

"I'd rather not," she said. There was no blood beneath the bullet holes that marred the sheet. She didn't know whether she was insane to hold out any hope, but her instincts had gone into overdrive. Luc wasn't lying there, she was certain of it.

"Ah, my dear, you have no choice. Move away from the window, please.''

"Why?''

"Because I plan to spend the night here before setting the place on fire and heading back to the city, and I don't want there to be any bullet holes in the windows to let in the cold.''

He managed to distract her from her surreptitious perusal of Luc's supposed corpse. "You're going to kill me and then spend the night with our bodies?" she demanded, aghast.

Mr. Hassan shrugged. "I'm not squeamish. It's a long trip back to the city, and I don't drive well in the dark. You know how it is with aging eyes.''

"Not particularly," she said. "And apparently I'm not going to have a chance to find out." Was that a shadow in the corner, some tall, dark shape that she hadn't seen before? Or was she grasping for hope where there was none?

"I'm afraid not," he said sadly. "Move away from the window."

The moment she moved he would shoot her, she knew it. She needed to figure out a way to distract him, long enough for Luc to get to him. If that shadow was only her imagination she had nothing to lose.

"Er...do you mind if I put on some clothes before you kill me?" she asked politely. "I won't be able to hold this towel around me once I'm dead, and I'd rather not lie here naked."

"Trust me, dear lady, I won't be interested," Mr. Hassan said gravely.

"Please?" she asked prettily. Not that she had anything handy to put on—her clothes were scattered all around the room.

"No. Away from the windows, now. You can make this difficult or you can make it easy. You can die instantly, like your friend in the bed there, or you can die in great pain. Don't annoy me."

She didn't move, frozen. "I can't," she said in a raw voice.

"Very well." He lifted the gun, and she saw the barrel pointing at her, dark and shiny, and she knew the bullet was coming, and she would die.

"Hassan!" Luc emerged from the shadows, and Mr. Hassan turned instantly, the gun directed at Luc's belly.

Emma didn't hesitate. She flung herself at him, knocking him flat as the gun exploded harmlessly in the air. A second later she found herself plucked off the struggling Hassan and tossed against a wall. The breath was knocked from her, and she collapsed, struggling for air, watching as everything moved in slow motion. Luc pulled Hassan up by his shirt, looming over him like a dark avenger, clad only in his black jeans, and he slapped the man's face, hard.

"That's for sending your wife out to whore for you, and then sending her to her death," he said. He slapped him again, and Hassan's head whipped back. "And that's for trying to kill me." He slapped him again. "That's for your organization." He hauled him upright. "And this is for Emma." And he drove his fist into Hassan's stomach so hard the man crumpled in a heap on the floor.

Emma's breath came back in a deep, gulping rush, and the first thing she did was grab the discarded towel and wrap it around her while

Luc was calmly tying Mr. Hassan's hands behind his back. She watched in fascination as he worked with quiet efficiency, leaving his would-be murderer trussed up like a chicken.

"Who's in the bed?" Emma asked weakly.

He lifted his head to look at her. "A dummy. One of the many useful toys the Department let me take away with me. It's the first time it saved my life."

She staggered to her feet. "He could have killed me," she said.

"Yes, he could have, if I hadn't been fast enough. But I'm very fast. Why did you jump on him?"

"I was afraid he would hurt you."

Luc smiled, a slow, tender smile, and he crossed the room to her. The huge towel hung around her like a blanket, but the knot left something to be desired, and he unfastened it with his long, deft fingers, then reknotted it efficiently. "I'll take you back to the city," he said. "There are clothes under the bed. You'll swim in them, but at least they're warm and dry."

"What happens to Mr. Hassan?"

"I have a friend who will see to him. I expect

Maurey isn't very far away, even as we speak. We'll leave it up to him."

"Will he kill him?"

Luc shrugged. "I don't know. Do you care?"

She looked at the outline in the bed, with the two bullet holes marring the white sheet, and she shuddered. "I don't think so."

He laughed. "You may have the makings of a Frenchwoman after all." And she wasn't sure whether that was supposed to be a compliment or not.

She dressed quickly in his clothes. All black, of course. His black jeans were way too long and, unfortunately, not particularly loose, and the T-shirt and sweater were blessedly warm. By the time she emerged from the bathroom, Mr. Hassan was lying on the bed, glaring, furious, struggling against the knotted silk ties. Luc came in from outside, dressed in boots and his leather jacket. He needed a shave, he needed a haircut. He needed a woman to love him. He needed her.

"Maurey will be here in a few minutes," he murmured. "In the meantime I'll carry you out to the truck."

"I can walk," she said, suddenly shy.

"The snow is still almost a foot deep and you have no shoes on. I'll carry you."

He came toward her and she backed away, instinctively. He halted, looking at her quizzically. "What's wrong now?" His voice was very calm.

"Where are we going?"

"Where do you want to go?"

Anywhere, she thought. With you. As long as you ask me. But she said nothing.

His expression grew cooler. "Ah, I think I can guess what's wrong. You've had your night of passion with the spy, and now you're ready to marry someone sane and sensible, is that it? You've had your fling and now you've come to your senses."

"No."

"Because if... No?"

"No," she said. "Is anyone else going to come after you?"

He shrugged, uncertain of her. Score one for her, she thought. "They might. Hassan had something particular driving him—most people treat it as a business. They don't hold grudges, they don't come after people who retire. I had warning that someone was planning something. Unfortunately I thought it was you."

"You were right. I was being manipulated by your old enemy—it was no wonder you distrusted me."

"No wonder," he said, his gray eyes sliding down over her body. "You still haven't answered my question. Where do you want me to take you?"

"To New York," she said. "To your apartment. To bed."

A slow smile formed at the corner of his impossibly sexy mouth. "You haven't changed your mind?"

"What if I had?"

"I'd have to change it back for you," he said, utterly self-assured. "If I were a good man I would send you away, back to one of your safe, boring men, and maybe you could teach him to make love to you properly. But I'm a bad man, a selfish man, and I need you. More than you need me, I expect, but you do need me as well. Don't you?"

"What do I need you for?"

His smile broadened into something deliciously sexy. "You need me to make love to you, day after day until we're both too tired to move, and then we'll sleep and wake up and do it again. You need me to keep you from doing silly things like sending love notes and poisoned chocolates to dangerous men..."

"The chocolates weren't poisoned!" she protested.

"Where did you get them?"

"From Mr. Hassan...oh," she said.

He shrugged. "You need me to look out for you, keep you safe. You need me..."

"I need you," she finished for him. "I need you to love me. Can you do that?"

Her breath caught as she waited for an answer. It would make the difference between emptiness and a future, between love and despair. She had asked him, all he could do was answer.

He cupped her face with his hands, tilting it up to look at him. "I need to marry you and give you babies and love you," he whispered. "I barely know you, and I need to know you for the rest of my life."

Her smile came slowly, spreading across her face like a sunrise, and she was about to tell him she loved him when she was distracted by noise from the bed.

"God, you make me want to puke!" Hassan shouted, finally having had enough. "Get out of here, or shoot me, I don't care what at this point.''

''Shut up, old man,'' Luc said ruthlessly, sparing him a glance. ''Can't you see I'm proposing to my lady?''

Hassan's response was suitably obscene. Luc ignored him, concentrating instead on Emma. ''Yes,'' she said simply.

''Yes?''

''Yes,'' she said again. ''I'm crazy and I don't care. I need to be with you. I'm in love with you.''

''Oh, God,'' Hassan groaned. ''Take pity on me. Leave me in peace.''

Luc kissed her eyelids, one at a time, a slow, lingering, incredibly erotic gesture that blotted out the sound of Hassan's curses. And then he smiled, looking down at her with a tenderness that caused her heart to ache in response, as his thumbs stroked her cheeks. ''Lots of babies,'' he murmured. ''If you want.''

''I want,'' she said. And she kissed his mouth, suddenly very certain.

He scooped her up in his arms, heading out into the snowy night. In the distance they could hear Hassan shouting after them, but Luc

kicked the door shut behind them and all was
silent.

He carried her to a battered pickup truck with
New York plates. It was black, of course, so it
had to be his. He put her on the seat with great
tenderness, fastening the seat belt around her
and then moving back to the driver's seat. She
could just barely see the tire tracks from when
they arrived, and there was no sign of Hassan's
vehicle.

It didn't matter. The truck was small, and she
could move next to him, even restrained by the
seat belt. He put his arm around her and she
nestled against his chest as he drove off into the
snow. The clock on the dashboard said 11:56,
and she realized the day was almost over, a new
day ready to begin.

Then she remembered what day it had been.

"Happy Valentine's Day," she murmured
against the side of his neck.

His laugh was soft and faintly cynical. "I
don't usually celebrate Valentine's Day."

"You will, darling. From now on, you will."

Once Upon a Mattress
Vicki Lewis Thompson

For Larry—
Happy Valentine's Day to the Father of the Bride
from the Mother of the Bride

Dear Reader,

If you grew up reading the same magazines I did, then you got the message that attracting a certain guy meant you had to *do* stuff, like choosing the right hairstyle, clothes, makeup and mannerisms that would make him ask you out. You had to research his likes and dislikes and figure out what would arouse his interest when you just *happened* to run into him. It was a lot of work.

That's what makes the concept of a secret admirer so delicious. What a thrill to discover that you've made a conquest *without even trying*. Even better, apparently the man likes you exactly the way you are. Best of all, there's an air of mystery about someone who adores you from afar without revealing his identity.

As you can tell, I loved the concept behind this anthology and thought it was perfect for Valentine's Day. But of course I had to give the concept a twist and send gorgeous but misguided Will Murdoch after the wrong woman. As for the Bedroom Fantasies store, I made it up. I've never heard of a commercial venture like it, but if someone wants to go into business, let me know!

Happy Valentine's Day,

Vicki Lewis Thompson

Chapter One

HE SURE LOOKED GOOD on a mattress.

Amelia Townsend leaned in the doorway of the storeroom and gazed at her delivery driver sprawled on his stomach, fast asleep. She smiled. Smart man—he'd chosen the deluxe pillowtop for his little nap. Probably stayed up all night studying for an exam and decided shuteye was more important than lunch.

She'd have to wake him—staff discipline would go to hell if she started allowing workers to sleep on the merchandise. But for a few precious seconds she could admire him without anyone catching her at it. He moved slightly, causing his snug University of California T-shirt to ride up and expose a strip of tanned skin above the waistband of his jeans. The idea of Will Murdoch shirtless under the California sun—now there was a tune she could dance to.

Will played a lot of tunes she could dance to, if she dared. Ever since she'd opened the store five years ago she hired college kids to make deliveries—strong young guys who loved telling their friends they worked for a place called Bedroom Fantasies. But Will was no kid. When he'd appeared last fall in response to the notice she'd put on the campus bulletin board, she'd stammered like an idiot when confronted by his rugged beauty, and hired him on the spot.

Now, six months later, she understood the problem she'd created for herself. His presence made her salivate. If she happened to be around when he muscled a mattress onto the truck, she nearly swooned. But she was the boss, and with sexual harassment suits thick on the ground these days, she couldn't risk asking an employee for a date.

He would have to ask *her*. Yeah, that would happen. He was on the shy side, which was one of the things she liked about him. Amelia was also shy, although her business contacts would never guess it. When it came to promoting the interests of Bedroom Fantasies, she'd been compared to a female Bill Gates, but her personal life was a different story. Actually it was a blank book.

With a sigh, she pushed away from the doorjamb. Time to wake up Sleeping Handsome and send him up to La Jolla. The Donaldsons expected to spend tonight enjoying Medieval Magic, complete with red velvet swooping from an iron bed frame and a suit of armor standing in the corner of the bedroom. Amelia loved watching her business flourish, but sometimes in the midst of creating exotic boudoirs for her customers, she longed for a make-believe world of her own. And a man who would make her dreams come true.

WILL WAS ENGROSSED in a great dream featuring an unidentifiable woman and the Jungle Fever bedroom suite. He'd never made love on leopard skin before, and although this was a fake version, he anticipated a satisfyingly primitive experience with this lady, whose face was mysteriously unclear.

Just as he was ready to shuck his clothes and draw aside the mosquito netting to slide onto the leopard skin with the willing woman, the dream began to dissolve. He moaned in frustration. If he wasn't getting any in real life, he ought to be allowed a little fun in his dreams. He shrugged away the hand shaking him awake and tried to bring his fantasy lover back into focus.

"Will," murmured a soft female voice as someone gripped his shoulder again. "Will."

A female voice. He hadn't been awakened by a female voice in many moons. He could smell her perfume, too—a spicy, erotic scent that mingled nicely with his jungle fantasy. Groggily he turned his head to gaze at a pair of nylon-covered knees. The woman crouched beside him was wearing one of those slim little skirts that slipped right up to midthigh in no time. The view from his angle was outstanding. Maybe he was still dreaming. If so, he was willing to forgive the loss of the leopard skin.

"Will, you have to get up. The Donaldson delivery needs to be made within the next hour."

He was at work. His military training kicked in, and he was on his feet before his brain was fully engaged. When the gears in his head meshed, he ran a hand over his eyes and groaned. Amelia would be within her rights to fire him, and he didn't have time to look for another job with midterms coming up. He glanced down at her. "Hey, I'm really sorry about that. I didn't mean to—"

"Don't worry about it." She stood up and smoothed her peacock-blue suit. "It's not a huge problem. But I'll have to ask you not to sleep on the mattresses. It sets a bad precedent.''

"Right.'' He looked at a point over her shoulder and tried not to think about the fact he'd just been staring up his boss's skirt and enjoying every minute of it. The warmth of arousal hadn't completely left, either. "I understand,'' he said. "And it won't happen again. I only meant to rest my eyes, but I must have conked out.''

"Tough exam this morning?''

She wasn't going to fire him, he realized. The tension eased from his shoulders as her compassionate tone drew his gaze to hers. The material of her suit made her eyes look turquoise. He'd never noticed what a beautiful color they were, especially now when they were soft with understanding. He basked in that tender look, hungrier for a woman's sympathy than he'd realized. "Yeah,'' he said. "My seven o'clock anatomy class. I pulled an all-nighter to study.''

She nodded. "That's right. You're premed. Have you decided what field you're going into?''

He thought it was damned nice of her to make small talk to get them over the awkward-

ness he'd created by sleeping on the job. But
he wasn't surprised. She was a good boss.
"Yeah, I have. Pediatrics."

"Really? Little kids?"

"Yeah." He smiled. "I happen to like kids.
I remember this terrific doctor I used to have.
He took most of the scariness out of being sick.
While I was stationed up in Alaska I had lots
of time to think about my future, and I decided
that would be a decent way to make a living,
helping kids get well without scaring them to
death."

"It's a very decent way." She glanced
around the storeroom crowded with exotic furniture. "In contrast, you must think this is
pretty frivolous."

"Are you kidding? I think it's a dynamite
idea! People spend a third of their lives in bed.
Thanks to you, they can fix things up so they're
excited about it. They'll get a better night's
sleep, and they'll probably enjoy sex more...."
He swallowed. "I mean—"

"Don't apologize. That's part of what we
sell, after all." Her cheeks flushed a becoming
shade of pink. "I named the store Bedroom
Fantasies on purpose. As we all know, sex is a
terrific marketing hook."

"Yep." For the first time since he'd started working for her he wondered how she'd come up with this idea. Someone would have to have an erotic streak to think of it, wouldn't they?

Yet she never acted as if she had those kinds of thoughts. She never told off-color jokes in staff meetings or made suggestive references. He knew nothing about her personal life, not even whether or not she had a boyfriend. Not that it mattered. She ran a highly successful company that was about to be franchised, while he was a very broke premed student. And she was also his boss. He needed to stop staring into her eyes and imagining scenes that would never take place.

She broke the contact first and cleared her throat. When she glanced back at him the softness had left her expression. "I'll go round up Gabe from the lunchroom so you two can get on the road. It'll probably take you the rest of the afternoon to set up the Medieval Magic grouping for the Donaldsons."

He mimicked her businesslike attitude. "Right. I'll check the order form and make sure we haven't forgotten anything."

"Thanks." She turned to leave.

"I'm the one who should thank you. For not firing me."

She turned back, astonishment making her look very young. "Fire you? It never occurred to me."

"Well, it occurred to me, and I'm glad you didn't."

"It would take a lot more than an unauthorized siesta to make me fire you, Will. Now get busy."

"Yes, ma'am." But as she walked briskly out of the storeroom he delayed checking the order and watched her go. Nice. Very nice. He could think of a couple of things he could do that would definitely get him fired, but they might almost be worth it. He wondered how he'd missed seeing what a great body lurked under those sensible suits of hers.

Of course she had a steady guy. With looks like hers and the creative talent to mastermind this business, she must have men lined up around the block. He located the Donaldson order and started checking off items, but his mind was only partly on the job. He kept returning to his original thought—that in order to conceive of a store dedicated to exotic and sexy bedrooms, a woman would have to have some personal leanings in that direction.

In spite of himself he started imagining Amelia Townsend lying on one of her fantasy beds, maybe the one in the showroom window decked out in white lace and red ribbons for Valentine's Day. In his vivid mental picture she was definitely not wearing a business suit.

"Hey, baby doc!" Gabe sauntered into the storeroom. "Ready to outfit the castle for Lancelot and Guinevere?"

"You bet." Will gestured with the clipboard. "You're in charge of our tin-skinned buddy there."

Gabe grunted and walked over to the rigid suit of armor. "Talk about heavy metal. It's like one big chastity belt. By the time you shucked this outfit, the chick would be asleep from boredom."

Will looked up from the clipboard and grinned. "Is that all you think about?" Talk about the pot calling the kettle black.

"How can a guy help it in this job?" Gabe lifted the armor and started out to the loading dock where the delivery truck stood open and ready. "We spend all our time handling beds."

Will picked up a carton labeled *Velvet Drap-*

eries, Red. "Beds are for sleeping, too, you know."

"Yeah, and someday in the far, far distant future, that'll be the first thing I think of when I see a big, cushy mattress. But right now, when I'm in the prime of my studly manhood, when I'm known as *the* babe magnet of El Cajon, I think of something quite different, my friend." He secured the suit of armor with a strap. "I'll bet you a beer after work that you do, too."

"You lose. Sleep's number one on my list." And most of the time that was the truth, Will thought as he stowed the drapery box.

"Poor boy. I think you froze your brains up there in Alaska. Or some other part of you." Gabe winked and picked up one end of a carved wooden chest. "Use it or lose it, man."

Will lifted the other end and they headed out toward the truck. "I don't have time." Yet he wondered if he should make time, considering the dream he'd had today, and his recent inappropriate thoughts about his boss.

"Nobody's that busy," Gabe said. "How long's it been, anyway?"

"You don't even want to know."

"Sorry to hear it." Gabe didn't say anything else until they'd loaded the chest and were walking back into the storeroom. "Have you checked out Leanne recently?" he asked casually, glancing at Will. "I heard she broke up with her boyfriend. Needs a shoulder to cry on."

A familiar anxiety tightened Will's stomach. He could pretend that he was too busy to date, but that was only part of it. He'd never been very comfortable with the game, and after being stationed in a remote part of Alaska for two years, he was downright rusty. "How about your shoulder, Mr. Babe Magnet?"

Gabe shook his head and looked smug. "I'm pretty much booked up." He clapped Will on the back. "Thought I'd pass this one on to you."

"What a guy." As they carried an iron bed frame out to the truck, Will thought about Leanne, the store's top saleswoman, a high-energy blonde who always had a joke to tell, a smile to flash. He'd lay odds she'd been a cheerleader in high school. She was probably exactly what he needed, but the thought of asking her out intimidated the hell out of him.

"You can't drag your heels on this," Gabe warned. "Troy's already sizing her up. He's got a girlfriend, but I don't think they're getting along all that good, so he may be available any day now. In fact, knowing the Troyman, he might start testing the water now, so he'll have a place to jump if he breaks up with his girl.''

Will laughed. ''You're really up on everybody's social life, aren't you?''

''This is what I'm talking about. All these beds. Romance is in the air around this place. I just pick up on what's happening.''

''Not me.''

Gabe strapped his end of the bed frame into place. ''I noticed. That's why I'm giving you a tip. I could tell you wouldn't figure this out on your own.''

''That's for sure.'' Will concentrated on adjusting the other strap and tried to sound neutral. ''So tell me, if you keep tabs on everybody, what's up with the boss lady? Is she involved with anyone?'' When Gabe didn't answer, Will glanced up at him.

Gabe was shaking his head as if Will had lost his mind.

''Hey, she's a good-looking woman, too, in case you hadn't noticed.''

''Well, sure, if you go for the anal-retentive, career-driven type.''

''Are you sure that's all there is to her? I

mean, she thought all this up, with the fantasy bedrooms and everything, so I figure that under all that efficiency she might be pretty.. ."

"Hot?" Gabe shook his head. "Not necessarily. This could be just a great business idea, like assembly-line hamburgers were for Mr. McDonald. Maybe he really liked six-course gourmet dinners, but he knew a great concept when he came across one."

"Maybe. But she wears this perfume that's—"

"Whoa, buddy! You're going around sniffing her perfume? Get a grip, man. She's gonna be rich any day now, whereas you..." He grinned. "Let's just say I've seen what you drive."

"Okay, okay. I get the picture."

"Leanne's more your speed, baby doc. If you want to get back in the action, take my advice and start with her. She's sweet and uncomplicated. And besides...." He winked and picked up his side of a king-sized mattress. "She told me she thinks you're cute."

Chapter Two

HER HEART STILL POUNDING from the close encounter with Will, Amelia sought the refuge of her office. She closed the door, something she never did, and sank into the swivel chair behind her desk. God, she was trembling like a teenager who'd just touched the hem of Leonardo DiCaprio's sleeve.

Her office wasn't much of a refuge, considering her state of mind. On the wall next to the door hung a framed publicity photo of her Hayloft Hanky-Panky collection. Oh, to tumble with Will into that nest of calico pillows. Swinging her chair around, she faced another publicity shot, this one of Harem Heat—a scarf-and jewel-draped bed to delight a sheik and his concubine. Amelia thought of Will's dark eyes and gripped the arms of her chair.

On some level she'd known that the bedroom designs said something about her erotic nature, but she'd downplayed that aspect, working instead to project the image of a hardheaded businesswoman so that she and her project would be taken seriously. It had worked like a charm. Franchising was only a few steps away.

Through it all, the sexual pull of her designs had never seduced her before, despite knowing that she was playing with fire each time she dreamed up an exotic new bedroom setting. Now she needed nothing more exotic than a mattress thrown on the storeroom floor. If Will had taken her into his arms and pulled her down on that pillowtop....

She closed her eyes, leaned her head back and drew in several long, steadying breaths. He was just a guy, for heaven's sake. Ah, but she hadn't left much time in her life for guys while she poured all her energy into Bedroom Fantasies. Maybe she'd known this could happen— that given the right chemistry she could be enslaved by a consuming passion. Besides, she hadn't had much in the way of temptation until now.

A neighbor in her condo complex had tried several times to take her out for coffee before he'd given up, and the leasing agent for the store had suggested a dinner that wasn't ''strictly business.'' She'd diplomatically refused, not wanting to take any chances on jeopardizing the deal she had for the property, which was ideally located for the urban professionals who were her customer base. And her neighbor simply hadn't been her type.

Had those been her only offers recently? The only straightforward ones, probably. Once in a while she'd been aware of a bedding company rep or a fellow chamber of commerce member poised on the brink of asking for a date. She'd always turned the conversation in a different direction, and they'd taken the hint. The men had seemed unremarkable, and she hadn't wanted to be sidetracked from her goal for some pointless dating exercise that could go nowhere.

But with Will, nothing seemed pointless. She wanted him so fiercely that her body throbbed with a sensation bordering on pain.

She'd been perilously close to telling him exactly that. His eyes, warm and dark as espresso, affected her as if she'd been drinking gallons of the stuff. How humiliating it would be to spill her guts and have him stumble through some explanation about a girlfriend, or worse, gently indicate he had no interest in her beyond their working relationship.

For a moment she'd imagined an answering spark in him. But she was burning so vigorously she could easily have mistaken reflected heat for interest on his part. No, she'd better cool it or risk the destruction of all she'd tried to build. What if she allowed her feelings to show and he told the other employees that the boss had come on to him?

Suddenly the designs she created, the groupings they were expected to sell and deliver, would take on a whole new meaning. They'd be viewed as the evidence of a thirtyish woman's sexual frustration, not the brilliant ideas of a savvy MBA. She had to control this desire for Will.

Yet she wondered if she'd ever forget the warmth of his muscled forearm under her hand, the appeal of his hair tousled by sleep, the lure of his mouth curved in a sensuous smile. Intuition told her he'd been dreaming of a woman.

He probably had a girlfriend. How could he not, going to college classes filled with beautiful young coeds, relaxed girls in shorts and minis, laughing and tanned, ready for anything? Amelia couldn't even remember where she'd put her bathing suit, and her last trip to the beach had been to supervise the shooting of a TV ad for the store.

Someone tapped at her office door. She got

up to open it, feeling guilty for the time she'd hidden in here analyzing this ridiculous crush. She prided herself on her availability to her staff, and no adolescent fantasy was going to change that pattern.

She opened the door with a smile and found Leanne Fairchild on the other side. Fairchild. So appropriate. Leanne was truly a golden girl, an uninhibited free spirit. Everything Amelia was not. Probably just the type Will would like. The thought drove an ice pick of pain through her temple.

"Are you feeling okay?" A frown wrinkled Leanne's otherwise perfect brow.

Amelia should have known the closed office door would be noticed. Her employees were a tightly knit group, which was exactly the way she had intended things to be. "Just a slight headache, but I took something for it and put my feet up for a few minutes."

"Good for you." Leanne looked relieved. "Sometimes I wonder if you're driving yourself too hard."

"Oh, you know me. I thrive on challenge."

"Good thing. I have one for you. One of my clients, Herb Morgan, is here, and he wants to trade in Highland Fling for Tahitian Temptress, and the Morgans are only three months into their lease.''

"And you're certain when you sold them the grouping they understood that the furniture couldn't be traded for a new theme for at least six months?''

"Absolutely certain. His wife was nuts about the theme, and so was he after I had a crack at him. Now he is back here, complaining.''

Amelia's headache got worse. Leasing theme furniture in six-month increments was the unique feature of her store, the one that had interested the potential franchise buyers the most. Customers had the option of exchanging one grouping with another so long as nothing had been damaged. The store could then sell the customer a new set of coordinating sheets and accessories, generating more revenue.

Amelia had researched and test-marketed the concept until she'd determined that six months was the most cost-effective time period and had the most consumer appeal. Amelia had proudly told the franchise prospects that she'd never had a customer who'd wanted a trade in less than six months. Now that was no longer true.

She massaged her forehead. "What's the problem?''

"Morgan says he's allergic to wool. He says the plaid accessories are giving him a rash."

Amelia stared at Leanne. "But he doesn't get to exchange the bedding and accessories. Just the furniture. Does he know that?"

"I told him. He says that's not the point. The theme isn't working, and he wants it gone. I tried to jolly him out of the idea, but he just got louder and more demanding."

"I'll talk to him." Amelia started out into the showroom.

"Peterson's out there, too. He came in right after Morgan showed up."

"Jonathan Peterson?" The New York financier was her best hope for a franchise east of the Mississippi.

"Yep. Said he didn't necessarily need to talk to you, just wanted to poke around, become more familiar with the merchandise. Troy's been trying to keep him busy and away from Morgan, but I'm sure he knows there's a problem."

"Great. Just great." Amelia unclenched her jaw with an effort and managed a smile by the time she entered the showroom. She waved in Peterson's direction and headed toward the belligerent-looking man standing beside the Tahitian Temptress display, his crossed arms resting on his potbelly.

She held out her hand. "I'm Amelia Townsend, Mr. Morgan. Leanne tells me there's a slight problem with your Highland Fling grouping. How can we help you?"

The hand he offered her in return was damp with perspiration. "I need a change," he said abruptly.

Amelia looked past the defensive stance and saw the anxiety in his gray eyes. Coming here today had probably taken enormous courage. "Why don't you tell me about it?" she asked quietly.

"It's...uh...the bagpipes."

"Excuse me?" Amelia couldn't remember including a set of bagpipes in the grouping, although it would make an interesting wall sculpture.

"Bertrice loves the sound. Well, she loves Mel Gibson, and the bagpipes make her think of him, which is why she wanted Highland Fling, because when she thinks of Mel Gibson she gets really—" Morgan stopped speaking as his ears reddened. "I mean, she thought it would set the mood, so to speak. And she thinks bagpipe music should be part of...what we're doing.''

''And you don't care for bagpipes?'' Amelia was determined not to laugh.

''I just don't know how a guy can be expected to get it up with that caterwauling!'' Morgan turned the color of a beet and looked away.

Amelia gazed at the floor until she had control of her urge to giggle. Finally, she looked up and cleared her throat. ''Have you mentioned this to Mrs. Morgan?''

''Not on your life,'' he muttered. ''The woman's seen *Braveheart* about a hundred times. How can I admit to her that I'm no Mel Gibson?''

Amelia studied the floor again. ''Won't she be upset if you change the bedroom theme without consulting her?''

''Not if I set it up right. Our honeymoon thirty-eight years ago was in Hawaii, and our anniversary's this weekend. I could tell her that's why I did it, and buy her a lei, and some ukelele music.''

She had to admire his inventiveness. ''Will this...work for you?''

''Are you kidding?'' He smiled for the first

time, giving her a glimpse of the dashing bridegroom he must have been thirty-eight years ago. "I'm ex-Navy." He gestured toward the tropical bedroom setting. "One look at this and I'm thinking *shore leave.* That's all it takes."

"Then I guess we'd better get you fixed up, Mr. Morgan. Come with me." Amelia walked over to the showroom sales desk and took a new contract out of the top drawer. She'd known from the moment he'd explained his real problem that she would do this. She just had to come up with a compromise that would benefit the store, as well. "Because this is against our normal policy, would you be willing to sign a one-year lease on Tahitian Temptress instead of the standard six-month one?"

"No problem. I'd be willing to buy the stuff outright, if you want."

Amelia started initialing the changes on the standard contract. "I don't advise that until you've lived with it a year." She pushed the contract across the desk for his signature. "Maybe your wife will want to trade for something else after that."

Morgan winked. "Not if this pans out the way I figure it will. She might want to redecorate the whole damn house this way."

Ten minutes later Morgan left the store a happy man.

"Beautifully handled," Jonathan Peterson said, coming over to the sales desk.

There was no point in trying to cover up what had happened, Amelia thought. He'd obviously heard most of it. "Thanks, but I can't brag anymore that nobody's wanted an early trade."

Peterson shrugged, lifting the padded shoulders of his hand-tailored suit. "So you institute a new policy. Early trades mean signing a year's lease. You haven't lost a thing. In fact, you've gained a few months." He rubbed his chin and gazed at her. "What sort of inducement could I offer you to come to New York and supervise the opening of my franchise?"

She was taken aback. "I don't know. I hadn't ever considered such a thing."

"Your staff is extremely capable. I'm sure you could leave the mother ship for a couple of months. I'd like you to hire and train my employees. Name your price."

She felt slightly breathless. "Then you've definitely decided on the franchise?"

"If you'll come east and help me get it going, I have. I suspected you were a key ingredient of this operation's success. After watching you deal with a customer, I'm sure of it. Who knows? I might even persuade you to find a manager for this store and stay on in New York.''

"Oh, I doubt that." Amelia's mind raced. A successful store in New York could ensure the future of Bedroom Fantasies. As the song said, if she made it there, she'd make it anywhere. But she thought there was a personal undercurrent in Peterson's invitation. Or maybe her preoccupation with Will was affecting her perceptions.

If Peterson was interested in her, she should be flattered. The man was both attractive and rich. Unfortunately those things didn't balance against Will's raw sensuality. But she wasn't going to pursue Will. In fact, she was going to avoid him at all costs. Traveling to New York would facilitate that.

She glanced at Peterson. "I'll consider it. Can you give me twenty-four hours to make up my mind?"

"Of course. I've lined up a potential space on Fifth Avenue. Once you decide if you can help me, we can start ordering. I'd need you in New York by March first."

Fifth Avenue. Amelia had never dreamed of such exposure. "I'll let you know tomorrow."

"Fine. Just leave a message at my hotel." He held out his hand. "And congratulations on this business. It's a credit to your creativity."

She shook his hand and wished bells would ring and angels would warble the way they had when she'd gripped Will's shoulder this afternoon. Silence. Damn. "Tomorrow," she said.

"Tomorrow."

AT SIX THAT EVENING Amelia was the last one in the store, as usual. She closed at six on weeknights, nine on Friday and Saturday or the day before a holiday. She didn't work all the hours the store was open—just most of them. Christmas Eve she always took a late flight to San Francisco to be with her parents and little sister, but on December twenty-sixth she was back at the store. Success was a powerful aphrodisiac, and she'd become hooked on it, she realized. But she was young and could work through that after she'd made her first million.

"Amelia?"

She glanced up from her desk to see Will standing in the doorway. Talk about aphrodisiacs. He wore a black nylon jacket over his T-shirt, but it only emphasized his broad shoulders and well-developed chest. He'd been well-muscled when she'd hired him. After six months of moving furniture he deserved to be sculpted in bronze. She really needed to take that New York offer and get out of temptation's way for a while.

Belatedly she realized he might have encountered a problem with the Medieval Magic grouping this afternoon. Otherwise he'd have gone home after returning the truck. The other possibility, that he'd arranged to be alone with her on purpose because he was attracted to her, tickled at the back of her mind. She couldn't think about that or she might have trouble breathing.

"Everything go okay at the Donaldsons'?" She straightened papers on her desk that didn't need straightening.

"Yeah." He grinned and leaned against the doorjamb. "By the time we left, Mrs. Donaldson had changed into a long flowing dress, and she had on one of those tall pointy hats with a scarf trailing from the top. She showed us the tights and puffy short pants she'd bought for Mr. Donaldson. Maybe you should open up a costume shop, too."

"Maybe I should." It wasn't a bad idea, she thought. Maybe after she got the New York store launched she'd look into it. But if everything had gone well at the Donaldsons', that wasn't the reason he'd appeared at her office door. Her heart beat a little faster.

Will cleared his throat and shifted his weight. "I came by after everybody left because I had something personal to discuss with you."

Her throat constricted. "Oh?" *He was attracted to her. Maybe she'd forget about New York. Maybe...*

"I probably wouldn't have dared before, but you were so nice about catching me sleeping, that I—well, if this is out of line, just tell me, but—"

"I'm sure it's not out of line," she said in a breathless voice. She clenched her hands into fists to stop them from trembling. Her dream was coming true. He was about to admit his feelings for her. Maybe he'd had them for months, as she had. Maybe he was just as frustrated and wild with unexpressed passion as she was. And here they were, in a store full of beds.

"I...well, this is hard to admit, but after being stationed in Alaska for so long I feel as if I've forgotten how to approach a woman."

"Don't worry." She struggled to keep her voice steady. "I'll help you."

"You will? God, how did you know that's what I wanted? Especially with somebody like Leanne, who's used to guys with a smooth line. I thought maybe—"

"Leanne?" She hardly realized she'd spoken as her dreams became a ball of fire that crashed to earth in a shower of hot sparks.

"You sound surprised. You probably don't know that she broke up with her boyfriend. I didn't either, but Gabe told me. I wouldn't ask her out otherwise. Anyway, with Valentine's Day coming up, I thought I'd try that old secret admirer routine, leaving her notes and little presents."

Amelia didn't know it was possible to hurt this bad when she'd received no physical wound. "I see."

"But I doubt I know her as well as you do, and I could use some help. I'll bet you've never had an employee ask you to play matchmaker, huh?"

"No." Despite her efforts to stay calm, her voice had an edge to it.

He looked a little startled, and then he

frowned. "Hey, it's a dumb idea. I don't know what I was thinking. Forget it. I can just—"

"No, no." She had no idea where she summoned the reserves, but she smiled at him. "I'll be glad to help. Give me the night to think about it. Tomorrow we can make some plans."

"Really? You're sure it's not too much of an imposition?"

Whereupon Amelia told the biggest lie of her life. "Of course not."

Chapter Three

WILL COULD HAVE SKIPPED his evening lab session for all the information he got out of it. He sat in a hard plastic chair staring into space and thinking what a complete idiot he'd just made of himself. Tomorrow he'd talk to Amelia, claim that lack of sleep had made him temporarily insane, and ask her to forget anything he might have said regarding Leanne, Valentine's Day and secret admirers.

Amelia was a busy woman, a woman on the rise. The last thing she needed was to help him with some stupid romantic stunt that would probably turn out bad. He'd let Gabe influence him too much, and when he'd admitted he was nervous about approaching Leanne, Gabe had suggested this dumb idea.

While he and Gabe had been setting up the Medieval Magic grouping and joking around, Will had thought the secret admirer route was brilliant. He should have slept on it instead of barging into Amelia's office so soon. He'd been afraid he'd lose his nerve, but he'd never forget the look on Amelia's face when she finally understood what he wanted. She was deeply disappointed in him, and she had every right to be. He shouldn't have bothered her with this.

The hell of it was that once he'd stopped in the doorway of her office, he'd had trouble concentrating on Leanne. He'd spent a few moments just watching Amelia, her brown hair falling in a shiny curtain past her cheek as she tackled the paperwork on her desk. Once again he'd thought of how young she looked, too young to have the kind of responsibility she'd taken on.

He'd wanted to walk behind her chair, massage her tense shoulders and find out if she'd bothered to eat today. What a laugh, that he'd have protective urges toward a woman who needed his protection about as much as Gabe needed a blind date.

Then Will had spoken her name, and she'd looked up at him with those incredible turquoise eyes. He'd almost said, *You look tired. Let's go grab a bite to eat.* Funny, but he didn't feel any anxiety about asking her out—the one person in the vicinity who would be most likely to turn him down.

Then she'd asked him about the Donaldsons, and that had reminded him that she was the boss and he was the hired help. Gabe was right. Leanne was more his speed. So he'd braved it through, and it had been a big mistake.

When the lab ended, he glanced at his watch and realized he didn't have to wait until the next day to square things with Amelia. He'd call her right now. She'd supplied her employees with her phone number and address in case any emergencies came up at the store when she wasn't there. Her trust that no one would misuse the information had been one of the things that had impressed him from the beginning. And in return the staff gave her complete loyalty.

He found a pay phone and started to put in his money. Then he gazed at the card again. She didn't live that far from here. Maybe he needed to explain in person, so he'd have a better chance of letting her know how sorry he was to have involved her. Yeah, he'd go see her and say that he was calling the whole thing off.

AMELIA EASED INTO A BUBBLE BATH scented with lavender and almost groaned out loud at the pleasure of it. With a sigh she leaned her head against the terry inflatable pillow positioned at the end of the oversize tub and reached for her glass of chilled chardonnay. Lush symphonic strings poured from the mini stereo unit on her marble counter. In summer she left her bathroom window open so she could hear the surf while she bathed, but February was a little cold for that, so she settled for music.

Okay, so today had been a total disaster. But at least she'd have no trouble deciding on the New York offer, and the sooner Peterson needed her there, the better. Maybe on his home turf Peterson would shine a little more than he did out here in California. Maybe she'd finally get rid of this obsession with Will Murdoch.

The wine was an indulgence she didn't allow herself on very many evenings. She often brought a stack of paperwork home in her briefcase, but tonight she hadn't been able to face it. Tonight she felt wounded and vulnerable, ready for a hot bath and a cool sip of wine. Her favorite white lace and satin robe lay ready on a tufted stool, along with the Egyptian cotton towel that was soft as a lover's touch.

She shouldn't have hired Will in the first place. "Take a memo, Suzette." She gestured toward an imaginary secretary with her wineglass. "To Amelia Townsend, CEO and nincompoop. Amelia, darling, never hire anybody you want to date. Never, never, never. Because he won't want to date you. He'll want to date some perky woman in sales and ask you to be the go-between."

She lifted the wineglass to her lips just as the doorbell chimed. Well, it figured. Some days were like that. Couldn't even take a decent dunk.

She considered ignoring the caller, then remembered it could have something to do with the store. What if she'd been robbed, or the place was on fire, and someone had come to take her there, not wanting her to drive when she was upset? She'd expect that kind of thoughtfulness from her staff.

Setting down the wineglass, she left the warm tub with reluctance and dried herself cursorily before pulling on the satin robe. The doorbell chimed again as she padded barefoot to the door. When she checked the peephole to see who was there, she nearly choked.

Hands trembling, she unlocked the door and opened it just as Will started to walk away. "Will?"

He turned, and his eyes widened. Then he

looked chagrined. "I've disturbed you. I'm sorry. Today just isn't my day."

"Or mine," she said, shivering both from reaction and the chill of the night air on her still-damp skin. Will was making her dreams come true, but it was like looking at them through a fun-house mirror. She'd often imagined him at her door, and her outfit was certainly appropriate to those fantasies, but he probably only wanted to talk about Leanne again. "What is it?"

"Never mind. Please go back to...whatever you were doing. I really apologize. At this rate I'll get myself fired yet."

"Nonsense." Amelia clenched her jaw to keep her teeth from chattering. "Come on in and tell me why you came. I'd discuss it here but I'm freezing to death."

He backed away. "No, really. I can—"

"Will Murdoch, you're taxing my patience. Come in."

"You're, uh, alone?"

"As a matter of fact." She realized he was afraid he'd interrupted something torrid. As if.

"All right, then. Just for a minute." He walked past her, bringing in the scent of cool salt air and a faint trace of aftershave that triggered her memory of earlier today when she'd crouched next to him in the storeroom.

She swallowed and closed the door. Her head knew he didn't want her, but her body reacted as if any minute he'd turn and take her into his arms. What garbage.

"I assume this has something to do with Leanne?" she asked.

He faced her, his eyes dark and mysterious, his hands clenched at his sides. "Yes, it does."

Of course, you idiot, she chided herself. *Did you imagine he'd had a change of heart and rushed over to tell you he wants you instead?*

TO HECK WITH LEANNE, Will thought. She might be cute, but on her best day she wouldn't compare to the elegant beauty standing in front of him.

"I suppose you'd like to get started on your campaign right away," Amelia said.

"To be honest, I—"

"I don't blame you. Let me give you a couple of ideas to get you going."

He needed to tell her to forget the whole project, but then he'd just have to leave, and he wasn't ready to do that yet. He was too busy taking in all the solid evidence that she was the sensuous woman he'd imagined her to be. Her living room was full of romance, with carved wood and flowered upholstery. Classical music drifted in from another room.

From the looks of things, she'd swept her hair back with a ribbon and stepped into a bubble bath not long ago. She smelled wonderful and her throat was still damp, along with a few strands of hair that had slipped loose from the red scrap of ribbon.

That was another thing. Most women he knew used an elastic piece of material to hold their hair. Amelia preferred ribbon. She also preferred satin and lace against her skin, and Will had a strong premonition she was wearing nothing underneath that carefully belted white robe. He'd noticed the thrust of her nipples against the smooth material when she'd stood in the chill of the doorway.

He should be used to that sight after spending so much time on a campus where women seemed to have given up wearing bras. And he *was* used to it in the free-spirited atmosphere of UCSD. But Amelia wasn't a free spirit, at least not in public. This was his first glimpse of her private pleasures, and it drove him wild.

Without her makeup she looked like a teenager, but no teenager would choose a robe as sophisticated as this. A drop of moisture gathered in the hollow of her throat. He watched it shimmer there a moment before it slipped gently over her collarbone and down into the shadowed cleft just visible between the robe's lace lapels. His body tightened as he imagined drawing back those lapels.

"So, is that enough to begin with?" she asked.

He blinked. He'd been so engrossed in imagining her naked breasts he hadn't even realized she'd been speaking. "Uh, maybe you'd better go over it one more time."

Amelia gazed at him and shook her head. "If you don't get more sleep soon, you're going to become a danger to yourself and others."

"Right." He'd take the excuse she'd given him and be glad for it.

"Okay, now pay attention. She likes chocolate, but not just any kind. White chocolate."

"Who?"

Amelia's exasperated sigh made her breasts quiver under the satin. "Maybe you should go home and sleep and we'll discuss this tomorrow. One day won't make that much difference."

Leanne. With an effort he forced himself to concentrate on something besides Amelia's soft skin underneath the robe. He was supposed to be organizing a secret admirer campaign to get a date with Leanne. He'd come here to tell Amelia to forget it, because he thought she wouldn't really want to help. But instead she seemed to be really behind the idea, so backing out now might be worse for his image than continuing with the plan.

Although he might love standing here weaving fantasies about Amelia, she wasn't for him. He needed to give this situation with Leanne a chance. He liked Leanne. Away from work she probably wasn't quite so gung ho. Maybe she enjoyed things like walking hand-in-hand along the beach looking for shells. Maybe she wouldn't insist, as he'd often imagined, on jogging along the wet sand wearing a Walkman and swinging hand weights.

Amelia touched his arm. "Go home and get some rest, Will. You're in a complete fog. I'll jot down my ideas and give them to you tomorrow."

He shook his head. Selfish as it was, he wanted to prolong this moment. He'd probably never be back in this room, never see Amelia in such a seductive outfit again. "No, now is the best time, if you're willing. I've already interrupted your evening, so unless you want to throw me out, we might as well get something accomplished."

She gave him a rueful smile. "You're a glutton for punishment, aren't you?"

"I guess so." It was sweet punishment, though, being here with her even if he couldn't follow his instincts. He couldn't remember when he'd felt more at home than he did in this room.

"As long as you're not going to go home and sleep, would you like some coffee and a sandwich?"

Now she was making him feel guilty. "No, no. That's okay."

"Well, I'm having some. We can talk in the kitchen. I haven't eaten yet."

"Well, in that case, okay. I skipped dinner, myself."

"So I figured. No wonder you're in a daze, with no sleep and no food in you. Just give me a minute to change." She started out of the room. "This isn't exactly my company outfit."

Disappointment shot through him. "Hey,

don't bother with that. This is your home, after all, and you look comfortable.''

She turned back to him. ''You don't think this is unbelievably casual and unprofessional, to entertain an employee in my bathrobe?''

''I never even noticed what you had on,'' he lied.

HE WAS IMMUNE TO HER, then, she thought as she brewed coffee and put together a couple of sandwiches with some leftover chicken. If only she could say the same about her reaction to him. But as long as she focused on his reason for being here—to orchestrate a date with Leanne—she could maintain her masquerade as his buddy.

So she hadn't changed from her silk robe into something more appropriate. If he hadn't even noticed, why worry about it? That he hadn't been the least interested in the fact she wore nothing underneath the robe was insulting, though. He probably thought of her as some sexless creature who lived for her quarterly profit reports. Okay, she did live for those, but not so much since Will had come to work for her.

She'd decorated the kitchen like a Parisian

café, complete with a bistro-sized table and two chairs. Perfect for one, very intimate for two. Whenever she had company she served meals in the dining room, but Will had already taken a seat at the little table, so she put their mugs of coffee there.

"You're sure I can't do anything?" he asked for the second time. "I feel bad putting you to this trouble."

"It's no more trouble for two than for one." She finished setting the table and put the plate of sandwiches between them. "And besides, this is a practical move on my part. You probably eat junk half the time, which will eventually lower your immune system. If you get sick, I'll lose my driver until you recover. So I need to keep you healthy."

"So this is a business dinner?"

"Absolutely." She sat down and accidentally bumped his knee with hers. "Sorry."

"No problem. These look great." He picked up a sandwich and bit into it.

Apparently being around her when she was half-naked was no problem for him, she thought with some irritation. Here they sat knees to knees, hers bare most of the time because her robe kept slipping, and he was oblivious.

It wasn't fair that she should be so obsessed with him and he didn't feel a thing. The sheer injustice of it made her reckless. She leaned forward a little, just enough to reveal a bit of cleavage. "I hope you like breast of chicken."

He swallowed the bite he'd been chewing. "I do. Thanks."

She gazed into his eyes, hoping to see a spark there. "Some people prefer thighs."

"I like those, too." His dark gaze remained unreadable. "I'm pretty easy to please."

Apparently, she thought. Leanne was a great saleswoman and very personable, but she was about as deep as the Victorian birdbath Amelia had out on her bedroom balcony. Oh, well. It made the secret admirer plan easier to set up. No subtleties required.

"As I mentioned when you were spaced-out a while ago, I think you should send Leanne something every day, along with a note," she said. "I'd start with chocolate."

"A box of chocolates? This could get expensive."

"That's why you don't send her a box. Just one piece. A good piece of white chocolate."

Will finished half of a sandwich and picked up another. "White chocolate, huh? Me, I like the dark stuff. The richer and stronger, the better.''

"Truffles," Amelia said, almost tasting it on her tongue. "Dark chocolate and espresso."

"Mmm." He met her gaze. "Dark chocolate and caramel."

She smiled. "Dark chocolate with a fresh raspberry center."

"Unless you have some chocolate in this house you'd better stop tempting me."

She looked into his eyes. Too bad the glow she saw there was motivated by candy. "I don't."

"Too bad."

She indulged herself in the warmth of his glance for another moment before returning to business. "Okay, elegant single pieces of white chocolate. Send them for three, maybe four days. Then you could start sending other little gifts, nothing expensive, but something with meaning for her."

"Such as?"

"She's a big Disney fan. That should help you."

"I guess so."

"Then for the last two or three days, you can get into the flower routine. I'd send single blooms at first. She seems to like yellow and orange. Save your money for that final delivery of a dozen red roses and the invitation to dinner on Valentine's Day. And that should do it. Secret admirer revealed, romance begins.'' What a depressing thought. Amelia hoped she'd be buying a ticket to New York by then.

''And you'll help me get this stuff to her so she doesn't know it's me sending it?''

''Sure, no problem.''

''And you think this will work? She'll want to go out with the guy who does all this?''

Amelia leaned her chin on her hands and gazed at him. She couldn't imagine that he didn't know how gorgeous he was. ''I think she'd go out with you if you walked up and asked her, Will. You probably don't need to do any of it.''

He put down his coffee mug. ''Yeah, I do.''

''Why?''

He gave her a sideways glance and looked away. ''Because it's been a while. If you tell me she's excited about meeting the guy who's sending her stuff, that will really help my confidence level.''

She was astounded that he felt he needed a crutch. ''But Will, you're—'' She caught herself before she said the word *gorgeous.* "You have all sorts of things going for you. Why wouldn't she want to date you?"

"Because I'd bungle the part where I asked her. I'm not good at making jokes and small talk like Troy and other guys I know. Never have been. With someone like Leanne, I don't want to hang everything on simply asking her out for a cup of coffee."

"This date matters that much to you?"

He gazed at her. "I guess you could say that."

Amelia's heart sank. He was already in love with Leanne.

Chapter Four

WILL WASN'T SURE how much longer he could hang on to his control. He'd nearly lost it twice—when she'd leaned forward and asked him if he liked breast of chicken, and when they'd been comparing notes on chocolate. She probably didn't even mean to tantalize him. After all, who was he but some guy she'd hired to move furniture?

Still, just in case he was wrong and she had been sending him a subtle invitation, he decided to do a little probing. He'd polished off two sandwiches and was on his second cup of coffee. He needed to go home soon, but she didn't seem in any hurry, so maybe she was enjoying the company.

He took another sip of the coffee. Good stuff. "I've been wondering something ever since I started work at Bedroom Fantasies," he said.

"What's that?" She cradled her mug in both hands.

He'd enjoyed noticing little things, like her

clear nail polish and the antique setting of the opal she wore on the ring finger of her right hand. "Where did the idea for the fantasy bedrooms come from?"

She hesitated and finally shrugged. "I just thought it would be cool."

"It is. I just thought...I don't know. I picture you and some special guy dreaming it up."

"Nope."

He dared a little more. "I'll bet your boyfriend likes the whole concept, though. I mean, you're the owner, so you could change your own bedroom any time you wanted."

Her smile was secretive. "I don't change my bedroom."

"You don't?" That surprised him. "Now I'm curious."

She pushed back her chair. "Come on. I've served you dinner in my bathrobe, so you may as well get a tour of my bedroom." She glanced at him. "I'll keep your secrets if you'll keep mine."

"That goes without saying." His heart raced, and it was only partly from the recent dose of caffeine. He wondered if he was up to this, if once he stepped into her bedroom his control would snap for good and he'd haul her into his arms, strip off that robe and...

No, he couldn't let that happen. For some reason she'd let him into her confidence, probably because he'd admitted his vulnerability where Leanne was concerned. Amelia couldn't know how she affected him as she made these personal revelations. One thing was for sure, after seeing her bedroom he'd know whether she had a steady guy or not. A woman in love nearly always kept a picture of her man on the bedside table.

He followed her down the hall.

"I decided to design one bedroom grouping that would be mine alone," she said over her shoulder. "The store designs will eventually have hundreds of copies all over the country, especially if Jonathan Peterson opens a franchise on Fifth Avenue. I wanted something unique for myself."

"Fifth Avenue, huh?"

"Yes, on the condition that I go back there and open the store for him."

The hair on the back of Will's neck rose as a primitive instinct sensed a rival. What a laugh. Will wasn't even in the running. "Is Peterson

an old guy?'' he asked, even if he had no right
to.

"Somewhere between thirty-five and forty,
I'd guess.''

He absorbed the information with a sense of
foreboding. "And rich.''

"Very.'' She stepped aside. "Here it is.''

He glanced through the doorway and sucked
in a breath. With luck she hadn't noticed his
gasp, and with even more luck he wouldn't de-
velop an erection just looking at her incredible
bed.

It was drenched in a heady, heavy sensuality,
strengthened by its lack of color. The massive
headboard, footboard and canopy were intri-
cately carved and enameled to look like polished silver. Tasseled ropes gathered thick ivory
draperies at each supporting post, and swags of
the same brocade hung in luxurious layers
around the edge of the canopy. Embroidered in
white, the coverlet and pillows glowed with the
richness of satin.

"What do you think?'' she asked.

What did he think? That he'd better get the
hell out of there. The woman, the bed and the
scent of lavender from the marble bathroom vis-

ible through an arched doorway had kicked his sex drive into high gear.

"I call it *Surrender*," she said.

"It's...really something." He sounded as if he'd been running a marathon. "And you know what? I really should get going. Get some of that sleep you think I need."

She gave him a puzzled look. "It's okay if you don't like it. I designed it for myself, so I can't expect other people to love it the way I do."

"Oh, I like it," he said, backing down the hall. "That big old bed just reminded me of how much sleep I need, and I'm suddenly beat."

"Sure. I understand." She sounded disappointed again, the way she had when he told her about his idea for Leanne.

He was sorry about that, but if he didn't leave her place within the next five minutes, he'd have even more to be sorry for. "Thanks for everything, Amelia," he said. "You're one in a million."

"You're welcome. See you tomorrow."

"Right." Grabbing his jacket from a chair, he made a quick exit out the front door. He didn't realize until he was halfway home that there had been no one's picture on her bedside table.

THE NEXT MORNING Amelia found an unmarked package on her desk. Inside was a small box with Leanne's name on it. Amelia held it to her nose. So Will had managed to find a chocolate shop open after he left, she thought. And he'd pretended to be exhausted. Well, love could revive even the most tired fellow.

She went into the lunchroom when no one was around and set the tiny box inside Leanne's Minnie Mouse coffee mug. Then, feeling enormously depressed, she returned to her office, called Peterson and agreed to open his Fifth Avenue store. He was delighted, he said, and invited her to dinner that night so they could celebrate. She forced herself to accept.

She had no trouble identifying the moment Leanne found her chocolate. Her squeal of delight could be heard throughout the store. A few minutes later, Amelia wandered out into the showroom. After Troy finished with a customer, she walked over to him.

"Cha-ching!" he said with a grin. "And a Hedonistic Greek model goes to the couple from Laguna Beach."

"Laguna Beach? That must mean our expanded ad campaign is working."

"It sure is. And that sale puts me ahead of Leanne for this quarter. Luckily for me, she was so busy trying to figure out who her secret admirer is that she missed seeing that couple come through the door."

Amelia pretended surprise. "Secret admirer?"

"Oh, yeah. Some guy must have sneaked into the lunchroom and put a piece of chocolate in her coffee mug. She even thinks it might have been me. I wish it had been. Damned good idea. Women love that kind of mystery."

"Aren't you already involved with someone?"

Troy frowned. "She moved out last night."

"Hey, I'm sorry."

"It's been coming for a long time." He glanced at Amelia. "But I think I'll finally trade in the Irish Milkmaid grouping she begged for and get the Sex in Space that I wanted all along."

Amelia smiled. The kid in Troy was one of the things customers found so appealing about him, and why he'd sold so much of her fantasy furniture. "Then if you can locate a woman who likes traveling in a rocket ship to galaxies far, far away, you're in business.''

"See, that's why I wish this secret admirer guy hadn't shown up. I happen to know Leanne likes Sex in Space. She's even talked about trading in her Wild, Wild West grouping for it.''

Amelia's brain threatened to go on overload. Will wanted to date Leanne. Troy wanted to date Leanne. It was a miracle that Peterson had asked Amelia to dinner instead of asking Leanne. Amelia decided she should be grateful that at least one man on the planet wasn't mooning over the lovely Ms. Fairchild.

She patted Troy on the arm. "Cheer up. Space is in vogue these days. I'm sure you'll find lots of women who want to help you command the bridge, so to speak. Anyway, congratulations on selling another Hedonistic Greek.'' Out of habit she glanced toward the white-columned bed with its distinctive dome rising from the canopy frame. The cobalt-blue bedding was quite rumpled. "Better go make the bed again, Troy.''

"Yeah.'' He grinned. "It's a great sales tool, letting them crawl onto the mattress and imagine themselves owning the setup. You should have seen the way the guy looked at the woman once they were lying there together. I had a feeling if I turned my back, they'd go right to it.''

"It's happened before." Amelia laughed. "Four years ago, soon after I'd opened the store, I walked out of my office one afternoon and found a couple rolling around on the Wild, Wild West bed, and clothes were starting to come undone. I swear to God if I hadn't showed up they were about to christen it."

"I believe you." Troy's eyes sparkled. "And you can't blame them. You've primed the place so that's what they start thinking the minute they come in the door. Why, before you hired me I had planned to become a priest, but you ruined me."

"Oh, sure."

"It's true!" He lapsed into a bad brogue. "When I broke the sad news to me family, me poor mither cried her eyes out, she did."

"Oh, Troy, will you cut that out?" Leanne approached them carrying a small box Amelia recognized instantly. "You've been sleeping in that Irish Milkmaid bed *way* too long."

"So I've decided." Troy waggled his eyebrows at her. "Gonna get me a Sex in Space as soon as Amelia can arrange the delivery."

"Whoa. Think you can handle something that snazzy, Troy-boy?"

"Are you offering to help me handle it?"

"That depends." She balanced the small box on the palm of her hand. "Want to own up to this?"

"Wish I could."

Leanne glanced at Amelia. "I don't suppose you happened to see who put this in my coffee mug this morning?"

"My lips are sealed."

"Aha!" Leanne smiled. "But you know who it was, don't you?"

Amelia just gazed at her without speaking.

"Aw, come on. Just a little hint. This is driving me crazy."

"If I told you, your admirer wouldn't be secret anymore, would he?" Will's plan was working, Amelia thought. Leanne was intrigued, and after a few more days she'd accept any invitation just to find out who her secret admirer was. "Did you like what was inside the box?"

"Are you kidding? I ate it already!" Leanne opened the box and displayed it. "See? Nothing in there but the note. I licked the bottom of the box, the chocolate was so good.''

Troy glanced at her. "I'm really sorry I missed that.''

"It *is* you, isn't it?'' Leanne turned toward him. "This would be just like you, to pull a crazy stunt and not admit it. But I'll be watching you from now on.''

"Cool.''

"What did the note say?'' Amelia asked with all the nonchalance she could muster.

"I memorized it.'' Leanne's brown eyes grew dreamy. "It was so romantic, which is the only reason I don't think you're the guy, Troy.''

"Thanks a bunch.''

"It said *Lucky is the chocolate that knows the touch of your lips. Your Secret Admirer.* Leanne sighed and carefully put the top back on the box. "I've never had a man write to me like that before.''

"Who knew you'd like it?'' Troy grumbled.

"All women like it.'' Amelia heartily wished she hadn't asked Leanne what was in the note. Now it would haunt her. Well, she could report to Will that his plan was a raging success. And she'd been the idiot who had agreed to help him put it in motion.

WILL MANEUVERED the delivery truck through morning traffic as Gabe fiddled with the radio.

"Nothing but commercials." Gabe shut the radio off in disgust.

"Well, I did it." Will said.

"No joke?" Gabe stared at him. "The secret admirer thing? Excellent!"

"Amelia's helping me."

"Get outta here."

Will shrugged, as if Amelia's part in the plan was inconsequential. Never mind that he'd dreamed about her the entire night, and most of the dreams had been connected with that silver and ivory temple of a bed she owned. "I needed somebody to plant the stuff so I wouldn't be caught doing it," he said. "I figured it should be a woman, and I don't know the new lady in sales very well."

"Me, neither. She's married."

Will grinned. "You say that like she has a terminal disease. Are you only friends with single women?"

"It's safer that way," Gabe said. "No point in yearning for something I can't have, if you know what I mean."

Will did know. He'd done his best to control his daytime thoughts, but he couldn't seem to do the same with his dreams. "Anyway, I asked Amelia if she'd help me do this, and she seems happy to."

"You know what, I'm not surprised," Gabe said. "She's a real standup lady. The kind you know you can count on. I can't imagine you asking her, though, considering you're scared to ask Leanne for a date straight out."

"I'm not *scared*. I'm just not good at it. I know myself, and I'd make a mess of the whole thing. For some reason I can talk to Amelia, probably because I have no intention of asking her out."

"I guess that makes sense. So what'd you start out with? An X-rated video? An extra-large condom?"

"You're romantic clear to the bone, aren't you, Gabe?"

"Only kidding, dude. Don't get touchy. Seriously, what was your first move?"

Will told him about the single piece of expensive white chocolate and that he planned to follow that with more goodies in the days ahead.

Gabe nodded. "Not bad. Sounds like you're on your way to a rendezvous with the luscious Leanne. Congratulations, buddy."

"It's all your fault."

"You'll thank me on some night in the near future, when your long dry spell is about to come to an end."

"Hey! You think this is all some sort of calculated setup to get Leanne into bed?"

"It isn't?"

"Hell, no. All I'm thinking about is a date, to see if we get along. I've never even touched her."

"That's not my fault. And I keep telling you she thinks you're cute, so you're halfway there already."

"Yeah, but how do I know if the chemistry's right? Maybe we'll be all wrong for each other, and—" He stopped as he became aware that Gabe was laughing. "What's so funny?"

"You. You haven't been with a woman in God knows how long, and you're worried if the *chemistry* will be right? Hell, you won't care if she has purple eyes and green hair and uses bug spray as her favorite cologne. Just get you alone with an available woman, any available woman, and you'll be *ready,* man. It's almost a shame to waste Leanne's charms on you, sort of like giving *cordon bleu* to a starving man, but you're lucky enough to be in the right place at the right time, so *bon appétit*.''

Will frowned and cleared his throat. ''Okay, so maybe I am easily aroused these days. Leanne's going to have to want to, you know. And she just might not.''

''And she just might. The word is that the guy she broke up with was very bright but sort of a zero in the bedroom. Had some sort of religious hang-ups she thought she could work around, but no dice.''

''Where *do* you get all this stuff?''

Gabe smiled. ''I'm a good listener.''

Will had a horrible thought. ''You haven't told anybody that I've been sort of...without action for a while, have you?''

''No, buddy, I haven't. I like to see all these affairs turn out well, and I can't imagine how that would help your cause, if Leanne thought you'd take the first woman who smiled at you.''

''That's not true, dammit.''

''If you say so.''

Will decided that the more he argued the point, the less Gabe would believe him. But surely Gabe was wrong. He hoped he was wrong. He'd hate to think that his reaction to

Amelia the night before had been based on nothing more than deprivation.

Maybe he needed to test himself and find a private time to talk with Leanne. If he felt the same cravings when he was alone with her as he had the night before with Amelia, then he'd know that Amelia probably wasn't the most astounding woman he'd ever met. His current state of mind had only made her seem that way.

Chapter Five

THE DAY SLIPPED AWAY from Amelia before she realized it, and she'd intended to give Will some feedback on the success of his campaign, plus suggest a better place for him to leave his daily gifts. Okay, so she was pathetically eager to see him, even if they had to talk about his interest in another woman. In fact, she looked forward to spending a few minutes in conversation with Will more than spending an entire evening with Peterson. Bad sign.

Late in the afternoon she went to the storeroom looking for Will and found Gabe instead.

"Greetings," Gabe said, flashing his brilliant Latino smile. "What can I do for you?"

"Has Will gone home yet?"

"I don't think so. He said something about grabbing a cup of coffee in the lunchroom before he left."

"Thanks." As Amelia returned Gabe's smile and headed for the lunchroom, she thought about what a good-looking guy Gabe was, yet she'd never been in the least attracted to him. He even hauled furniture around like Will did, and she supposed he had a good body, although she'd barely noticed. She wondered what made the difference with Will. Maybe it was his shyness, or his incredible eyes, or the cute way his mouth turned up at the corners when he was amused. And maybe there was no analyzing an attraction this strong. It just *was*.

She found him in the lunchroom, all right, and wished she hadn't. Her imagination had created enough pictures of him with Leanne to make her thoroughly depressed. She hardly needed a dose of the real thing.

He stood with his broad back to her, his head slightly bent as he talked with Leanne. Although she couldn't see Will's face, she caught a glimpse of Leanne's as she gazed up at him with a friendly smile. Too damn friendly to suit Amelia.

"I love the beach, too," Leanne said. "Just me, the waves and my Walkman. I get the best workouts jogging there."

"So you don't stroll along looking for shells," Will said.

"Nah, I'm really not into shells. I collect Disney memorabilia, though. Just last month I

bought a big glass case to—'' She stopped
when she spotted Amelia. "Hi, Amelia. I told
you about that display case I found for my
Mickey and Minnie collection, right?''

Will turned quickly, almost guiltily, as if he'd
been caught doing something illicit.

"Yes, you told me," Amelia said. "It
sounded like a real bargain to me. Listen, I
didn't mean to interrupt, but when you're finished here, Will, would you please stop by my
office for a minute?''

"Sure.''

Leanne tossed her blond hair back. "Hey, if
you two have something private to discuss, I'll
just take off. Troy's on floor duty tonight, so
I'm a free woman, and I have about fifty er-
rands to run and an appointment for a massage
at six.''

Amelia knew she should feel some remorse
for interrupting a cozy little chat between future
lovers. "Okay," she said breezily without the
least bit of regret.

Leanne picked up her purse. "I also need to
get home and find out if my VCR is working
right. I've decided to record all the *Seinfeld* re-
runs and I think there's something wrong with

my machine, but I'm not sure." She glanced at Will. "Do you like *Seinfeld?*"

"I guess I would if I ever had time to watch TV. But lately—"

"I can't imagine never getting to watch TV." Leanne shook her head. "You must be one of those disciplined, dedicated types I envy so much. Well, see you two tomorrow." She glanced back at Will. "Maybe I'll get another message from my secret admirer."

"Yeah, could be," Will said.

After she left Amelia made herself apologize. "Sorry about that. I should have left as soon as I saw you two were alone in here."

"It doesn't matter." Will rubbed the back of his neck. "You know, this is probably a huge mistake. I don't have time to watch TV, so I won't be able to connect with her on that, and I'm really not up on Disney stuff, either."

"Maybe you could give her a massage."

He gave her a narrow look. "And what's that supposed to mean?"

A devil had hold of Amelia's tongue. "I can't help wondering what you two have in common, besides the obvious."

His dark eyes probed hers with compelling

intensity. "So you think this is just about sex, too?"

"Too?" Somehow she managed to carry on the conversation, although her pulse rate increased several notches as she looked into his eyes. "Is someone else in on this campaign?"

"Gabe. He suggested the secret admirer deal in the first place."

"I see. Well, it was a brainstorm. She's loving it."

"Yeah?"

"Oh, yeah. The candy and the...note were a big hit."

"She showed you the note?"

"She showed everybody the note."

"Oh." Red crept up his neck. "I didn't count on that. I guess I thought she'd keep the note to herself. It was private." He glanced at Amelia. "Of course, you could have read it before you gave it to her. I didn't seal it up or anything."

"I would never do that."

He studied her for a moment. "No, I suppose you wouldn't."

She met his gaze for longer than was wise and found herself wanting to tell him she'd never show a love note to anyone, that a walk on the beach to collect shells sounded like heaven and she didn't have time for TV, either. But so what if all that was true? Obviously she didn't have the physical attributes he was looking for in a woman and Leanne did.

She might as well do the matchmaking job she'd agreed to. "I don't think anybody noticed that box on my desk this morning," she said. "But one day they might, so why don't you leave your gifts in my top desk drawer? No one opens that except me. I'll just check the drawer every morning and make the transfer when no one's around."

He took a deep breath. "Listen, before this goes any further, let's get something straight. I'm not doing this just because Leanne has a great body and I want to get her into bed."

"Okay."

"You don't believe me."

"You're the one who said you couldn't imagine what the two of you would talk about."

He ran his fingers through his hair and glanced away. "That's because I'd probably have trouble knowing what to talk about with any woman I took out."

"I find that hard to believe. You don't seem to have any trouble talking to me."

He gazed at her. "No, but we're not dating, are we?"

Amelia swallowed, disappointment clogging her throat. He could talk to her because he didn't find her sexually attractive. "No, we're not."

"In my early twenties I overcame my shyness with women, but then I was shipped off to Alaska, and I seem to have lost all the ground I'd gained. I have to remember that two people don't have to be exactly alike to get along, and Leanne can probably talk enough for both of us. She's a good beginning for me." His smile was crooked. "Sort of a date with training wheels."

"I see." Amelia hoped to hell the time spent in New York would ease the ache building steadily in her heart. To salvage a little of her pride, she glanced at her watch. "Whoops. Gotta go. I need to change before I have dinner with Peterson."

Will's eyes narrowed. "You're having dinner with him tonight?"

"Yes." It was unworthy of her, but she couldn't help it. "We have to discuss the timetable for my trip to New York. He's providing

me with an apartment, and I think he'd like me
to consider a permanent move.''

''You wouldn't do that, would you?''

She took satisfaction in his sudden concern,
although he probably only cared about losing
her as a boss. ''I don't know,'' she said. ''Peterson can be very…persuasive.''

''But New York's so cold, and—''

''Warp speed!'' The swinging door on the
lunchroom slammed open and a little boy hur-
tled through. He came to an abrupt stop and
looked shocked to see anyone in the room.
''Alien life-forms!'' he gasped. ''Gotta alert the
crew!'' He spun around and started to run back
out.

''Hey, captain.'' Will reached down and
gently gripped the boy's shoulder.

The little boy tensed and opened his mouth
as if to scream.

Will crouched down next to him. ''Don't lose
your head, captain,'' he said. ''We're crew
members, too. An evil force has changed us into
the horrible creatures you see before you. We
need your help.''

His eyes wide, the boy turned to look at Will.
He stared at him for several seconds before he

started to giggle. "I was just playin', you know."

"Jeremy, you can't go back here." Troy pushed open the door, his expression weary. "Oh. I see you've got him, Will."

"Yeah, he was just checking out the place," Will said. "He didn't mean any harm. Right, Jeremy?"

Jeremy gave Will a grateful glance. "Right."

Troy looked at Amelia. "Sorry. His mother and I were getting the paperwork finished up and Jeremy took off. I've never seen a little kid move so fast. Ran all through the store, knocked over a couple of things, but I don't think anything's broken."

Jeremy's lip began to quiver. "I didn't mean to break stuff."

"Tell you what," Will said. He stood and held out his hand. "Let's take a walk through the store and make sure. That way you won't have to worry about it."

Jeremy nodded and put his hand in Will's. "I like the rocket ship bed," he said quietly as they started out. "Let's look there first."

"Okay. There's some cool stuff in here, isn't there?"

"Yeah," Jeremy said. "Real cool."

As Amelia watched Will take the child back out into the showroom, she pictured Will a few years from now, calming and comforting sick children. He would be wonderful at it. She wondered if he'd have children of his own some day, and the ache in her heart became even harder to bear.

"Jeremy's mother's getting a divorce," Troy said. "That's why she's buying a new bed, so she doesn't have to sleep in the one she shared with her ex."

"She said that in front of Jeremy?"

"Unfortunately. Then she told him to wait with me while she went out to the car to get her checkbook. That's when he took off like a bat out of hell. You can tell he hates having his parents split. Will sure handled him, though, didn't he?"

Amelia felt a warm glow of pride. "He's going to be a pediatrician."

"Good choice. Well, I'm sure the mother is back and wondering what happened to me. She's leasing Midnight Lace."

"*That's* what she chose, with a little kid in the house?"

"Yep. Want me to refuse to sell it to her?"

"You know we can't do that." Amelia thought of the red-and-black lace that decorated a black lacquered bed that was almost X-rated in its blatant sexuality. More than one customer had said the grouping belonged in a brothel, and it usually sold to single men. "He's probably too young to get the significance of the decor, anyway."

"Let's hope so."

After Troy left, Amelia returned to her office. She really did have to leave the store and get ready for her dinner with Peterson. But she paused for a moment and glanced out into the showroom, where Will was holding Jeremy up so he could get a better look at the futuristic canopy on the Sex in Space bed.

Amelia had assumed she'd marry and have kids some day, but she'd been so focused on her business that she hadn't given the matter much thought. Even her crush on Will had been a craving for physical satisfaction with no wish for commitment. Ironically, she'd wanted him for exactly the same reason she'd assumed he wanted Leanne—for sex.

Yet her focus was changing. Oh, she still

wanted him for sex. That would probably never change. But he was also making her consider what sort of man she'd like to spend a lifetime with, what sort of man she'd like to be the father of her children. Will was that sort of man.

WILL TRIED TO TELL HIMSELF that everything was going great. His gifts to Leanne continued to be a hit according to the office gossip supplied regularly by Gabe. Will stopped composing the notes he included once he realized they'd be circulated as faithfully as an interoffice memo. Instead he quoted poetry, which seemed to do about as well. Once he even quoted Mickey Mouse, which according to Gabe, caused Leanne to pledge her undying love to this secret admirer.

"She wants you bad, man," Gabe said one afternoon as they were returning to the store after delivering and setting up Troy's new Sex in Space bedroom grouping. "When are you gonna pop the question about dinner?"

"Tomorrow." Will knew he should be more excited about the prospect, but for some reason he felt detached from the entire operation.

"Cool. Where are you going to have her meet you?"

"She might not meet me, you know."

"Oh, she'll meet you. That's one curious lady. She can't figure out if it's you, Troy, me, or the new sales guy Amelia hired right before Christmas. She even suspects the mailman because he always talks to her when he gets a chance. The suspense is killing her."

Will parked the truck behind the store. He noticed with irritation that Peterson's rental car was sitting in the space next to Amelia's Subaru. The guy couldn't park out in front, like everybody else. He had to pull in back here, as if he had special privileges. Will kept thinking of Amelia's massive silver bed and wondering if Peterson had seen it yet. He sure as hell hoped not.

"So you're not going to tell me where?" Gabe asked as they climbed out of the truck.

"What?" Will looked at Gabe in confusion.

"Where you're going to set up the meeting with Leanne. You've sure been distracted lately, baby doc. Got a big test coming up?"

"No, I mean, yeah, kind of." Will always had tests coming up, so it was a good cover story. "I'm going to make a reservation at that little Italian place I like and tell Leanne which booth I'll be in. How's that?''

"Perfect. Intimate, not too showy. She'll love it.''

"Yeah, but I wonder if she'll love seeing me sitting there. Sure you don't want to take this one, Gabe?''

"After all your work? I wouldn't think of it. Besides, I have a date for Valentine's night. And she's cooking at her place.''

Will grinned at him. "Sounds promising.''

"When a woman invites you into her kitchen and fixes you a meal, you're most of the way home, buddy.'' He climbed the steps to the loading dock. "That's in case you've forgotten the signs.''

As Will followed him up the steps he thought of the night Amelia had invited him into her kitchen and fixed him a meal. But it hadn't meant anything. "What are some other signs?'' he asked.

"Oh, if she takes you on a tour of her place and makes sure you see the bedroom,'' he said. "But I think even you could figure that one out.''

Will nearly choked. But Amelia had made

the whole gesture seem so commonplace. Surely she hadn't been implying…no, of course not. He walked with Gabe through the large open door into the storeroom and heard voices coming from behind a wall of stacked boxes.

"…thought you wanted to see the new Erotic Egypt shipment," Amelia said.

"I do," said a man who sounded a lot like Peterson. "In a minute."

Will grabbed Gabe's arm and motioned for him to be quiet.

"Jonathan, we've discussed this," Amelia said. "I don't think it's appropriate for us to—Jonathan, that's enough!"

Will started forward instinctively, but Gabe stopped him. As they stood there, Amelia marched out from behind the stack of boxes, her head high and her cheeks rosy. She glanced quickly at Will and Gabe but said nothing as she continued on toward the door into the showroom.

"Amelia!" Peterson called out. "Don't you think you're being a little—" He walked out from behind the boxes, spied Will and Gabe and paused. "Gentlemen," he said with a curt nod.

Then he, too, walked through the door into the showroom.

"Will, are you okay?" Gabe peered at him in concern.

"Uh, yeah." Will discovered he was breathing hard from the effort of restraining himself. He wanted in the worst way to go after Peterson and tell him to keep his damned hands off Amelia. But mixed in with his protective urge was the satisfaction of knowing that she didn't want Peterson, after all.

Gabe put a hand on his shoulder. "You haven't totally given up that fantasy, have you?"

"Sure I have."

"Couldn't prove it by me. You were ready to take that guy apart. Listen, buddy, you're looking to get your heart broken with that one. She's going to New York. She may not want Peterson, but he's only the first of many guys just like him who will be happy to wine and dine our Amelia. That's going to be her world now. There's talk she may not even come back to San Diego. Either Troy or Leanne may end up running the store for her."

Will took a long, shaky breath. Then he

dredged up a smile for Gabe. "So you're telling me that Leanne could be my boss in a few weeks? Then I could have the same damn problem!"

"Not a chance. In a few weeks, it won't matter if Leanne's in charge or not. You'll already have established your...shall we say, new position with her." He grinned. "And I guarantee sweet Leanne will make you forget all about the boss lady."

Chapter Six

WILL HOPED THAT GABE WAS right and going out with Leanne would make him forget Amelia. He also hoped that once the secret admirer campaign was over he'd get better at remembering the pesky details in his life. He was becoming more absentminded with every day that went by. Between daydreaming about one woman and angling for a date with another one, plus trying to keep up with his course work, he was constantly forgetting the simplest things.

Case in point—he'd left his only jacket at the store, a fact he didn't realize until he came out of his night lab and a cold rain sliced right through his T-shirt. The store would be locked up by now, but he had a key to the back, as all the employees did. Rather than suffer through the rest of the night and his early class in the morning, he decided to swing by the store and pick up his jacket.

When he pulled into the back parking lot his heart started to pound. Amelia's Subaru was still there. Of course she might have gone to dinner with Peterson and left her car here, but after the scene he'd witnessed the other day, he doubted it. Still, he knew she wanted that New York franchise, so maybe she had to continue placating the jerk with a dinner date now and then.

Much as Will hated admitting it, he sort of identified with Peterson. Will knew how the guy must feel, wanting Amelia so much he could taste it. But Will's fantasies were probably more specific than Peterson's. Will had seen Amelia's silver bed and had thought a lot about the title of *Surrender* that she'd given it.

And unlike Peterson, Will had spent an evening with Amelia when she wore only a satin and lace robe and the scent of lavender clung to her damp skin. His dreams had been filled with images of her untying the robe and allowing it to fall into an ivory heap at her feet. Then she would beckon him toward that bed, slide onto those cool ivory sheets and lie back, waiting.

Will passed a hand over his eyes and wondered how long he'd been sitting in the parking lot behind the store, car engine running, windshield wipers flapping, headlights on. And an erection in the making. If the security guard happened along he'd probably want to take Will in for suspicious behavior. Damn. Valentine's Day was almost here, and he wondered how in hell he'd pretend to be infatuated with Leanne when Amelia was the only one he wanted.

Maybe he should drive away and forget about his jacket. Being alone in the store with Amelia might not be such a bright idea right now. Then again, what difference did it make? He wasn't the kind of guy to force himself on a woman, or even push the issue as Peterson had apparently tried to do. Amelia had no interest in him. He could simply go in, call out to her so she'd know who it was, get his jacket and leave.

In spite of that little speech to himself, his pulse quickened as he opened the back door. "Amelia?" he called out in a loud voice. "It's Will. I forgot my jacket." He flipped on the showroom light and started over to the wall where his jacket hung on a hook.

"Will?"

He turned toward the open showroom door and his heartbeat went off the Richter scale. The light from the showroom teased its way through the thin silk of her blouse and skirt, giving him a dim but arousing view of her body.

"Are you in a hurry?" she asked.

Not anymore. "Uh, not particularly." He swallowed. "Do you need...some help with something?"

"I've started a project that I may not have the ability to finish." She beckoned to him. "Come on. I'll show you."

"Okay." *Oh, yeah.* She wasn't beckoning him into her bedroom, but she was taking him through Bed City. He'd have to remember that the front of the store was glass, and with the lights on it became a theater for anyone driving by.

"I'm not satisfied with the way the Valentine grouping has been selling," she said over her shoulder. "All that white lace is pretty, but it may look too virginal, don't you think?"

"Well, I—" Whatever comment he'd been about to make flew out of his mind when she opened the door to the front display window and stepped inside. The shades were pulled down, concealing the window from the street. Once he stepped through the door and joined her there, they'd be shielded from the world.

Rain spattered against the glass, increasing the sense of intimacy.

For one crazy moment he wondered if she'd done this on purpose, to seduce him. What a truckload of wishful thinking that was. She'd had no idea he'd be coming by the store tonight. Obviously she wanted to rearrange the display in private, knowing that the fantasy element would be destroyed if customers happened to drive by and see a bare mattress or mismatched bedding.

"So far I've changed the sheets to red satin with an ermine throw across the foot of the bed," she said. "I don't have the matching canopy on yet, but what do you think? Is it too obvious?"

"Uh…" He wondered how he'd get through this without making a fool of himself. When he looked at the bed, the top sheet tossed back in invitation, the white fur begging him to lay her naked body across it, his groin tightened painfully. But looking at her was no better. His fingers itched to undo the silk-covered button at the vee in her blouse and find out for sure what he suspected, that she wore the kind of under-things that drove a man wild.

"It's too much," she said, grabbing up the

white ermine and clutching it to her chest. "I was afraid it was, but sometimes I don't know where to draw the line."

He stared at the soft fur pressed against the triangle of creamy skin between the lapels of her blouse and almost groaned aloud. How he wanted to press his mouth to that exact place. And that was just the beginning of what he'd like to do. "I...don't think it's too much," he managed to say. "I'm sorry. My brain's fried right now."

She gazed at him. "I'll bet you just got out of class and want nothing more than to go home and go to bed."

She got two out of three right, he thought. He had just left class and he'd love to go to bed, but he had no intention of going home. "I'm not really that tired," he said, forcing a normal tone into his voice. "What can I do to help you?"

Her expression brightened. "So you really think it looks nice? Well, not *nice*. I guess I'm going more for naughty."

Oh, God. "I think you're getting there."

"Great. Then what I need from you is to help me angle the bed a little more. I stood outside and looked at the display from different perspectives before I decided to make this change, and I think the bed should be turned so it's on a slant instead of straight across the window. I think you'd get more of the effect of the turned-back sheets, more of a desire to climb right into that bed.''

"Just show me where you want it.'' He wondered if she had any clue what this whole conversation in the cozy, curtained window was doing to him. Probably not. He was nothing more than an obliging furniture mover to her. Well, if that's all he could be, then he'd be the best damn furniture mover she'd ever had in her life. He'd shift and adjust and realign this bed a million times in exchange for the chance to breathe in the scent of her perfume and once in a while be rewarded with an approving glance from those amazing blue-green eyes.

AMELIA KNEW SHE WAS playing a dangerous game, but if Fate was going to send Will to her tonight, she'd get whatever thrills she could out of the situation. Between the pressure of his studies and his preoccupation with Leanne he probably missed the erotic nature of what they were doing as they fooled around with a bed dressed in red satin while the display window curtains were drawn. The rain tapping on the window only added to the sensuous nature of the setting.

But she really needed his help, she rationalized. She couldn't have moved the massive white canopied bed by herself, and she honestly had decided it needed to be moved. She just hadn't pictured watching Will do the job.

As he lifted, she lusted, shamelessly positioning herself for the best view of muscles bunching and straining to perform the task she'd assigned. The beauty of his body in action made her light-headed with desire. After he'd moved the bed, she inspected the angle with great seriousness and guiltlessly asked him to shift it several inches to the right. Then she had him put it back again. When he broke a sweat and his T-shirt began to adhere to those well-tuned muscles, she closed her eyes and offered a brief prayer of gratitude that he'd decided to come back tonight to retrieve his jacket.

Leanne would have him soon enough, Amelia rationalized. Before long she would be in New York, far away from the glory of his dark eyes and sculpted physique. She asked him for another adjustment of the bed's position. As a woman about to be deprived, she deserved this.

Of course she was also torturing herself with what she couldn't have, like a kid with her nose pressed to the candy store window. She could almost taste that candy, too. "Another couple of inches more to the left, and that should do it." She crossed her arms to still the fine trembling that had overtaken her.

He grinned and wiped his forehead on his sleeve. "If I didn't know better I'd say you're enjoying this."

Her heart hammered at the sexy quality of that grin. "Of course. Women love to coax men into moving furniture for them. It's been going on since some female ancestor of mine asked her guy to rearrange a couple of boulders in the cave." *Her guy.* That had slipped out. Will was Leanne's guy, or soon would be. And she needed to end this interlude before more slipups crept into her routine.

Will moved the bed to the spot she'd indicated, then straightened and rolled his shoulders. "How's that?"

Mighty fine. "Perfect." Now she'd bid him

good-night, and that would be that. The hour of midnight was striking for Cinderella.

"Want some help putting the new canopy up?"

She told herself to refuse and finish the job herself with a stepladder. But temptation snared her once again. "Thanks. That would be great. If you'll take down the white lace one, I'll get the red satin."

She returned to the storeroom and located the box containing the canopy. On her way back to the showroom she noticed his jacket hanging on the wall. Some people said there were no accidents in life. In that case, he'd unconsciously forgotten to take the jacket tonight so that he'd have to come back and see her again. But that made no sense. He hadn't known she'd be here.

She sighed. No matter how she twisted things, she couldn't come up with any evidence that he was the slightest bit interested in her. She walked over to the wall where his jacket hung and slid her hand along the material, but touching his clothing ran a poor second to what she really wanted. Feeling sinful, she took the jacket off the hook. The scent of his aftershave reached out to her, and she held the collar up to her nose and breathed in. Warmth transformed to heat, and heat built into the insistent pressure of need.

Stop this, she commanded herself. Replacing the jacket on its hook, she carried the canopy box into the showroom and through the door into the display window.

Will stood with the folded lace canopy cradled in his arms. "Where do you want this?" he asked.

The sight of a brawny man like Will carefully holding a frothy bundle of lace was an enticing contrast. She wondered what he'd look like holding a baby, his baby. A virile, child-loving man like Will would have children, and some lucky woman would get to be the mother of— Amelia put the brakes on her thoughts. "If you'll start putting on the new canopy I'll take the other one back to the storeroom."

During the exchange she was very aware of each time his hand brushed hers, but if she hoped that he'd pause, gaze into her eyes and say something significant, she was doomed to disappointment. He handled the whole episode with businesslike efficiency. Back in the storeroom she reboxed the lace canopy and took the opportunity to draw in several long, calming breaths. There. Now she was ready to send him on his way with a smile and a friendly handshake.

She marched back into the showroom and through the door into the display window. "I really appreciate this, Will. I'm sure you need to be getting home. I can finish up."

"I almost have it." He reached up and positioned the fourth corner of the canopy. "Besides, I owe you this, after all you've done for me with the Leanne business."

She wished to hell he hadn't brought that up. "The big day is almost here, isn't it?"

"Yep." He adjusted a flounce on the red silk.

At least he had the good grace not to sound as eager as he probably felt. But his mentioning Leanne had sure spoiled the erotic haze she'd been moving in for the past half hour. She was even alert enough to notice that the canopy wasn't hanging evenly on the rail.

She moved over next to him and reached up to tug on the material. "This isn't quite right."

"Does it need more over here?" He leaned around her to work the material from the top.

"That's better." Somehow in the process she

became bracketed between his outstretched arms. She basked in his heat, reveled in the scent of healthy male and the sweet sound of his breathing until her knees began to quiver with reaction. But he probably didn't even know they were practically embracing. "Now, if you'll just—" She gasped softly as his arm nudged the side of her breast.

"Just what?"

There was something new in his voice, something rough-edged and untamed. Heart pounding, she slowly released her hold on the canopy and turned around in the tight space between them. He gripped the canopy rail with both hands, effectively imprisoning her against the bed. She thought he'd excuse himself and back away. He didn't move. Slowly she lifted her gaze. And forgot to breathe.

All this time she'd thought he was unaware of her. She'd thought he didn't feel the electricity, didn't feel the heat. Didn't want her.

She'd been wrong.

A MAN COULD ONLY TAKE so much. He'd been maintaining until she invaded his space. And now…now her mouth was so close…so full, as if she wanted this. Her eyes were the hot blue of an August sky, and her perfume drifted toward him, making him dizzy. The rain drumming against the window echoed the pounding of his heart. He gripped the rail harder in one last effort to keep control.

Yet the promise of her drew him closer, and closer still. Her eyes widened, darkened. He waited, heart beating so fast he could barely breathe, for her rejection. It didn't come. "Time's up," he murmured. Still gripping the rail over her head, he closed his eyes and touched his mouth slowly, gently to hers.

Still he thought she'd pull back. Knew he should. But she didn't, and he couldn't. The soft pressure of her lips was too sweet, too new. He lifted his mouth and sought a better angle. She met him halfway, her lips slightly parted.

His heartbeat throbbing in his ears, he edged her mouth with his tongue, coaxing, exploring, sure that any moment she'd push him away. Instead she clutched his shoulders…and gave him what he sought.

With fierce joy he took full possession of her mouth. So lush. So hot. So ready. *Amelia.* He lifted his head to gaze down at her and saw everything he wanted to see in her dreamy eyes. Keeping one hand on the canopy rail for balance, he wrapped his other arm around her, relishing the sensation of silk warming under his embrace. He drew her close, delighting in the fullness of her breasts, the narrow span of her waist, the swell of her hips. Her body and his were a perfect fit.

Still gazing into her eyes, he released his grip on the rail and guided her down to the bed. The mattress at her back must have awakened some caution in her, because she opened her mouth as if to protest. *Too late, Amelia.* With a smile and a shake of his head, he slipped his arm under her knees. Her shoes fell to the floor as he lifted her completely onto the satin sheet. He followed her down, not giving her his full weight but pinning her to the bed, nonetheless.

Instinct directed him as he held her motionless and looked deep into her eyes while he combed his fingers through her silky hair. She'd designed a bed for herself and called it *Surrender*. From the moment she'd told him that, he'd known her fantasy. And maybe, just maybe, she'd let him give it to her.

He had no illusions the fantasy would last

beyond tonight. He wasn't the man she envisioned spending the rest of her life with. And she might be so embarrassed to have him around after this that she would fire him. He didn't care. For her this might be an illicit episode never to be repeated, but for him it was the culmination of a dream, and he would have no regrets.

He watched as indecision clouded her gaze. Then, in a moment so brilliant it took his breath away, the indecision cleared and her eyes grew luminous. With a groan he lowered his mouth to hers.

He'd never been met with such hunger. Once she'd given herself up to him, she held nothing back, kissing him with the sort of abandon he'd only dreamed of but never expected to find. And at last he acknowledged that Amelia was his ultimate fantasy—contained and prim on the outside, never letting on that on the inside she was a blazing inferno.

As he unfastened each covered button of her navy blouse, he raised his head to gaze at the tailored garment giving way slowly beneath his fingers. True to his fantasy, the conservative blouse covered navy lace worthy of a centerfold, a delicate garment that cupped and lifted her breasts while barely concealing them. Her quick, excited breaths added to the temptation, and just gazing at her he grew very hard and very needy.

But rushing to undress her would be the same as ripping open an elegantly wrapped gift. He glanced up and found her watching him, her lips parted and her eyes the color of twilight. As rain continued to batter the window he slipped his finger under the front clasp of her bra. Instead of undoing the clasp, he stroked his finger up and down between her breasts in subtle suggestion. She gasped softly and he took her mouth again, teasing her with his tongue.

He took his time kissing her, and when he finally lifted his head and opened the catch of her bra, he used such care that the lace cups stayed in place, still supporting her fullness. Slowly he smoothed away the material from one breast, turning the motion into a caress. As his palm slid across her warm, silken skin and encountered her taut nipple, he closed his eyes and sucked in a breath. Trembling with pleasure, he gazed down at her breast cradled in his hand.

''Please,'' she whispered.

Desire raged through him at her soft request, making him long to wrench the rest of her clothing away and expose every inch of her to his gaze, to his caress. But he had much to gain if he savored each step along the way, if he took the time to burn every sensation into his memory, for he could never expect to be allowed to touch her this way again.

Churning with anticipation, he leaned down slowly to take what she offered.

Chapter Seven

WILL MIGHT BE SHY out of bed, but once in it there was nothing shy about him, Amelia thought. He seemed to read her mind, seemed to understand the secrets buried deep in her soul. Then his mouth found her breast and she lost whatever remained of her reason. "Yes," she moaned. "Oh, yes."

Crazy to get her hands on him, too, she tugged his T-shirt from the waistband of his jeans and slid her palms up the muscled expanse of his back. Oh, to feel the bunch of those muscles as he continued to pleasure her! She kneaded his warm skin with the ecstasy of a kitten.

With a soft growl of satisfaction he shifted and took her other breast while he continued to stroke the damp nipple he'd just left. She writhed against the satin sheet, wild with joy to discover that he wanted her, even if he was acting on impulse. She would take whatever Will would give her and be grateful.

With a leisure that excited and frustrated her at the same time, he kissed his way down the valley between her ribs. The tumult of her heartbeat nearly drowned out the rasp of her skirt zipper, but when he gently tugged at the material, she raised her hips, wanting the skirt gone, wanting everything gone and Will buried deep inside her. She ached for him to be there.

"Perfect," he murmured, tracing the outline of her lace garter belt. Then he expertly unfastened the hooks securing one stocking.

As he rolled the silk down over her bent knee, he followed his progress with nibbling kisses that made the ache inside her almost unbearable. By the time he'd finished with the other stocking, she was molten lava, ready to erupt.

He tossed her stockings on the floor and returned to kiss her fully on the mouth. *Soon,* his kiss seemed to say. *Very soon.* But when she reached for the snap on his jeans, he caught and held her hand.

His ragged breath mingled with hers as he lifted his lips a fraction from hers. "We can't."

Can't? Her dazed mind refused to understand. And her body refused to be denied. She struggled against his restraint.

"I don't...have anything with me." He tightened his grip on her hand.

Her whimper of disappointment gave away her neediness, and she wished she could take that small, vulnerable sound back. She kept her eyes closed, not wanting to look at him when she felt like such a fool. Of course he wouldn't be prepared.

"It's okay." He dropped quick, feverish kisses on her lips. "We can't," he murmured, sliding his hand down to the drenched triangle of silk still covering her, "but you can."

Her eyes flew open and her heart began to pound with a new rhythm.

He gazed down at her and smiled softly as he slipped his hand beneath the material. His voice was husky. "I wouldn't start something I didn't mean to finish."

As his fingers tunneled through her damp curls, seeking her heat, she tried to tell him to stop, that it wasn't fair for only one of them to be satisfied, but for the life of her she couldn't speak. Her whole body seemed to have liquified, and nothing mattered but his touch. There. *There*.

She gasped at the first quiver of release.

"Surrender, Amelia," he whispered, kissing

her throat, her cheeks, her mouth. "Surrender to me."

And surrender she did, giving up everything in one spectacular, cataclysmic moment. She cried out, and he caught the cry against his mouth as he held her tight, absorbing the tremors of her climax. The power of it caught her completely by surprise as wave after wave washed over her, leaving her panting and dazed, but so safe, so warm in the shelter of his arms.

As she sank back against the bed, cocooned in the bliss of completion, she was oblivious to the world. He had to tell her that someone was knocking on the back door and ask her what to do about it.

She gazed up at him with a silly smile on her face. "I have absolutely no idea."

He smiled back. "It could be the security guard."

"Could be."

"Both our cars are parked out there. He'll expect somebody to come to the back door. If we don't…"

She touched his cheek. "Are you trying to protect my reputation?"

"Yeah." His glance was tender. "How about

if I go tell him we're involved in a complicated floor move?''

''I think we're involved in an earth move. At least it did for me.''

He kissed her, his mouth already wonderfully familiar. ''I'm glad.'' Gently untangling himself, he climbed off the bed and tucked in his T-shirt as he headed out the door of the window display.

After he left Amelia's euphoria lasted about two seconds. Then she covered her face with her hands and moaned softly. What had she done? Had she just stolen Leanne's secret admirer? Or would he continue with his campaign and go out with Leanne? Was this just ''one of those things'' that they would both try to forget ever happened?

Except that she would never forget. With shaking hands, she began to dress herself. My God, she'd allowed herself to be undressed and thoroughly fondled in the front window of her store by an employee who might not be interested in a relationship with her and might have been motivated only by the seductive nature of the moment.

Or worse yet, maybe she'd looked so needy that he'd thought he'd better cooperate or risk losing his job. She didn't know if she could face that sort of humiliation. But even if he really was attracted to her, she'd loused up a budding romance between two of her employees and compromised her authority beyond belief.

Terrible as all that was, however, she could live with it, deal with it somehow. All those horrible possibilities were worth facing in exchange for the glory she'd found in Will's arms. But she also had to consider that she might never experience that glory again. She didn't know if she could live with that.

WILL STEPPED OUT onto the loading dock to talk to the security guard and hoped the dim light and cold air would minimize his aroused condition. He could smell Amelia's perfume and knew if anyone came too close they'd figure out he'd recently been very chummy with her. With luck, the wind and rain would take care of that, too, and the security guard wouldn't get suspicious.

If the guard had any doubts about Will's claim that he was helping Amelia with a floor move, he didn't say so. "Just thought I'd check," he said, turning up the collar of his slicker. "Thought I heard a cry for help, and after all, that's my job."

"I'm sure Amelia appreciates your alertness," Will said. "You probably heard her yell when she almost fell off the ladder. Fortunately she caught herself in time." He knew she'd be mortified if she suspected that the guard had heard her cry out in the moment of climax. Will decided not to tell her exactly what had brought the guard to their door.

"I'm glad you're here helping her," the guard said. "I think she works down here by herself too much of the time, and with all those sexy beds she could easily draw the attention of some psycho."

"Good point. I'll tell her." Will made a note to tell her in no uncertain terms that she shouldn't stay down here late at night by herself anymore, and not just because the security guard didn't like it. Will didn't like it.

"Plus, I'm sure the lady's got bucks. Somebody who needs drugs could get ahold of her and force her to write them a big fat check."

"That too." Reality began to descend upon Will. He had no right to tell Amelia not to work late at the store. He was her employee. She was his boss. Now that he wasn't blowing her mind with sexual satisfaction, she was probably starting to remember that fact.

"Guess I'll continue making my rounds," the guard said. "Have a good night."

"Thanks." Will figured he'd had all the good night he was going to have. Now he had to face the consequences of what he'd done. Besides overstepping his boundaries with his boss, he'd also forgotten all about Leanne in the excitement of finally holding Amelia in his arms. Amelia must think he was a real piece of work. For days he'd been dreaming up tempting gifts for Leanne, and he'd already ordered a dozen roses to be delivered to her at the store on Valentine's Day.

But in the meantime he'd grabbed a chance to seduce his boss. Yeah, Amelia must think he was a prince, all right. He couldn't back out of the dinner with Leanne, and he hated the idea that he'd led her on only to let her down. Because he would have to let her down. Whether or not Amelia wanted anything more to do with him, he couldn't pretend an interest in Leanne when his whole being was consumed with thoughts of Amelia.

With a sigh he walked back into the storeroom and closed the door behind him. Then he stood staring at the floor, hands shoved in his pockets, as he tried to figure out what to say to Amelia that wouldn't sound completely lame. He should never have let himself get involved with her while he still had unfinished business with Leanne. He'd really screwed up this time.

AMELIA FINISHED DRESSING and belatedly wondered if she should have sent Will off to investigate alone. She'd never had a problem with a break-in, but San Diego had its share of criminals. Of course, burglars usually didn't knock before breaking in.

Running her fingers through her hair, she ventured out into the showroom. She heard indistinct voices coming from the loading dock and relaxed a little. Will must be out there talking to someone, probably the security guard, just as he'd thought. She edged closer to the door leading into the storeroom. Then she heard the guard leave. Will came back inside and closed the back door.

She stepped into the storeroom, intending to thank him for being so gallant and allowing her to get herself together while he dealt with the guard. The sight of him staring at the floor, shoulders slumped, brought her up short. *Oh,*

God. He regrets everything. Pain hit her midsection. She clutched her stomach and closed her eyes against the onslaught of shattered pride. He was trying to figure out a gentle way to let her down.

Although her insides felt shredded to bits, she straightened her spine and forced brightness into her voice. "And Bedroom Fantasies claims two more victims. I can't believe we allowed that to happen, can you?"

His head came up. For a brief moment he looked uncertain and confused. Then he glanced away, and by the time he turned back to her he wore a mocking grin. "Just shows you what a little atmosphere can do. I guess you'd have to say your Valentine display works."

"Yes, I guess I would." She cleared her throat. "Listen, as far as I'm concerned, this never happened."

He nodded. "Gotcha. I mean, we were both tired, not thinking straight."

"That's so true. You've been stressed with school, and I've had this franchising thing preying on my mind."

"Are you going to New York?"

She tried to detect any hidden meaning in the soft-spoken question. He'd probably be relieved to see her go. "Yes. Yes, I am. And you…will have your date with Leanne in three days."

"That's right."

She hurt so bad she wondered how much longer she'd be able to stand upright. "She's a great gal."

"Yeah." He gazed at her for an agonizingly long time. "I'd better take off."

"Of course. I've kept you long enough." The stock phrase sounded ridiculously impersonal, considering that only moments ago he'd been— no, she mustn't think about that.

"Amelia…"

She held her breath, foolish enough to hope she'd misread his dejected posture just now.

"Do you…want me to quit?"

Hope died. "Don't be silly. We can be adult about this, can't we?"

He studied her for several seconds. "Yes," he said. "See you in the morning."

"In the morning." No doubt he'd leave another gift for Leanne in her center desk drawer. And she would deliver it, no matter how much it hurt, because that's what adults did with obligations they'd agreed to carry out.

He walked over to the door and opened it, letting in the scent of rain.

When he paused and turned back, her heart-beat kicked into high gear again. She was such an eternal optimist. Maybe he'd cross the room and take her in his arms again. Maybe he'd confess that he couldn't live without her. Maybe—

"Please lock this behind me," he said. Then he closed the door with a firm click.

"LOOK OUT, MAN!" Gabe grabbed the wheel of the delivery truck Will was driving and jerked it to the right. The truck swerved back into the right-hand lane, narrowly missing oncoming traffic. "Pull over," Gabe snapped.

Shaking from the near collision, Will did exactly that, swinging into the parking lot of a seafood restaurant. He braked the truck and sat clutching the wheel and taking deep breaths.

"Get out and let me drive," Gabe said.

Without replying Will climbed out of the cab and walked around the front of the truck.

Gabe met him halfway, blocking his path. "What's up with you?"

Will just shook his head and tried to move around Gabe.

"Oh, no, you don't." Gabe held out both arms. He wasn't very tall, but he was muscular, and at the moment he looked determined not to let Will get by until he explained himself.

Will wasn't going to wrestle his way past Gabe. He didn't have the energy. "Nothing's wrong," he muttered.

"The hell it isn't. You've been driving like a zombie all morning. I didn't say anything when you almost backed into that Jaguar, and I didn't mention the stop sign you ignored. I was cutting you some slack, figuring you were low on sleep. But you just about got us killed, and that gives me the right to find out what's eating you."

Will took off his sunglasses and massaged the bridge of his nose. He hadn't had much sleep, but he'd learned to function without it. No, sleep wasn't his problem. He replaced the glasses, using them as a shield as he looked at Gabe. "I'm sorry about the way I've been driving. You're right—I have no business being behind the wheel. If you'll take over, we can still make the delivery to the Hamiltons on time."

"I don't give a rat's ass about being late for that delivery. Something terrible has happened to you. Is it school? Did you flunk out?"

"No. Listen, Gabe, I—"

"Money? I got a few bucks put aside, if you need a little help."

The one thing Will didn't need was this kind of compassion. It only made him weaker. "Thanks, but I'm fine. Can we get on with it?"

Gabe ignored him. "Then it's women. That's the only thing left. I know for a fact that Leanne's looking forward to her dinner date with her secret admirer, so that's not the problem." Gabe stroked his chin. "So it's gotta be the boss lady."

Unconsciously Will stiffened. Once he realized that his body language was giving him away he forced himself to relax, but it was too late.

Gabe nodded. "Uh-huh. I thought as much. I've been watching you for the past few days. In spite of all my excellent advice you've gone and developed a megacrush." He shook his head. "Not very bright, baby doc."

"You're telling me."

"So obviously you don't want to go out with Leanne, considering you're hung up on the boss lady."

"It's a nightmare," Will admitted. "I need to stop this farce now, before Leanne walks into that restaurant to find a guy who has no interest in being there with her because he's…"

"In love with someone else?"

Will's gut wrenched at having the truth laid out so plainly. Yeah, he was in love, for all the good it would do him.

"Your silence speaks volumes, as they say." Gabe stared off into the distance. "Look, I can't take care of your problem with the boss lady. That's up to you to figure out. But I think I can fix things so Leanne won't have to spend her Valentine's Day crying her pretty little eyes out."

Will grabbed at the first hopeful thing he'd encountered recently. "You'll go to the restaurant in my place?"

"Not me. But I think the Troyman might be persuaded."

Will winced at the idea of his personal screw-ups being exposed to Troy. "How much would he have to know?"

"Only that the secret admirer had a change of heart. I'll tell him that the way's clear and he can step right in and be a hero."

"Yeah, but if he's supposed to be the secret admirer, wouldn't I have to describe the gifts and give him copies of the poems I sent along?'' The thought of such a discussion with Troy wasn't the least bit appealing.

"Are you kidding? Leanne's boasted about every gift and read aloud every poem to whoever would listen. Troy's been paying attention. In fact, he took some notes the other day. I figure he plans to steal your material to use on some other woman.''

Will felt the weight on his heart lighten a little. "Then I guess that's the answer.''

"I can probably even get him to pay for the roses you ordered for tomorrow.''

"No, that's okay. I've already paid for them, and it's a small price for being let off the hook. I owe you one, Gabe.''

"Nah. I got you into this, so I feel responsible for getting you out. But are you sure, now? Really sure? Because you're throwing away a great chance with Leanne, and she just might make you forget this other insanity of yours.''

"You know, Gabe, if I thought she could, I would be the happiest guy alive. But I know there's not a chance in hell of that happening.''

Gabe stared at him. "You got it bad, boy.''

Will didn't need Gabe to give him that particular news flash. It had been running through his brain relentlessly ever since he'd left Amelia at the store that night. He'd thought of little else. As for Amelia, she showed no sign of strain. She'd greeted him the next day with a cool, impersonal smile. As near as he could tell, she'd put the whole thing completely out of her mind.

Chapter Eight

AMELIA WAS UNLUCKY enough to be in the showroom helping a customer on Valentine's Day morning when the bouquet of red roses was delivered to Leanne, so she couldn't avoid the spectacle of Leanne's response. No one in the store could avoid it, in fact.

"Oh, I'm in *love!*" Leanne waltzed through the displays holding her vase of roses like a dance partner. "My secret admirer has such wonderful taste." She giggled. "But of course he does. He picked *me*."

The woman Amelia was helping smiled benevolently at Leanne. "How sweet. A secret admirer. That's such a romantic idea."

"Isn't it?" Amelia gritted her teeth. "Now, Mrs. Delaney, you understand that the Jungle Fever bedroom grouping is on a six-month lease. If, after that time, you decide to switch themes, then—"

"Troy, read this note," Leanne said, excitement raising the pitch of her voice until it carried throughout the store. "He's asked me to be his Minnie. Can you believe it? He really knows what I like."

Amelia thought she might throw up. *His Minnie?* How could he? Especially after...but that night had meant nothing to him, obviously. Fool that she was, she'd kept hope alive by imagining that he'd reveal himself to Leanne and tell her it was all a mistake, that he'd started the secret admirer campaign before he realized his strong attraction to Amelia.

The arrival of the roses had pretty much killed that hope. Will obviously planned to go through with the dinner, and with whatever might happen after dinner. Amelia wanted to scream.

Mrs. Delaney touched her arm. "Excuse me. Is there a problem with my contract?"

"What?" Amelia glanced at the woman and realized she'd forgotten all about her. "No, no problem. Sorry. I was distracted there for a minute."

"I just wondered. You looked rather... upset."

"Just a touch of indigestion," Amelia said. "Now, let me make sure we've gone over everything." It had been a banner day for sales, she reminded herself. Holidays were usually great for business, and Valentine's Day, catering as it did to couples, was a natural for the store. Peterson seemed impressed with the holiday surge and would probably open the Fifth Avenue franchise even if she refused to encourage a personal relationship.

She needed to focus on what was going right in her world. Unfortunately, the one part going wrong seemed to blot out everything else.

Mrs. Delaney offered to pay extra to have the bedroom suite delivered that afternoon as a Valentine surprise for her husband, so Amelia excused herself and went back to the storeroom to find out if Will could work the extra delivery into the schedule. She caught him just as he and Gabe loaded the last piece on the truck for an order that was due out on Coronado Island by noon. As usual he looked like a California god dressed in his snug T-shirt and worn jeans, his sunglasses on a cord around his neck. Thank heaven she would soon be going to New York and wouldn't have to torture herself this way much longer.

She decided it was safer and less personal to direct her statement to both of them. "I can offer you guys a bonus if you can work a delivery and setup of Jungle Fever into your schedule this afternoon.''

Will leaned one hand against the side of the truck and wiped his forehead on his sleeve. "Where does it go?''

"Pacific Beach.''

Will glanced at Gabe. "Are you up for that?''

"I can always use the extra money, but I gotta be finished by six. I don't want to be late to Gina's.''

"I think we can work it all in,'' Will said. "I don't want to be late tonight, either.''

Because he had to hotfoot it over to the restaurant to meet Leanne, Amelia thought bitterly. "Shall I tell the customer we can do it, then?'' she asked.

"Sure.'' Will put on his sunglasses and gave her a brief smile. "Wouldn't want to disappoint someone on Valentine's Day.''

She stared at him. Was he really that callous, that he'd throw his date with Leanne in her face? And to think she'd imagined he was sweet and sensitive. She lifted her chin. "No, we certainly wouldn't.'' Fighting tears, she turned and walked quickly out of the storeroom and straight to her office.

In the doorway she stopped, her mouth dropping open at the stunning bouquet of flowers sitting in the middle of her desk. Whoever had sent them hadn't been satisfied with traditional red roses as a Valentine's Day tribute. Someone had decided that the occasion demanded orchids.

Amelia had a bad feeling that Peterson had done this. She'd thought she'd made herself clear, but a man like Peterson might enjoy the challenge of trying to change her mind. He certainly had the money to spend on orchids.

Breathing in the delicate scent of the flowers, she pulled an envelope from its plastic holder and read the name written there to make sure the bouquet was for her. No use getting excited if an overburdened florist had made a mistake today.

But there was no mistake. The flowers were in the right place. She had to admit the gesture was classy, but there was no way she'd ever be interested in Jonathan Peterson. Only one man claimed a place in her heart, and he was completely out of reach. She glanced at the card, fully expecting Peterson's name to be at the bottom. It wasn't.

As orchids seek the fire of the sun, so I must seek the fire in your eyes, my love. Watch for me tonight.

Your Secret Admirer

Amelia crumpled the card and held it to her chest. Peterson couldn't know how impossibly cruel his note was. No doubt Leanne had told him, along with half the free world, about her secret admirer. He probably thought it would be cute to try the same thing with her, not realizing that for her the term *Secret Admirer* conjured up a picture of the one man she was trying to forget.

She tossed the card and envelope in her wastebasket. Peterson could show up at the store tonight if he chose to do so. She couldn't very well prevent him from doing that. His approach had been imaginative and the wording of his message quite beautiful—she was somewhat surprised that he'd managed to be so poetic. But all the orchids and poetic phrases in the world wouldn't change the fact that he left her cold.

IT HAD BEEN THE MOST successful Valentine's Day promotion in the history of Bedroom Fantasies, Amelia noted as she tallied up the receipts after everyone else had left. She turned off her computer and glanced at her bouquet of orchids. To her surprise, Peterson hadn't come to the store, after all. She'd never invited him to her condo, but he had the address, so maybe he imagined he'd show up and be asked to come in. If so he was going to be disappointed.

She took the orchids home with her. They'd caused quite a bit of comment during the day, and everyone had agreed with her that Peterson was the likely candidate. Leanne had even said that she was sure he'd thought of it because of all the talk about her secret admirer.

Amelia knew Leanne didn't have a malicious bone in her body and hadn't meant to imply that Amelia's admirer was a copycat with no imagination. All the same, the comment rankled. Probably anything Leanne said would have rankled, considering that she was about to spend the evening with Will. Amelia would spend the evening alone—at least once she got rid of Peterson.

The orchids looked fantastic on her coffee table, almost as if Peterson had seen the color scheme of her living room and chosen them for that reason. Lucky guess on his part, she thought. And no matter how thrilled she was with the bouquet, he still wouldn't be invited in. After the incident in the storeroom she avoided being alone with him.

If he was offended and withdrew his franchise offer, she could live with that. Lately the thought of going to New York had only been appealing because she'd escape seeing Leanne and Will as a couple. In fact, her usual interest in promoting her business seemed to have waned considerably.

She longed to change into the soft terry loungewear she'd bought herself not long ago, but she didn't dare when Peterson might show up any minute. So she settled for taking off her suit jacket and her shoes, and pouring herself half a glass of chardonnay.

"Happy Valentine's Day, kid," she toasted herself as she stood in her living room admiring the orchids. "You're one hell of a businesswoman, and you even have orchids from a secret admirer." The usual congratulations she gave herself after a banner day of sales comforted her not a lick, and the orchids gave her little pleasure because they'd come from the wrong man. Her thoughts went inevitably to

Will, and what he might be doing with Leanne at this very moment.

Amelia stared into the pale liquid in her glass and admitted to herself that she'd give every dime she'd made from Bedroom Fantasies if she could trade places with Leanne tonight. Her precious business that she'd nurtured so carefully over the years meant nothing if she couldn't have the man she loved.

And she loved him. Once she'd thought of her feelings as a crush, a passing episode of lust. But this was more than a mere physical craving. She could find physical satisfaction elsewhere, but there was only one Will, and without the prospect of having him in her life, all that she'd worked for seemed meaningless.

She finished her half glass of wine and stood there wondering if she dared have any more. She'd need to be clearheaded when Peterson came to her door to take credit for his orchids. She ought to fix herself something to eat, but she wasn't the least bit hungry. As she weighed her options, the doorbell chimed.

Here we go. Amelia grimaced. Sliding her feet into her shoes, she set her wineglass on the coffee table next to the bouquet of orchids. She refused to feel guilty about the flowers. Peterson could probably write them off as a business expense. He probably had some secretary in New York make up that phrase about orchids seeking the fire of the sun, considering that he didn't strike her as a wordsmith. Preparing herself for the sight of Peterson looking smug, she gazed through the peephole in her door.

At first she thought she was hallucinating. Desire had driven her crazy enough to think she was seeing the man she wanted standing outside her condo. She blinked and looked again. His sport coat, navy slacks and open-necked dress shirt added to her disorientation. She'd never seen him dressed like that.

Her heartbeat picked up speed as she finally acknowledged that Will was not a figment of her imagination. Had his date with Leanne gone wrong? She hardly dared hope such a thing. Maybe Leanne was waiting out in the car while Will came to the door to ask if they could both have tomorrow off. She braced herself for yet another round of blows to her heart as she unlocked the door.

Hands shoved in his slacks pockets, he gazed at her without speaking for several seconds.

She swallowed. They hadn't faced each other

alone since the incident in the display window. "Is…something wrong?"

"No." He sounded a little hoarse. "May I come in?"

She forced herself to be gracious. "Is Leanne out in the car? She's welcome to come in, too. I was just having some wine, if either of you would like a glass."

He looked confused. "Leanne?" Then his expression cleared. "No, she's not out in the car."

"Where is she, then?"

He glanced at his watch. "She might still be at the restaurant with Troy. Depends on whether they decided to have dessert."

Amelia stared at him. He was making no sense. Finally she stepped back from the door. "I guess you'd better come in and explain what's going on. I seem to have lost my place in this story. Why is Troy at the restaurant with Leanne?"

Will didn't answer her question as he walked past her. Instead he glanced at the orchids. "Nice flowers."

"They're from Peterson. I thought you were him, as a matter of fact. Now why on earth did you include Troy in your dinner?" She was still prepared for Will to ask her for tomorrow off. Maybe at the last minute he'd taken pity on Troy's dateless situation and invited him to tag along to the restaurant, although that seemed like a truly bizarre thing to do when this was the night Will was unveiling himself as Leanne's secret admirer.

"Is that offer of wine still good?" he asked.

She was totally confused. "Uh, sure. I'll...get you a glass." As she hurried toward the kitchen she tried to imagine why he would sit here with her and drink wine, leaving Troy and Leanne at the restaurant. Maybe...but she dared not speculate. Her heart was too fragile to take another roller coaster ride.

When she returned with the chilled bottle and a second glass, she found him seated on the couch. He leaned forward to stroke one finger over an orchid petal. Desire slammed into her as she remembered the pleasure of his touch on her heated skin. She gripped the cold wine bottle and pushed the memory away.

"So these are from Peterson?" he asked.

"I'm afraid so." She sat on the couch but put a decent distance between them. He wouldn't catch her giving him that needy look ever again. "I've tried to let him know I'm not interested in a personal relationship, but I doubt he's used to taking no for an answer.'' She poured a glass of wine for each of them and handed him his glass.

He took it and raised it in her direction. His dark gaze held hers. ''Here's to those who seek the fire.''

The glass slipped from her fingers and bounced on the carpet, splashing wine over her legs and Will's slacks. She opened her mouth, but nothing came out. There was a roaring in her ears and she began to tremble.

Will paid no attention to the spilled wine as he continued to look deep into her eyes. Slowly he put his glass on the table, but he made no move to touch her. ''So there it is,'' he said softly. ''Troy's taking my place tonight because I couldn't go. Not after what we…'' He paused and took a shaky breath. ''What happened between us was more than just a chance encounter for me, Amelia. I can't pretend otherwise. If that's all it was for you, then I'll walk out of here and you'll never have to trouble yourself about me again.''

She shook her head violently, but her vocal cords still refused to work. She felt as if she'd just emerged from a dark cave into blinding light, and she was so dazzled that she couldn't comprehend where she was. *Will had sent the orchids.*

"Obviously I've made you speechless with this little revelation." He smiled faintly. "I wish I could tell if you're speechless with happiness or horror."

That tiny smile of his wrenched her heart, but she didn't realize she was crying until he leaned over and brushed his thumb across her cheek.

"Hey," he murmured. "Don't—"

With a moan, she flung herself into his arms and began kissing his mouth, his cheeks, his nose.

"Oh, God." He grabbed her face in both hands and held her still so that he could capture her mouth with his. His kiss tasted of longing and triumph. Still kissing her, he slipped one arm around her shoulders and the other under her knees before he stood upright, bringing her with him.

She knew exactly what he had in mind as he carried her back to her bedroom. Joy rushed through her. He would be the first and only man to make love to her in the bed that was her ultimate fantasy, the bed she'd designed, unconsciously, for this moment of surrender to the man she would love for the rest of her life.

WILL WONDERED WHEN he would wake up. Any minute now the warm, sensual woman in his arms would disappear, along with the ivory and silver bed where they lay. The rapid sound of her breathing would be replaced by the buzz of his alarm clock and he'd roll over and realize he was late for class.

But, by God, until that happened, he was going to enjoy himself. He would caress her in ways that turned the light in her eyes into a blaze of desire, and then he'd taste and nibble his way over her body until she moaned with pleasure. For the space of this dream she was his—her silken skin glistening with the dew of passion, her touch as eager as his.

She abandoned herself completely to him, becoming his fantasy woman filled with unrestrained passion. No shyness, no barriers stood between them as he pushed the boundaries and found her to be his willing partner in anything he asked. The possibilities were endless, and he wanted to try them all, but finally she begged him for that final joining. As she pleaded, the white-hot need to sink deep into her quickly blotted out everything else.

As he rose above her, he decided to risk everything. He might as well make this dream perfect in every way. He gazed into her eyes. "I love you," he said. "Marry me. Have children with me."

"Yes." Her smile trembled and her eyes filled with tears. "Yes."

Perfect. He pushed deep, expecting that moment to be the trigger that would jolt him awake. Instead he gasped at the intensity of the connection. He looked into her eyes and saw the same shock of recognition, as if she, too, had found what she'd been seeking all her life.

"I love you, Will," she whispered. "I'll always love you."

Dazed by the force of what he was experiencing, he stayed locked against her for a moment. Then he drew back and slid home again, finding the same sense of completion. And again, and again, as she rose to meet him and held his gaze captive.

He saw her climax building in her eyes, felt his own match her rhythm. As if their bodies vibrated with the same frequency, her shock waves sent him over the edge, and through it all they held each other's gaze…and drank of each other's soul.

Slowly the trembling stopped, yet Will couldn't look away. "I'm dreaming this," he murmured.

"No. It's real."

He shook his head. "I know a dream when I see one. I have to say this is the best so far, but it fits right into the pattern of my dreams about you, so I'm sure it's not real."

Her mouth curved into a smile. "You've been dreaming about making love to me in this bed?"

"Ever since I saw it. And now I'm going to wake up, and—ow! You pinched my—"

She chuckled. "Now do you believe you're awake?"

He stared at her in disbelief. "No! Amelia, you just said you'd marry me!"

"Which I absolutely intend to do."

"Look, this can't be real."

"Want another pinch?"

He reached behind him and grabbed her hand. "No, thanks." He brought her hand to his mouth and kissed her fingers. "Amelia…I'm a poor college student, and you're a rich businesswoman, and you're going to New York, and—"

"I'm not going to New York. I have a wedding to plan. And lots more love to make."

"Now wait a minute. You have a chance at a very important franchise on Fifth Avenue. You can't give that up just because of me."

"Now you wait a minute." She pulled free of his grip and cradled his face in both hands. "You're the first person to notice that this business is a walking advertisement for the kind of person I am, deep inside. It may look as if all I care about is the bottom line, but in reality, all I care about is finding a man to love, a man who will share my fantasies. I don't give a damn about a franchise on Fifth Avenue. It was only a substitute until you came along."

"But you're throwing away—"

"Nothing. Unless you didn't mean it when you asked me to marry you." Her eyes clouded. "After all, you were operating under the assumption this was all a dream."

The words came easily, as if he'd learned them before he was born. "My dream is to spend the rest of my life with you."

Her lower lip trembled and she sniffed. "Oh,

Will. I want to spend mine with you, too. Now kiss me.''

His voice grew husky as he leaned down, his lips close to hers. ''I love you.''

''And I love you. We're going to have a wonderful time, Will.''

He brushed his lips over hers, still hardly believing that he'd be allowed to do that until they were old and gray. ''Do you...think I should resign?''

''Resign?'' She traced his lower lip with her tongue. ''Just when I'll finally be able to stroll back to the storeroom and ogle your buns with a clear conscience? I think not.''

He smiled. ''Does it work both ways? Because I have some ogling to catch up on, myself.''

''Really?''

''Really.'' He leaned down and nibbled her earlobe, breathing in her perfume as desire stirred in him again. ''In fact, I was just wondering what grouping you're planning to use in the display window, now that Valentine's Day is over.''

''I thought I'd use that new collection that just came in, Erotic Egypt.'' She paused as the meaning of his question finally occurred to her.

"Would you like to help me arrange it some evening this week?"

He lifted his head and looked into her eyes. "I'm your man."

She smiled and drew him down to her waiting mouth. "I like the sound of that."

Special Deliveries
Marisa Carroll

Dear Reader,

For young lovers, Valentine's Day has always been the most romantic day of the year. But we can remember what a special holiday it was for two little girls growing up in Ohio. In our part of the country, February is a gray, bleak month, and the excitement of decorating shoe boxes with red and white and pink crepe paper, and buying valentines for all our classmates, made the cold winter days go a little faster.

Like our nine-year-old character, Dani Jensen, we would spend hours choosing just the right cards for each of our classmates—the prettiest ones for special friends, and the ugliest ones for yucky boys! And then, a few years later, choices reversed, and a boy might rate one of the nicer cards. Soon we realized that Valentine's Day was about romance, and the same realization strikes Dani and her little sister, Kara. Dani knows that sometimes romance needs a push. She knows her dad must have thought Christy Herter was special all those years ago, and she has a plan....

We hope you enjoy Dani's and Kara's attempts to bring romance into their lonely father's life as much as we enjoyed writing about them.

Happy Valentine's Day,

Marisa Carroll

Chapter One

CHRISTY HERTER SMILED at her guests. "Welcome to Rosewood House, my dears," she said, in her best imitation of a gracious Victorian hostess. "Come right this way. You can leave your things in the Blue Bedroom, and then we'll find you all something very special to wear." She made a stiff little curtsy, necessitated by the corset she was wearing beneath her high-collared lace dress, and flicked open the painted ivory fan she'd been practicing with for an hour. The half dozen eight- and nine-year-old girls all giggled nervously as they trailed her through the dining room, the hard soles of their shoes tap-tap-tapping on the parquet floors. Under their multicolored parkas and knitted caps they were wearing everyday clothes, sweatshirts and jeans, but they'd worn party shoes for the special event.

Christy's Aunt Sarah hosted Victorian tea parties in her century-old home in Otsego Rapids, Ohio, and Christy, on leave of absence from her job in an Atlanta hospital emergency room, had volunteered to come home and run the Rosewood Tearoom while her aunt was in Costa Rica doing six weeks of missionary work for her church.

"You may each choose the dress you wish," Christy said, throwing open the doors of the big walnut armoire. The theatrical flourish revealed a dozen formal dresses in a rainbow of colors, and was greeted with an assortment of *oohs* and *ahhs*. This was the third little girls' birthday tea party she'd hosted in the past ten days. She was starting to get the hang of it. Little girls' parties involved dressing up. Grown-up ladies' tea parties did not, although Christy was fast learning that some of her older guests would have liked to dress the part of Victorian ladies, as well.

"When you've found the perfect dress, you may choose a hat and gloves and jewelry to go with it. They're over here." She moved across the room to a smaller armoire that was filled with sliding shelves of vintage hats and drawers of pearl ropes and glittering faux gems, brooches of every shape and size, white gloves, and long dangling earrings to put the finishing touches on the tea ensembles.

The girls remained where they were standing

by the bed, suddenly too shy to come forward—especially the birthday girl, eight-year-old Mandy Peterson.

"Go on, Mandy. It'll be fun," her camera-wielding mother and grandmother urged from the doorway.

Christy held out her hand. "Come, Mandy. You choose first. It's your birthday."

"Hurry, Mandy. Choose." The words were accompanied by a little push from the tallest of Mandy's birthday guests, a willowy girl with short, sleek hair the color of wheat and sunshine, a breathtaking smile, and mink brown eyes with a glint of pure devilry sparkling in their depths.

Danielle Jensen, Del's daughter, who might have been Christy's daughter, too, if things had turned out differently ten years ago.

"Yes, Mandy. Pick one. I see just the dress I want," another girl urged.

"Blue," the littlest of the girls piped up. "I want a blue one." Kara Jensen, Dani's sister, was not quite seven, younger than the other guests. Her hair was longer and lighter in color, almost silvery in the light of a dull February afternoon, and her eyes were blue like the Ohio sky on a midsummer's day. But the mischief that sparkled within those blue eyes matched Dani's to a T.

"Pink," Mandy said shyly, pointing to one of the dresses. "I want a pink one." Christy took the dress from the armoire and, with another flourish, spread the organdy skirts across the blue Dahlia quilt on the canopy bed that gave the room its name. "This one, my lady?"

"Yes," Mandy giggled. "That one." Pink lace and organdy, it had been someone's prom dress five years earlier. Now shortened and altered in the bust line, with adjustable pull-apart fastenings instead of a zipper down the back, it would fit almost any little girl, transforming her, for the next two hours, into a Victorian young lady at high tea.

"Take off your coat and hat," Christy instructed while she went to one of the deep low drawers of the armoire and produced a pile of silky shifts for the girls to wear under the dresses. "Then come behind the screen and I'll help you put it on."

Mandy, already out of her coat and hat, stepped behind the chintz screen and pulled her sweatshirt over her head. "When all the girls have their dresses on, you may take pictures. And, of course, a formal portrait is included with the tea party,'' Christy said, smiling at Mandy's mother.

''I've got the camera right here.'' Mandy's mother hurried to the armoire to help Mandy choose a hat, while Christy took the next little girl and her choice of aqua satin behind the screen.

''Which dress do you want, Dani?'' Christy asked fifteen minutes later. All the other little girls, including Kara, had made their choices, and were busy admiring themselves in front of the peer glass in the corner of the room by the big window.

Kara came to stand by her sister, carefully gathering the skirts of her robin's-egg blue satin gown in one gloved hand. ''Dani likes green, like that one.'' She pointed to an emerald green sheath with a matching jacket, once a mother-of-the-bride dress, Christy guessed, sleek and unadorned, and not very popular with the little girls, at least the ones that had attended the parties Christy had hosted so far.

''Yes, green. But no ruffles or lace,'' Dani said, her lip curling into a sneer. ''I'm not into that kind of stuff.''

''Then let's try this one.'' Christy took the mother-of-the-bride dress out of the armoire and led Dani behind the screen. The little girl took off her sweater and stepped out of her jeans. Christy raised the dress over Dani's head and let it slide down over her nonexistent hips. Then she held the lace jacket and Dani slipped her arms into the sleeves. She was as skinny as a beanpole, as skinny as Del had been as a boy.

Christy tried not to think about Del Jensen. She hadn't seen him in over ten years, not even a glimpse of him in the grocery store or at the post office in the two weeks she'd been back in Otsego Rapids. And that's the way she wanted it to remain. Del Jensen had broken her heart ten years ago and she guessed, when you came right down to it, the child now standing before her had been the reason.

They went to the smaller armoire and Dani picked a hat, a twenties flapper hat of green velvet, with a tall, nodding feather. Then she took out a long rope of pearls and let Christy loop them around her neck two times. She put on the gloves Christy handed her and turned to the big mirror to have a look.

The little frown of concentration Dani had been wearing smoothed away. "Yes. This is just what I wanted. Not too girly, but pretty. Very pretty."

Christy smiled, she couldn't help herself. She had been like Dani at that age, a tomboy, an athlete, contemptuous of all things "girly," at least most of the time. "I'm glad you like it." She caught Dani's eye in the mirror and Dani smiled back.

Del's smile.

Christy watched her own smile fade and she turned away.

"You're a nurse, aren't you? I mean when you aren't living here in Otsego Rapids," Dani asked.

"How did you know that?"

"Your Aunt Sarah told me. I like her. Sometimes she lets me help her in her garden. We live just two blocks away. On Maple Street, past the school."

In Del's grandmother's Craftsman bungalow, if their address was Maple Street. She might not have stepped foot in Otsego Rapids for ten years but she still knew her way around.

"You're right. I'm a nurse in a big hospital in Atlanta, Georgia. I take care of people in the emergency room."

"But you're staying here while your Aunt Sarah is in Costa Rica to keep the tearoom open. Your Aunt Sarah told my Grandma Patty that you needed a rest.''

Christy hesitated. ''I...I needed some time away from my job.'' That wasn't true; she loved her work. What she'd needed time away from was the unsettling events that had occurred while she was a member of a jury hearing the trial of three gang leaders accused of dealing drugs and selling guns to minors. One of the defendant's brothers had tried to intimidate several jurors with obscene phone calls and threatening letters before he was caught and arrested. Christy had been one of those harassed. It had been a frightening experience.

''You know my dad, don't you?'' Dani asked her suddenly.

''Yes. I do.'' Christy stopped thinking about the trial. Had Del told his children about her? It hardly seemed likely. Their high-school romance had been a long time ago, a lifetime ago for Dani.

''I saw a picture of you with him in *The Warrior*,'' she said, smoothing her rope of pearls with her gloved hand. ''At a dance. A Valentine's dance.'' *The Warrior* was the Otsego High yearbook. Christy had that yearbook, too, stored away at her parents' place in Florida.

"Your dad took me to the Valentine Ball. But that was a long, long time ago. Before you were born."

"1989. A long time ago," Dani agreed. "Your dress was pretty. No ruffles. No bows."

It had been a beautiful dress. Black satin with an organdy skirt that floated around her like a dream. Del had worn a tux with a red cummerbund. He had given her a corsage of red roses.

Christy managed a smile. Nothing of what had happened that long-ago Valentine's Day was Dani's fault. "It was a very pretty dress." She turned away, still smiling. "It's time for tea, ladies. Please, won't you join me in the dining room?"

The girls giggled some more at being addressed as ladies, but fell into the spirit of the party and followed her out of the bedroom, noses in the air, skirts held daintily in their hands, across the hallway into the dining room. The big, high-ceilinged room was cozy with the warmth of the fire that burned in the small marble fireplace. The brass and crystal chandelier glowed softly overhead.

Each of the girls had a name card at her chair. Christy brought cushions for Kara and Lindsay Trainor, the two smallest, so that they could see over the edge of the big mahogany table, gestured Mandy's mother and grandmother to seats in the wingback chairs before the fireplace, then took her own place at the head of the table.

She picked up the small silver bell beside her plate and rang it. Hilda Westhoven, her aunt's friend who baked all the wonderful cakes and cookies they served and helped with the cleanup after parties to augment her Social Security checks, backed through the swinging doors from the kitchen carrying Sarah's heirloom antique silver tea service. In summer when the tourists descended on Otsego Rapids in larger numbers Sarah had three more helpers, but during the slack time of January and February there was only Hilda.

She was wearing a long black dress with a white apron and a matching cap set on her short gray curls, in keeping with the turn-of-the-century atmosphere of Rosewood House. Christy knew for a fact though, that she *was* wearing Nikes beneath the long skirts. She set the big pot in front of Christy and leaned close. "A water pipe in the utility room has sprung a leak. There's water everywhere," she whispered.

"Oh no," Christy whispered back. "See

what you can do. I'll be there as soon as I can.''
But it was over half an hour before she could
excuse herself from her guests. They ate their
fill of tea cakes and drank their sweetened raspberry tea. Christy sipped and smiled and told
them stories of what it would have been like to
be a little girl in this house a hundred years ago,
while all the time her mind was fixed on the
flood in her aunt's utility room. She posed
Mandy and her friends around a huge wicker
chair with a backdrop of ferns and velvet draperies for their portrait, and then turned the party
over to Mandy's mother while the birthday girl
opened her gifts in the formal sitting room at
the front of the house.

Then and only then did Christy excuse herself and hurry into the kitchen. It was a big
room and thoroughly modern, although the
cherry cabinets, the pegged oak flooring and
cheery flowered wallpaper had been chosen to
complement the character of the century-old
house.

She stuck her head into the utility room, a
windowless cubbyhole that had once been a
scullery and pantry. Now it housed the behe-
moth-like old hot water furnace, an industrial-
sized water heater, her aunt's state-of-the-art

washer and dryer, and shelf upon shelf of old canning jars and mismatched china that hadn't been used in years. The air was warm and redolent with the smell of wet wood. Hilda had mopped up the water and tied a towel around the broken pipe, but water was still dripping steadily onto the floor.

"We need a plumber. Now," Hilda said, mop in hand.

"Who do you recommend?" Christy held the long skirts of her vintage gown carefully out of the way. Sarah, so conscientious about everything else, hadn't left instructions on what to do if the plumbing went bad.

"The Christman boys are good. And, of course, there's Dick Allen at the hardware. But with this cold snap we've been having, I imagine they're all still really busy." Otsego Rapids was a small town. Their choices were definitely limited. Hilda took another swipe with the mop at the steadily advancing stream of water. "Lots of people got busted pipes when the temperature hit ten below the other night. Been keeping people real busy."

"My dad is a good plumber." Christy whirled around at the sound of Dani Jensen's voice.

"Dani, you should be with your friends watching Mandy open her gifts."

"I heard what Mrs. Westhoven told you at the table. About the broken pipes. My dad can fix it."

"Your father's an accountant." Her mother had told her so. Frances Herter had read that Del Jensen had passed his Certified Public Accountant exam in the *Otsego Flag,* and passed the news along to Christy when she had visited last spring.

"He's a plumber, too, and a fireman," Dani said with pride, smiling her gamine smile. "He says you have to be a jack-of-all-trades to make a decent living in Otsego Rapids. Do you want me to call him? I bet he can come over right away."

Chapter Two

"JENSEN ACCOUNTING SERVICES. Del Jensen speaking."

Del tucked the phone receiver between his ear and his shoulder and stared at the jumble of credit card receipts, Medicare forms and check stubs that Virginia Amos had dropped off last week. The elderly widow had made sure he earned his fee for doing her taxes this year. She hadn't kept track of a thing, just stuck all her business papers in a shoe box and delivered it to his office on her way to Florida. "I'll be back to pick it up April 14th," she said. "I'm not sending those crooks in Washington my hard-earned money a day before I have to."

"Del. Hi. It's Christy. Christy Herter."

Christy. He had wondered if their paths would cross while she was visiting in Otsego Rapids. The odds were good, of course, It was a small town, after all, but for almost two weeks she'd managed to stay out of his way.

"Hi, Christy." He cleared his throat. She'd

caught him off guard. He was prepared for small talk in the post office, or the grocery store. But he hadn't expected her to call him. "It's good to hear from you. What can I do for you?"

He waited, Virginia Amos's lackadaisical tax records forgotten, as Christy's voice, warm and rich with a maturity that hadn't been there when she was seventeen, stirred memories he'd buried so deeply he'd thought surely they were dead. Christy, with the auburn hair and hazel eyes, as warm and sweet and caring as her voice. Ten years ago, when they were both high-school seniors, he'd been falling in love with Christy Herter, and that heady and incredible state of affairs had lasted exactly six weeks, until he'd learned his old girlfriend was pregnant with his child.

"What can I do for you, Christy?" he repeated. "I hope Dani and Kara aren't misbehaving at Mandy's party." He didn't think that was likely. They'd both wanted to go to the birthday tea party very badly, and they were good kids, but being a parent had taught him always to expect the unexpected.

"Oh, no. It's nothing like that. Dani and Kara have both been fine, enjoying themselves.

They're adorable, Del,'' Christy said, her voice softening a little. ''It's…well,'' she laughed, and there was a hint of nervousness underlying the melodious sound. ''Actually, I'm calling on Dani's recommendation. I need a plumber. Badly.''

''A plumber?'' How had she known he was a plumber? Or used to be until he passed his CPA exam and got his accounting business up and running. And then he realized just how badly he'd been thrown off balance by her call. She knew he was a plumber because his daughter had told her.

''Yes. I've sprung a leak. At least Aunt Sarah's pipes have, and to be honest I haven't the slightest idea where the shutoff valve for the water is. Could you…would you mind helping me out? I wouldn't ask, but I'm afraid the water is going to get into the kitchen and ruin the floor.''

''I'll come over and see what I can do. It will save Mandy's mother having to drop the girls off after the party.'' They had to see each other sooner or later. It might as well be in the privacy of Rosewood House instead of in the middle of the produce aisle at Ron's SuperValue, or at the Volunteer Fireman's Pancake Break-

fast at the fire station Sunday morning, with half
the town looking on. "I'll be there in ten
minutes. In the meantime why don't you tie a
towel or an old rag around the pipe. That'll help
soak up the water."

"We've already done that. I know this is an
imposition—"

"No problem. I'm on my way." He hung up
the phone and sat staring at the wall.

Christy. He wondered what she looked like
after all these years. Was she still the prettiest
girl in the senior class? She wasn't married, he
knew that much from hearing about her from
his mother who still exchanged Christmas cards
with her parents. She was a nurse. She lived in
Atlanta. She hadn't set foot in Otsego Rapids
since the day she'd left for college, a few weeks
before Dani's birth, a month before he'd left
town to join the army.

Five years ago he'd come back to Otsego
Rapids to raise his children when his marriage
failed and his hitch was up. It had taken a long
time for Christy to return. He didn't have to
wonder why.

Del pushed his chair away from his desk and
stood up.

Dwelling on what had happened between

them ten years ago would only make their reunion that much more awkward. He vowed to
put it out of his mind, but it wasn't easy. Memories of Christy Herter had been insinuating
themselves into his thought processes off and
on for the past two weeks, and once or twice,
they'd even managed to sneak into his dreams.

THE TEA PARTY WAS BREAKING UP. All of
Mandy's gifts had been loaded into her
mother's van. Her Victorian young ladies had
changed out of their dress-up clothes, leaving
the past behind, turning back into modern children, talking more loudly, laughing more easily.
They put on their hats and parkas and said their
goodbyes as Christy stood in the doorway, waving and shivering in the cold.

She had forgotten how cold and damp northern Ohio winters could be. There were six
inches of snow on the ground and more in the
forecast. The temperature was supposed to dip
below zero every night this week. She was
lucky she only had a water leak to contend with,
and not frozen pipes.

Christy went back inside and headed straight
for the warmth of the gas logs burning on the
grate. Kara and Dani were sitting in matching

recliners in front of the fireplace in the small back parlor that was Aunt Sarah's favorite room. The little girls looked up at her expectantly. "Is my dad here yet?" Kara asked.

"He said he would come right over."

"Good. I don't want to miss *Rugrats* on *Nickelodeon*. Does your Aunt Sarah have cable?" Kara was round-cheeked, button-nosed and looked a lot like her mother. Christy and Ashley Walters had been friends in grade school but drifted into different circles in high school. Christy had been good at science and history and loved athletics. She was a jock. Ashley had taken business courses, played lead flute in the band and been a cheerleader and a member of the drill team. Christy's path and Ashley's seldom crossed. They had nothing in common until she started dating Del a few weeks after Del and Ashley broke up. Their romance had lasted six weeks, until Christy, until the whole town, learned Ashley was carrying Del's baby.

Kara was waiting for her answer, uninterested in Christy's memories of the past. "No, I'm afraid she doesn't have cable. Aunt Sarah doesn't like to watch television much."

"She likes to read books," Dani offered. "She told me so. So do I."

Christy smiled at Del's oldest daughter. "So do I." And so had Del. He was always reading a book. She wondered what he looked like now. His voice had sounded different on the phone, lower, deeper, a man's voice, not a boy's.

Kara looked pained as she slouched back in the chair, swinging her short legs. "I like TV best. I hope it doesn't take long to fix your broken pipe."

"I hope so, too. If you'll excuse me, I'm going to change out of this dress. Your father might need my help, and I don't want anything to happen to it." The tea gown was pale gray lace with an underdress of darker gray satin, and was too old and fragile to risk getting wet or stained.

"Yes, it's too pretty to spoil," Kara agreed.

Dani nodded wisely. "It's old enough to be an antique, isn't it? You have to be careful with antiques. Grandma has some. Dishes and stuff. She's always telling us to be careful around them."

"Yes, it's very old. And very fragile. I'm always worried I'll tear—" The doorbell jingled. It was an antique, too, a brass knob that was set in the middle of the front door and turned by hand.

Dani bounced up from her chair. "That's probably my dad."

"Then I think we'd better let him in."

"WHAT ARE YOU TWO whispering about?" Dani and Kara had been huddled together on the couch leafing through Del's old high-school yearbook since they'd returned home from fixing Christy's broken water pipe.

"Daddy, did you and Christy love each other?"

Del looked up from the newspaper. "No," he said, almost truthfully. "We were not in love."

"You look like you're in love in this picture." Dani held up his copy of the *Warrior*. His girls loved to look through his old yearbook, picking out photos of him in his basketball and football uniforms, finding their mother in the woodwind ensemble and clowning around at drill team practice. The candid shots of him and Ashley when they were still a couple had always been their favorites, and he'd let them spend as much time as they chose leafing through decade-old memories because he thought it helped them remember their absent mother in a good way. But lately, since Christy came to town, their focus had changed. Now Dani wanted to know all about the Valentine Ball, and why he'd taken Christy and not her mother.

"We weren't in love," he repeated. "It's getting late. Time for bed. There's school tomorrow." He'd known this day would come, when he'd have to explain everything to Dani, but he'd hoped it wouldn't be so soon. He wasn't ready for birds and bees stuff. He wasn't ready for her to grow up, period.

"You took Christy to the dance, but then you married Momma."

"Yes." He hoped Dani would lose interest in his one-word replies.

"Why?"

Del took a deep breath. "Because she was going to have a baby. You, our little girl. And I wanted us to be a family."

"Momma didn't want us to be a family. Or she wouldn't have gone to California without us." Dani got up off the couch and came over to stand beside him, still holding the yearbook. Kara followed her and crawled up into his lap. She was sucking her thumb, just the tip, something she only did when she was thinking about Ashley.

"No, she just needed some time for herself." For about the thousandth time Del wondered what had gotten into his ex-wife that she would desert their daughters to run off to California to "find herself." "She calls you whenever she can. She says she's coming home for a visit this summer." He didn't believe that for a minute. He hated having to defend Ashley's neglect this way, to make the best of her unforgivable conduct, and on his bad days he sometimes thought that was his punishment for having gotten her pregnant in the first place. He didn't care that she hated his guts. But he cared a lot that she was breaking their daughters' hearts.

"It's a long time to summer," Dani said, looking out the window at the snow swirling around the streetlight.

"It's a long time to anything," Kara said despondently.

"It's only a week until Valentine's Day. Have you got your valentines ready for school?"

"I do," Dani piped up. Last Saturday she'd spent nearly an hour at the drugstore choosing just the right valentines to exchange with her classmates. She'd been busy signing them every night this week after she got her homework done.

"How about you, Kara-mia-mine?"

"Dani's helping me. I'm almost done, too."

"Good. Then we can take the night off. It's been a busy day. Let's turn in early."

"I'm not sleepy, " Kara wailed, but the denial ended on a yawn.

"Yes, you are," Dani said in her bossy big-sister voice.

"You guys head to your room, and I'll get the lights and turn down the furnace." He'd rather read in bed than sit in his empty living room and stare at the TV. Especially when all he'd be thinking about was his awkward meeting with Christy Herter. And wondering why in hell he'd agreed to go back tomorrow and replace her Aunt Sarah's leaky copper water pipes with PVC tubing when it had been more than apparent she wasn't any happier to see him than he'd been to see her.

Except somehow he hoped he could find a way to explain to her what had been going on in his mind all those years ago, and ask her to forgive him for telling her he loved her, would always love her, and then just two weeks later marrying Ashley. The only way Ashley would let him be a father to their unborn child.

"GOOD NIGHT, GUYS."

"Good night, Daddy." Dani liked the way he always called them "guys" like that, making it sound special, like "honey" or "sweetheart," but not as hokey as those wimpy names. He knew being called names like that made Dani feel silly.

"'Night, Daddy," Kara mumbled. She was getting really sleepy.

Del shut their door most of the way. Good, they could talk now without him hearing them. "Kara! Wake up."

"What? I'm sleepy." Kara scooted over as Dani crawled into her bed. Kara put her arms around Dani and held her close. Kara was afraid of the dark and she said only Dani could keep her safe.

"I've got a plan to get Daddy and Christy together."

"What about Momma?"

"Momma's not coming home. You know that. I've told you that over and over." It was funny but it hardly hurt anymore when she said it. She thought if she kept telling Kara that too, she'd get tougher and quit crying every Sunday after Momma called or, even worse, when she didn't call.

"She is, too."

"Okay," Dani conceded. "Maybe she will someday, but she's not going to come back and live with Daddy and us. We know that."

Kara sniffed but nodded. "I know."

"Then we might as well find someone else for Daddy to love."

"Christy?" Sometimes Kara wasn't as dumb as most little sisters.

"Remember how they were looking at each other in that picture in the *Warrior?*"

"That's not how they looked at each other tonight."

Kara had a point there. "That's just because they haven't seen each other for a long time. And maybe because we were there."

"She likes us," Kara insisted.

"Yeah, I know that. But no one likes to have little kids hang around on a date."

"Fixing a leaky pipe isn't a date."

"Yeah, I know. But that's what we have to get Dad to do. Ask her out on a date."

"How?" Kara yawned again and snuggled up close.

"Dad can be her secret admirer." The other day Oprah had done a show about secret admirers. And Dani had thought it was great.

"Who are secret admirers?"

"People who like someone else but are too shy to tell them so."

"Dad's shy."

"I know." At least that's what he always said when Grandma wanted him to ask some lady out. He'd grin and shake his head and say, "Aw shucks, Ma," in a funny teasing voice, dragging the toe of his shoe across the floor. "I'm too shy to ask her out."

Grandma always "humphed" and giggled and shook her head, but it must be the truth because ever since their mom left town, a long time ago, almost two years, he hadn't had a date with anyone else.

But Christy was different. He'd already dated Christy. And they must have liked each other because they were almost kissing in the picture taken at the Valentine Ball.

"I've got a plan," she whispered. Kara was asleep, already snoring, but it didn't matter. Dani smiled into the darkness. She was going to send Christy some valentines…from *A Friend*—yeah, a friend. Then her *friend* would ask her out. It was a good idea getting her dad and Christy together. Just for a date, nothing else. She wasn't going to start thinking how Christy would make a great mom or anything. She didn't make silly wishes like that anymore.

But just a date. That was okay.

She'd get her grandma to bake heart-shaped cookies with red frosting. She had nine dollars and fifty cents in her jewelry box. They were advertising heart-shaped pizzas for Valentine's Day at the Pizza Pad. She could get one of those, a little one, and maybe have enough left to buy a heart-shaped balloon, or even a flower. A rose. Yeah, that was it, a red rose. Then their dad and Christy could eat the pizza and cookies, and share the bottle of sparkly wine that had been in the fridge since Christmas, and talk about the real old days. And he would give her the red rose.

And maybe, just maybe, Christy would have such a good time she'd want to go out with her dad again, and then she'd decide to stay in Otsego Rapids....

That's where Dani fell asleep and dreamed of what it would be like to be part of a real family again.

Chapter Three

THE DOORBELL CHIMED promptly at 6:30. It was Del. Christy could see his outline through the etched glass of the side porch door. No one used the elaborate carved double door of the front entrance except the tearoom guests. She took a deep breath and tried out a smile. This was only going to be awkward if she let it be.

"Hi, Del. Thanks for coming back this evening. I'm sorry it's taking so long to fix the leaky pipes." The girls were both with him. Christy was so relieved to see he wasn't alone, the smile turned genuine. The evening before, Hilda Westhoven had been there to act as a buffer against the past. Tonight, Del's children could do the same. "Hi, guys. It's good to see you again."

"Hi, Christy," Dani and Kara said in unison.

"Come in. You'll freeze to death standing there." She opened the door wider.

"It's supposed to be five below tonight," Dani said, her nose pink with cold. "Way cold enough to freeze you solid if you get lost in the dark.''

''Dani, that's enough. You're scaring your sister. You know she's afraid of the dark. Hello, Christy.'' Del was carrying a big red toolbox in one hand, and holding onto Kara with the other. He was wearing jeans and an old army coat and there was a shadow of a beard on his chin. He looked tired, she thought, and wondered how long a day he'd already put in. ''I'm sorry I had to bring the girls. I hope you don't mind. Mom has an appointment to show a house. She should be here to pick them up about seven-thirty. It's harder than hell to get a baby-sitter—''

''Dad, you owe us a quarter,'' Dani broke in. ''He's not allowed to use bad words around us,'' she explained to Christy. She held out her hand.

''Dani's picked up the notion that if I use four-letter words so can she. So we made a deal not to use them.''

''I'm winning,'' Dani bragged.

''You had better be,'' Del said, but there was a smile to go with the warning tone.

''I don't say bad words, do I, Daddy?''

''No, Kara-mia. But sometimes you do things that are just as bad, remember.''

"Yeah, like run off to Grandma's without telling anyone," Dani said.

"Did not."

"Did too."

"Girls." The edge of command in Del's voice silenced them, although he didn't raise his voice. "I promise they'll behave."

Christy knelt down to help Kara unzip her coat. "Of course they'll be good. Now what can we find to do while your daddy's working?" The words caused a funny little pain around her heart. A home, a husband, a family of her own. She wanted that as much as any woman. She let herself imagine, for just a second, what her child and Del's would have looked like before banishing the thought.

"Kara brought a video, if it's all right for her to use Sarah's VCR. And Dani has to practice her spelling words. She missed three on her test today. Like I said, they shouldn't be any trouble." Del's tone was slightly challenging, his eyes were a dark, unreadable blue. She wondered if he was remembering that Valentine's night so long ago when he'd told her that Ashley was going to have his baby. And because she was young and thoughtless and convinced he had just broken her heart, she'd urged him to tell Ashley to have an abortion or give the baby up for adoption so they could be together. He'd said no. He was going to marry Ashley and be a father to his baby. She'd called him a fool. She hoped he'd forgiven her. Somehow she didn't think he'd forgotten.

"I'll get them settled," she said. "If there's anything you need—" She knew as much about plumbing as she did rocket science.

"I'll have to turn off the water."

"That's all right."

He'd taken off his gloves. His hand brushed hers, warm and strong, as he handed her his coat. She remembered his hands touching her all those years ago. They had never made love, but she had meant them to the night of the Valentine Ball. Instead, she'd lost her virginity to a boy in college whose name she barely remembered.

"I'll get started, then. You might want to run some water in the kitchen sink, in case you need it."

"Of course." She hurried to hang his coat on one of the ornate brass hooks by the door. Surely, what she'd been thinking hadn't shown in her eyes or on her face. "Christman's delivered the tubing this afternoon. I had them put it in the utility room. I hope that's where you wanted it."

"Fine." He headed for the kitchen carrying his toolbox. She let herself watch him for a moment or two as he walked away from her. He'd matured from a good-looking boy into a handsome man. His hair was darker and shorter than he used to wear it. He was taller than she remembered, his shoulders beneath the dark-green plaid shirt broader, his legs longer and more muscled.

"Christy, can I watch my video, please," Kara said, tugging on her skirt.

Christy blinked and realized the path her thoughts had taken, a forbidden path that led to old heartache. She looked down at the little girl. "Yes. Of course you can."

"I'm hungry," Kara whispered, giving her a soulful look.

"Don't beg for food," Dani said. She took off her coat and handed it to Christy.

"I missed my snack at day care. I'm hungry," Kara insisted.

"We'll have supper at Grandma's. She'll be here real soon." In Otsego Rapids the evening meal had always been supper, not dinner. Dinner was the noon meal. Old ways. Country ways.

"Let's see what's in the kitchen," Christy said. She wouldn't have to be alone with Del if the girls were eating at the kitchen table.

"She can wait." Dani's tone was emphatic. "We're not supposed to bother Christy, remember. You promised Dad to be good."

"I am good. I'm good and hungry."

Christy laughed and took Kara's hand. "Come with me. I think there are some cheese sandwiches left from this afternoon's tea party."

"Can you make them toasted cheese?" Kara asked with a blinding smile.

"I don't see why not."

"Kara. Stop asking for stuff."

"It's all right, Dani. I think there's some little cakes and fruit tarts in the fridge. Aren't you just a little hungry, too?"

"Well..." Dani was obviously torn between good manners and the truth.

Christy made it easy for her. "I'm as hungry as Kara. I had so many ladies asking questions about the house at tea today that I didn't even get to taste the food."

"Okay, then. I guess it's all right if you're hungry."

"And Daddy, too. He missed dinner."

"How do you know that?" Christy asked.

Dani explained. "It's tax time. He schedules appointments for people during their dinner breaks so they don't have to take off work."

"That's good business."

"He works real hard. He takes care of us and we take care of him. Our momma went away. To California. That's a long way off." Kara's smile faded away.

"A very long way," Christy agreed. She got out a skillet and some butter and the remaining diamond-shaped tea sandwiches. She turned on the gas and buttered the bread as they talked.

Dani slid onto one of the high-backed chairs that surrounded the table Christy's great-great-grandfather had made from native walnut a hundred years ago. "She's finding herself." She spoke the words matter-of-factly, as though she'd explained her mother's absence many times before.

"It might take a long time," Kara added, and the longing in the little girl's voice almost broke Christy's heart. She set the plate of fruit tarts on the table with more force than necessary.

Christy hadn't thought about Ashley Jensen for a long time. Now she found herself wishing she could find Del's ex and shake some sense into her. What kind of woman left her children to go off and "find herself" two thousand miles away?

"What's going on in here?" Del came out of the utility room wiping his hands on a red cloth. "I told you two not to bother Christy."

"They're not bothering me. We're having supper." It was impossible to tell from the look on his face if he'd heard the girls telling her about Ashley's defection or not.

A frown creased his forehead. "My mother is making supper for them."

"We're hungry now. Starving," Kara whimpered.

"Sit down and have a sandwich," Christy said ignoring his frown, although her heart was beating just a tad too fast.

"You don't have to feed my children. I've made arrangements—"

Sarah's big gray tomcat jumped up onto the kitchen windowsill and began to howl at the top of his lungs. "Dani, Kara. Would you mind going to let Hannibal in? He's giving me fair warning. If we don't hurry, he'll claw the door to pieces.''

''Okay,'' Dani said, her eyes troubled as she glanced from her father's stony face to Christy's flushed one.

''Hurry.''

''C'mon, Kara.''

As soon as the little girls left the room Christy rounded on Del. ''Of course you can take care of your daughters. Anyone can see you're doing a great job. But what on earth is wrong with me offering to fix them a sandwich? Just because of what happened between us ten years ago, you don't have to take it out on those sweet, innocent girls.''

''I'm not taking anything out on the girls. Or you.''

Christy could have bitten off her tongue. Why on earth had she said that about their past? Del would think she had nothing else on her mind. It was too close to the truth to be comfortable. ''I...I'm sorry. Of course I have nothing to do with this. It's just, well, I like having your girls around, okay. They're cute and sweet and funny.''

''And motherless.''

"Now who's being defensive," Christy shot back.

"Touché." He pushed the rag into the back pocket of his jeans. "I'm sorry I barked at you like that. It's been a long day."

"You don't have to prove anything to me, of all people. You're doing a good job with the girls," Christy said quietly. "I think I knew you were going to be a great father from…from the moment you told me you were going to marry Ashley for the baby's sake. It was a long time ago but I'm still ashamed of what I said to you that night." There, she'd done it. Ten years of a guilty conscience laid bare. "I hope you've forgiven me."

He looked at her for a long moment. "I forgave you a long, long time ago. Have you ever forgiven me for—"

"Here's the cat," Dani announced loudly, carrying Sarah's huge, gray tom triumphantly into the kitchen.

"He's hungry," Kara said. "I can tell."

Christy forced her eyes away from Del's. "His dish is in the utility room. He'll probably be in your dad's way in there."

"That's all right. Let him go eat, Dani." He hesitated a moment. "I haven't really gotten started yet. If there's enough, I think I could eat one of the sandwiches.''

"There's more than enough.'' He was still watching her. She could feel his eyes on her and the knowledge warmed her skin.

"But only on the condition that you let me buy you breakfast Sunday morning.''

"It's the Fireman's Breakfast,'' Kara piped up.

"They make awesome pancakes. You can have all you want.'' Christy looked at Dani, still holding the big cat, and saw the slight frown between her brows. She must have known they were arguing.

"I don't know.''

"And my dad's the best pancake maker of them all,'' Kara seconded.

"You'll be cooking?''

"I offered you breakfast. I didn't say I'd be eating it with you.'' Del's grin was rueful. "Consider it a peace offering.''

"Please, Christy. Say yes. We can walk. We'll be here early so you don't get too hungry. It's only three blocks to the fire station. It'll be fun.'' Dani sounded so pleased Christy couldn't deny her.

"All right. I'll come." She let her eyes find Del's once more. "Thank you for asking."

"Great," Dani said, and her frown was replaced by a great, big smile.

"Can we eat now?" Kara wanted to know.

"Yes," Christy laughed. "Now we can eat."

DANI SETTLED INTO THE REAR of the police cruiser and looked at the back of her grandpa's head through the wire mesh that separated the prisoners from the policeman in front. Not that there were a lot of prisoners that rode in this car. Not too many people did anything to get arrested for in Otsego Rapids. Dani liked to think it was because her grandpa Gary was such a good Chief of Police. But he always said it was because most everybody in Otsego Rapids were good God-fearing people, and that made his job a lot easier.

"Turn on the lights and the siren, Grandpa," Kara begged. She loved to play police officer and ride in the back of the patrol car. *COPS* was her favorite TV show. She was a weird little kid, Dani thought.

"You know I can't do that, sweetie. It would scare people. Besides, your grandma's waiting supper for us."

"We already ate," Dani told him. "Christy fixed us sandwiches and we had fancy little pies and cakes from the tearoom."

"She did? Well, that was nice of her."

"They were real good."

"She's going to come to the Fireman's Breakfast with us Sunday," Dani said.

"She is?" Grandpa sounded interested. He looked at Dani in the rearview mirror. "Your grandma will like to hear that."

"Dad's going to cook her pancakes." She was smiling as she said it. This was working out better than she'd thought. For a minute back there in the kitchen she'd thought her dad and Christy were going to get in a fight, just like her dad and mom used to, and ruin everything. And right when she'd managed to slip her first secret admirer valentine into Christy's mailbox, too. It was an awesome card. It had a drawing of a shark with a big, toothy smile on his face and it said, *Love at first bite*. It was one of the ones she'd chosen for her classmates and she thought it was cool. Not girly at all. Christy was sure to think a grown-up man had sent it. Especially since Dani had printed her message on the computer and taped it to the card so her handwriting wouldn't give her away. *Save Val-*

entine's Day for me, she'd said. And signed it, *A Friend.* And then she'd walked in the room and they were acting all stiff and funny and her stomach had tied itself into a knot.

But then her dad had smiled and invited Christy to the Fireman's Breakfast, and Christy had smiled, too, and said yes, and everything had been fine.

Tomorrow was Friday. Valentine's Day was only a few more days away. She would ask her dad if she could go to her grandma's office after school, and then she'd sneak next door to the florist and check out how much the roses were. She settled back against the seat and listened to Kara making siren noises, and smiled some more. After she got her homework done she'd ask her grandma to help her bake some heart cookies and decorate them with red frosting and silver glitter sprinkles this weekend, and plan what to say on her next secret admirer valentine.

Chapter Four

SUNDAY MORNING WAS COLD and bright with no warmth in the winter sunlight. Christy dressed in wool slacks and a cowl-neck sweater, the warmest clothes she owned, added hat and coat and gloves and went outside to sweep the ice crystals from the front walk. She was hosting a bridal shower at two that afternoon and she wanted to be certain that the brick walkway was clean and dry. It would never do for the bride to stumble on an icy patch and sprain her ankle. The Methodist and Lutheran church bells were calling the faithful to worship as she finished her chore and turned back to the house to wait for her escort. She wasn't going to church this morning, an omission Aunt Sarah would surely have frowned on. Instead, she was going to the fire station to eat pancakes and sausages with Del and his daughters.

She stopped to give the treacherous herringbone patterned bricks one more swipe with the broom when a shout caught her attention. She looked up to see Dani and Kara running toward her, bundled up from head to toe against the February cold. Behind them, down the block and across the street, Del's mother, Patty Jensen, raised her hand in greeting as she got into the car with her husband. In Atlanta, Christy lived only two blocks from the hospital where she worked, but it was a rough neighborhood and she never ventured out alone. In Otsego Rapids, everything was much closer together, and it was safe to walk the streets. It had been that way when she was a girl and, thankfully, it hadn't changed.

She hoped.

Her eyes strayed to the mailbox beside the door. She'd found two unsigned valentines in there over the past few days. The first, the morning after Del changed the water pipes. The second, just yesterday with her mail. She hadn't known what to make of them. They were obviously the kind sold for children to exchange with classmates, although they weren't the traditional hearts and flowers pictures, but shark-like monsters with mouths full of teeth and aggressive sentiments. A message had been printed on a computer and taped to the back. The first had said: *Save Valentine's Day for Me.*

The second: *I Have Something Special Planned for You.* Both were signed, *A Friend.* Was it some odd kind of merchants' advertisement she couldn't decipher? A neighborhood custom? A child's prank?

Not for the first time, she wished she had mentioned it to Chief Jensen when he saw her out salting the sidewalk the day before, and stopped to say hello and welcome her back. But then she would have had to explain about the threatening phone calls and letters from the trial in Atlanta, and she just wanted to put that all behind her. So she had said nothing at all and let the opportunity slip away in five minutes of small talk. After all, this wasn't Atlanta with its gang wars and high crime rate. It was her hometown and no one here wished her harm.

"Hi, Christy," Dani called. "We stayed all night with Grandma and Grandpa 'cause Daddy had to get up at six o'clock to start cooking pancakes. Grandma said we could walk to the firehouse if you wanted to."

"Do you want to?" Kara asked. She was wrapped so warmly against the cold that nothing showed but the pink tip of her nose and her sparkling blue eyes. "I'm freezing. If you're cold, we can ride with Grandma and Grandpa in their car.''

''Or we could take my car,'' Christy offered, as the chief and his wife slowed to a stop in front of the house.

Patty Jensen rolled down the window and stuck her head out. She was a handsome woman with steel gray hair and eyes the same blue as Kara's. She had gained a few pounds it appeared, but otherwise looked much the same as Christy remembered. ''Are you sure you want to be saddled with these two?'' she asked. Her voice was as friendly as if it had been only ten days since they'd spoken last and not ten years.

''It's no problem at all. We'll catch up with you in a few minutes.''

''I want to ride,'' Kara pouted.

''No. It's only a few blocks. You need the exercise.'' Dani's tone was adamant.

''It's freezing.''

''It's good for you.''

Kara turned and started along the sidewalk in the direction of the fire station. ''When I grow up I'm going to live where it's warm all the time. I don't like winter.'' Christy hid a smile. Kara was so warmly dressed, when she walked she waddled like a penguin.

"You like Christmas," Dani said, pointing out the flaw in her sister's argument.

"They have Christmas where it's warm, don't they," Kara said over her shoulder.

"Yes." Christy propped the broom against the porch railing. She would have to remember to put it away before the bridal tea guests arrived. "With trees and lights and tinsel and everything."

"But it isn't the same," Dani said forcefully. "When I was a baby, my dad was in the army. He had to be in Saudi 'rabia at Christmas. He said it wasn't the same at all."

"Christmas in the south is very nice. It's not like being in a foreign country." She found herself picturing Del spending Christmas in a war zone, thousands of miles away from his wife and baby, and her heart went out to him.

Dani nodded wisely. "Christmas is always best at home."

"Look, the Petermans' new puppy is outside. Isn't he cute? I want a puppy. Daddy says we'll go the shelter and look for one after tax time, when he's not so busy and has time to help us potty train him."

"You don't potty train a dog. You housebreak a dog. Jeesh." Dani rolled her eyes.

"Whatever," Kara said. She bent over and petted the fat beagle puppy on the top of his head. "You're cute, puppy. I like you. My daddy likes you, too."

"Dad says it would be nice to have a dog to keep him company while he's working. His office is in a room in our garage," Dani explained.

"We have to be real quiet while he's working."

"You're not quiet. You're always running in there climbing on his lap for a hug, or asking for a snack."

"Nuh-uh," came the muffled but indignant reply. "I always ask him if I can come in and give him a hug, and he always says yes."

Christy felt another uninvited tug at her heart as she thought of Del stopping his work to spend time with his daughters. The more she saw of him, the more she realized what a good father he was. For a long time after they broke up, she had allowed herself to think the worst of him. Later, she had made herself stop thinking of him at all. Now it seemed he, and the two little girls with her, were always on her mind.

She knew it wasn't a good idea to let herself

get too close. In a few weeks she would be back in Atlanta and out of their lives. Del's children had lost too much. It wouldn't be fair to make herself important to them and then walk away as their mother had done. And she had her own feelings to safeguard. She loved children, and these children were Del's, which made them doubly precious. And doubly dangerous to her wary heart.

The thought brought them to the door of the firehouse and the realization that she should never have agreed to come. This was Otsego Rapids, not Atlanta. A woman didn't walk into the Volunteer Fireman's Pancake Breakfast with a man's children, a man she had been involved with, no matter how many years ago, without causing speculation. And when the thought of seeing that man again in a minute or two made her heart suddenly beat a little faster.

Christy stopped dead still. It was all she could do to keep from turning around and walking as fast as she could back to Rosewood House.

"Christy, what's wrong?" Dani asked, looking up at her with anxious eyes.

"Let's go inside. I'm freezing and I'm hungry," Kara urged.

The door opened. Christy found herself face-to-face with her old guidance counselor from high school.

"Mr. Whitmore."

"Christy Herter? Well, I'll be. I heard you were staying at your aunt's. Welcome back to town. Come in out of the cold." He peered at the girls over his bifocals. In high school she'd thought he was ancient, but now she realized he couldn't be much over fifty. "Who have we here? Aren't these Del Jensen's kids?"

"Hello, Mr. Whitmore. It's good to be back again. And yes, these are Del's children." Christy held her breath, waiting...for what? A snide remark? A wink and a nudge and a reference to old flames fanned back to life?

"I heard he was doing some emergency plumbing for you. Old houses like your aunt's and mine are always needing some sort of repair." Roger Whitmore and his wife lived in the oldest house in Otsego Rapids. It was down near the river with marks painted on the side to show how high the flood waters had been in past years. The original portion was a log cabin made from native oak and elm. Every eighth-grade Ohio History class in Otsego Rapids toured his house; Christy's had been no exception.

"It was good of him to help me out."

He nodded. "Del's a good man." His smile didn't alter. His brown eyes were kind and full of good humor. "Good morning, girls. Your dad's really outdoing himself on the pancakes this morning. I hope you're hungry."

"We're starved," Kara responded promptly.

"And you too, Christy? I hope you aren't so citified these days you can't enjoy a good country breakfast."

"That will never happen," Christy assured him, and laughed. Maybe this wouldn't be so bad after all.

HE SHOULD NEVER have invited Christy to the breakfast. He certainly shouldn't have given in to the girls' cajoling that they be allowed to escort her to the firehouse. His lack of foresight had left Christy open to all kinds of speculation from his friends and neighbors. In small towns people had long memories. They were probably all sitting there eating pancakes and sausage thinking back to how he had followed her around like a lovesick puppy day and night for

six weeks. Right up until he'd owned up to fa-
thering Ashley's baby and married her instead.

"Hey, Bob. Want to take over here? My
mom and dad are getting ready to leave and I
need to talk to them about taking the girls home
with them." He flipped half a dozen pancakes
on the griddle and slid them onto the warming
tray as he talked.

Bob Gresham, one of the other volunteer fire-
men, looked up from the pancake batter he was
pouring into a pitcher. He gazed past Del out
into the community room of the station where
about thirty people sat at long tables eating and
talking as cold winter sunlight filtered in
through the high, narrow windows that faced
the river.

Del felt himself tense, waiting for Bob to
make some kind of remark about him getting
rid of his kids so he could spend time with his
old girlfriend. He found he was gripping the
pancake turner he was holding so tightly his
knuckles were white.

"Sure, Del. Take a break. It'll be pretty slow
until Mass is over and the crowd from St. Al's
starts coming in. I can handle it myself."

Del felt like a fool. "Thanks, Bob. I won't
be long." Bob Gresham hadn't even lived in

town when Del and Christy were teenagers. He didn't know anything about Del and Christy's past. And the guys who did hadn't said a word beyond a friendly greeting to her when Kara and Dani had dragged her to the counter to pick up their plates of food.

They were old news, he reminded himself. Ancient history. A memory of only passing interest to everyone but himself.

Well, maybe not everyone. Attendance at the fund-raiser had been brisk all morning but, at the moment, there was a lull in the crowd and the only full table in the big room was the one where his parents, daughters and Christy Herter were sitting. Three of their old high-school classmates were seated there along with Jennifer Weber and her son.

Del ground his teeth as he untied the big white apron he'd been wearing over his flannel shirt and jeans. His old football teammates he could deal with. But not Jenny. She was a couple of years younger than he was, divorced and had a son Kara's age. Their backyards butted up to each other and the kids played together a lot. He'd made the mistake of sitting with her at one or two school functions and then agreeing to a home-cooked meal in exchange for helping her with some tax questions she had involving her divorce settlement. He'd found out after dessert that night that Jenny was ready to take the next step in the relationship. Del wasn't.

He walked over to the table and laid his hands on Dani's shoulders. Christy was sitting beside his oldest child and when she turned a little sideways to say hello he smelled her perfume, light and lemony and sexy as hell.

"Hi, Christy," he said as casually as he could manage. *Damn,* her smile still had the power to make the blood surge through his veins like a flash flood in springtime.

"Hi, Del," she said.

"Hi, kid," he said to Dani, careful not to call her anything too affectionate and embarrass her.

"Hi, Dad. The pancakes are awesome."

"Awesome," Kara echoed, her mouth full.

"Don't talk with your mouth full," he said at the same moment his mother did. Everyone laughed and Del sat down in the last empty chair. The one beside Jenny. Jenny leaned a little closer. Del wished he'd remained standing.

"It's sure good to see you again, Christy," Vince Pieracini was saying. He'd been the star quarterback of the Warriors football team a decade ago. Now he was the high-school science teacher, as well as the football coach, and in the middle of his second divorce. Christy had dated him once or twice in high school. From the look in his eye Del figured Vince was hoping he could talk her into dating him again.

"It's nice to be back, Vince," Christy said politely. "I hadn't realized how much I missed being here."

"There's no place like home," Mel Carter intoned. He had been a hell-raiser in high school. Now he was the town mortician and somber as a judge. He'd never married. And neither had Brad Melrose, the third classmate at the table. All of them were buzzing around Christy like bees around a flower. Del wished he could have her all to himself, and the need was just as strong here and now, as it had been when he was seventeen.

"I hope you'll come back in August for our class reunion," Brad grinned. "Ten years. Can you believe it?"

Christy turned her smile on Brad and color washed up his neck and ears. "I'll try, Brad. But I'm afraid I might not be able to get the time off. I...I'm using up all my vacation helping Aunt Sarah out."

"Oh, oh sure." Brad looked down at his plate.

"But I'm so glad I got to see you this morning. You haven't changed a bit."

Brad grinned and rubbed his hand over the bald spot on top of his head. "Just losing a little hair, that's all."

They all laughed. Jenny said something and put her hand on Del's arm, jolting him from his thoughts. He blinked and found Christy watching. She couldn't help but notice Jenny's proprietary gesture. "I'm sorry," he said, moving his arm from beneath Jenny's fingers. "What did you say?"

Jenny's eyes narrowed. It was obvious she hadn't forgotten that he and Christy had once been an item. "I said I'm looking forward to seeing Christy again this afternoon. I've been invited to Brittany Morris's bridal shower. She's Kyle's baby-sitter." Kyle was Jenny's son, as busy eating pancakes as Kara was.

Christy stood up. "It's my first bridal shower," she said, smiling at everyone and waving at the men at the table to keep their seats. "I want everything to be just right. So if you will all excuse me..."

"Don't go yet, Christy," Dani pleaded.

"I have to." Christy's smile softened. "I still have a hundred things to do."

"I'll help you."

"I thought you were going to the mall with us," Del's mother cut in smoothly. "And remember, we have Valentine cookies to bake for your school party."

"Oh yeah. I forgot. Sorry, Christy."

"That's all right. Thanks for offering."

"What if Momma calls?" Kara asked Del.

"Grandma and Grandpa will have you back early. Your mother always calls after supper." If she made the effort to call at all.

"We'll be back in plenty of time," Patty assured her granddaughters.

"Hurry and finish eating, Kara. Grandma and Grandpa are ready to go."

Bob Gresham came out of the kitchen carrying one of the insulated carriers they'd borrowed from the Pizza Pad down the street. "I've got a delivery here for old Mrs. Tussing. Del, can you take it? My car's blocked in."

"Sure. Just as soon as I get my coat."

Christy was still standing by her chair. Vince and Brad and Mel were all grinning at her like moonstruck calves. Jenny leaned sideways until her shoulder brushed Del's thigh and stayed there. Del held out his hand to Christy. "Violet's house is right down the block from your Aunt Sarah's. I'll drop you off on my way."

Chapter Five

CHRISTY DIDN'T KNOW whether to take Del's hand or not. If she didn't, it would embarrass him. If she did, would everyone sitting at the table start wondering if they were getting together again? She hesitated a moment, then laid her hand on his. She was being oversensitive. It was a friendly gesture, that was all. There was nothing more to read into it. But then, why was her palm tingling and her heart fluttering in her chest like a trapped bird?

Del kept her hand in his until they got to where their coats were hanging on the row of hooks along the wall by the door. He held hers for her to slip into, then took his down and put it on. She felt the tension radiating from him and wondered what had upset him. He didn't attempt to take her hand again after they left the fire station but shoved his free hand into the pocket of his coat. He wasn't wearing a hat. His thick, dark hair caught glints of winter sunshine in its depths and his breath made a cloud of smoke in front of his face. He stepped out onto the sidewalk and looked up and down the street. "Oh, hell. I forgot I parked my car in front of the hardware store. It'll be closer to walk. Do you mind? I need to clear the cooking fumes out of my head anyway."

She held out her hand. "Twenty-five cents, please."

"What?"

"That four-letter word. You owe me twenty-five cents. I'll give it to Dani the next time I see her." For a moment he looked confused and then he smiled. That wonderful, sexy smile of his that had always started her stomach doing cartwheels, and still did.

"I'll give it to her myself," he said. He angled his head just a little to look down at her. He was an inch or two under six feet. Not all that much taller than she was, and she liked that, had always liked that in a man, and realized it was a preference formed during the time they'd been together.

Christy caught herself up short. She would not admit that she'd measured every other man in her life by the standard of Del Jensen and found them wanting.

"No way, Jose." She laughed and wiggled her gloved fingers. "Pay up."

He pulled a quarter out of his pocket and folded it into her hand. He looked at her with dark eyes filled with shadows, and she found she wanted to make him laugh again and take those shadows away. "I'm sorry if I embarrassed you back there. It was a high-school stunt grabbing your hand that way." He stopped talking so abruptly she heard his teeth snap together.

It always came back to that, what had happened between them ten years ago. Suddenly she wished they had never had a past, had only been friends then, and could build on that foundation now without all the old and hurtful memories coming between them. She put the quarter in her pocket and started walking. Del kept the insulated carrier between them, a small but telling detail that showed his thoughts somewhat paralleled her own. "You didn't grab my hand, you offered yours. And I took it. It's as simple as that."

Del turned his head and looked at her. "Don't tell me it hasn't crossed your mind that everyone must be thinking back to when we were an item."

"Of course it has. But good heavens, it was so long ago. And if they do, so what? It was only a crush, after all." She used the word deliberately. A crush was not as serious as a love affair. For her, it had been love. Love as a seventeen-year-old virgin defined the emotion, perhaps, but something far more serious and more precious than a mere crush. And something that hurt far more when it died.

"Jenny hasn't forgotten."

"Does she mean something to you?" Christy surprised herself by asking the question. Del's love life was none of her business. It hadn't been for a long, long time.

"No," he said, his voice sharp. "I haven't given her any encouragement."

"She certainly encourages you." Now why had she said that? Because she didn't want to think about Jenny Weber in Del's arms, his lips on hers, his big, strong hands caressing her hair, her breasts. This time it was Christy who snapped her mouth shut. They waited for the red light at Elm and Cherry, even though there wasn't a car in sight.

Del looked at her and smiled ruefully. "Jenny is persistent. Got any suggestions on how to keep my distance?"

She smiled, too, as she stepped off the curb. Ten years ago she'd never been able to stay angry with him when he smiled at her that way. She still couldn't, it seemed. How easy it was to fall back into old habits. "No, I'm afraid I don't. I'm not much of an expert in the romance department."

"There's no one special in your life?"

She could lie and say there was, end this dangerously personal slant to the conversation with a single word, but she didn't. "No. There's no one special. My work is demanding. Most of the men I meet are overworked interns or married doctors. My life-style doesn't lend itself to romance."

"With me, it's school loans to pay off. Kids to raise. A business to get off the ground. And a failed marriage to throw into the mix. Things sure went wrong there," he said after a moment's pause.

"What did go wrong between you and Ashley?" Christy asked quietly. She didn't look at him, but straight ahead at her Aunt Sarah's house sitting proudly on its big corner lot, lording over the smaller houses on every side.

She didn't expect him to say, *I fell in love with you and that's what came between us,* and he didn't. "I don't know. It was rough at first. I was in the service. I was stationed in California. She hated being away from home. Then I got sent to Saudi during the Gulf War and she came back to live with her parents. When I got back we both worked hard to patch things up. Ashley got pregnant with Kara. I worked days and went to school at night. It was tough but I thought we were making it. Then." He lifted his shoulders in a shrug. "I don't know. It all went sour somehow. Ashley's parents moved away. She got restless, bored. She wanted a new house, more money. She hated working at the Toyota factory over in Ottawa, but she didn't want to go back to school. She blamed me for getting her pregnant with Dani, and ruining her life."

"It takes two people to make a baby, Del."

He nodded. "We were both too young and foolish. Ashley thought she knew when it was safe, and I was too stupid and embarrassed to buy condoms."

"I know I said some terrible things to you back then, Del. But believe me I admire the way you accepted your responsibility for the baby...for Dani."

"I love my kids with all my heart and soul,"

he said simply. "I thought Ashley did, too. I still believe she cares for them. But she was just so mixed-up about herself and her life she made us all miserable. Then one day she said she wanted a divorce, and God help me, I didn't try and talk her out of it. She left for California the day we signed the custody papers for the girls. She hated it while we lived there but she couldn't wait to get back to 'find herself,' whatever the hell that means. It's been over two years and she's still looking."

"Do you want her back?"

He didn't answer right away and Christy found she was holding her breath. "No," he said at last. "Not even for the girls' sake."

"I'm sorry." Christy knew she should say more than that. She should tell him she regretted his marriage hadn't worked out, but she didn't feel that way and she wasn't going to say so. Ashley had been a spoiled and willful child, a wild teenager, and she obviously had failed to mature into the caring and supportive marriage partner that a good man like Del deserved.

They crossed Maple and turned onto Oak. Rosewood House was just ahead, the windows glistening in the cold sunlight, smoke curling from the chimney. Del walked her to the side door, following her onto the small porch that sheltered it. Automatically, she opened the ornate brass mailbox and peered inside.

"There's no mail delivery today. It's Sunday." She swung around to find Del watching her with a quizzical frown between his strongly marked brows.

"I know." She closed the lid, breathing a little sigh of relief. The box was empty. There were no more of those disturbing unsigned valentines inside. "It's just that I...I know this sounds silly, but have you gotten any prank notes in your mailbox? Or maybe I shouldn't even call them prank notes. Odd advertisements? Valentines with monsters on them?"

"No," he said. "Nothing like that, but I take it you have."

She nodded and a cloud of his warm breath mingled with hers, coiling like lovers coming together after a long time apart, distracting her momentarily from her uneasy thoughts about the anonymous valentines. "Yes. Two of them. But I'm sure it's nothing."

"This being Otsego Rapids, I tend to agree with you. But from the look on your face, I'd say that's not going to be good enough. May I take a look at them?"

"I threw them away."

"Do you want me to ask my dad to keep an eye on the place for you?"

"No." She couldn't have him starting to look out for her. It felt too natural, too right. "I know I'm being silly. It's probably nothing. It's just that last year I sat on a jury in Atlanta. It was a gang-related case. Drug dealing and gun running. One of the defendant's brothers sent threatening letters and made phone calls to jury members, including me. The police caught him. He's already in jail, but...well," she managed a little laugh, "I guess I'm still kind of jumpy." She had been more than a little jumpy, she'd been frightened out of her wits, but she didn't want to tell him that for the same reason she didn't want him looking after her. It felt too right.

"I'll talk to Dad when he drops the girls off."

"Del, no. I'm sure there's some reasonable explanation. I'd rather not make a big deal out of it. I...I have the bridal shower and—"

"And you know I can be here in two minutes flat, if you need me."

"Thank you, Del." Her throat tightened. Once upon a time she had wanted nothing more in the world than for Del Jensen to be there for her. Part of her still did.

"Anytime," he said and smiled. "I should be going. Mrs. Tussing's going to be wondering what happened to her pancakes."

"Yes—" She couldn't seem to say any more.

He made no move to leave the porch. "Thanks for being so kind to the girls these past few days."

She welcomed the change of subject. "They're great kids. I enjoy having them around."

"And thanks for keeping me company."

"You're welcome." The words were a little forced, a little too breathy. Del was so close, only a step away, a heartbeat away. It was hard to concentrate on anything but the dark blue of his eyes and the curve of his mouth.

"Christy?" He leaned a little forward. His kissable mouth was only inches from hers. As a boy, his kisses had been unpracticed but exciting. As a man, she knew he would be a thoughtful but demanding lover, and the image that conjured curled her toes and sent waves of longing pulsing through her.

"Yes?" He was going to kiss her and she

wanted him to. She curled her hands around the doorknob to keep from flinging herself into his arms but she was only partially successful. She pushed away from the door, drawn to his heat and strength and the need to feel his lips on hers again after so very, very long. He was watching her with an intensity that excited her even more. He raised his hand to her cheek and touched her. The leather of his glove was as warm and supple as skin. A shiver went through her that had nothing to do with the cold. She closed her eyes and waited for his kiss.

A car drove by and the driver honked a greeting. Del straightened as though someone had jerked him backward by the coat collar. "I...I have to go." He looked a little dazed, as though he'd suddenly found himself in a different time and place than where he'd been a moment before.

Christy felt the same way, as though time had unraveled for a few seconds and they were seventeen and falling in love again. That they were going to kiss for the first time. She didn't dare let that happen. She couldn't face having her heart broken by Del Jensen a second time. She turned the doorknob and backed inside. She spoke the first words that came to her mind. "Mrs. Tussing's pancakes..."

Del didn't say anything for a moment, then nodded. At the bottom of the step he turned and looked back at her. "I'd like to see you later, if that's all right."

She shook her head. Her throat was tight but she managed to speak in her normal voice. "Oh Del, I'm not sure that's a good idea."

"Christy, I'm not going to say for old times' sake, but there's still something there. You felt it."

I felt it. "I'll think about it," she said and closed the door.

"WHY COULDN'T WE let Grandma drive us home? It's too cold to walk. We'll miss Momma's call."

"Be quiet, baby." Dani had a lot on her mind. Listening to her little sister whine made it hard to concentrate. And it was cold. After they got back from the mall, Grandma Patty had helped her bake cookies and, by the time they got the kitchen cleaned up, the afternoon was over. The sun had gone down a few minutes ago and the sky was a pale, icy blue with a few stars twinkling here and there, and clouds moving to cover the moon.

"It's so cold my cookie is frozen." Kara stopped to examine the heart-shaped cookie with red frosting and sparkly white sugar glitter she carried in a plastic bag. "How can I eat a frozen cookie?"

"I'll put it in the microwave for you when we get home. Now be quiet. You're making so much noise someone will hear you and notice us putting the valentine in Christy's mailbox. And hurry up. Dad's expecting us." Grandma Patty had let them walk home from her house alone since last summer but she always made Dani call her dad first and tell him they were on the way.

"Why don't we just give it to her? Tell her to come to our house for pizza Valentine's Day. It's only two days away, isn't it?" Kara was only in first grade and still had trouble keeping track of days sometimes.

"Because grown-ups having pizza with two little kids is not *romantic*." She'd read a whole bunch of mushy valentines in the drugstore. That's where she'd figured out what words to put on the notes. She'd watched all the candy and flower commercials on TV all week. She didn't know much about grown-up dating. She didn't even like boys. But she knew men and women needed time alone together. Everybody knew that.

She'd seen how her dad smiled at Christy this morning. And the way Christy had smiled back and taken his hand. It was almost the way they'd looked at each other in the old picture in the *Warrior*. They just needed some time together alone, and all she had to do to help that happen was make sure Christy didn't have any other plans for Tuesday night. She patted her coat pocket to make sure the note was safe. This one said: *I'll be with you on Valentine's Day.* And it had a giant octopus on the front.

"Come on, Kara. Hurry up. All the cars from the bridal shower are still parked at Sarah's house. Everyone's busy inside. No one will see me walk up and put the note in the mailbox."

"Is this the last one?" Kara asked plaintively.

"Nope," Dani said, looking up and down the street, relieved to find there were no cars coming and no one else walking along the sidewalk. "There's one more. It's an invitation. We'll give her that one tomorrow. I'll ring the doorbell so she finds it right away. I signed his name and everything. Right then Christy will know Dad's her secret admirer.'' She wasn't like Kara. She didn't think their mom would come home. And if they couldn't have their mom back, then Dani thought it would be okay if their dad found someone nice like Christy to love.

But first she had to get them together.

Chapter Six

IT WAS ALMOST NINE O'CLOCK by the time Christy finished putting the house back to rights after Brittany Morris's shower. She was tired, but also restless, an unsettling combination brought on by her long and busy day, and, if she was honest with herself, by the kiss she'd almost shared with Del.

She wandered through the house admiring the high ceilings with their ornate plaster moldings, and softly glowing walnut and cherry woodwork. Aunt Sarah had never married, never had children of her own. She'd worked thirty years at the Otsego Rapids State Bank and Trust before opening the tearoom. She was generous to her nieces and nephews, active in her church and community, but she lavished most of her love and attention on this house.

Sarah cared for her aunt deeply, but she didn't want to end up like her, alone with her cat in a beautiful but empty house that had been built for a large and lively family. She hadn't let herself look so far into the future for a long time. Not since her last serious relationship had ended two years before, and then she hadn't liked what she'd seen. Tonight she relished the prospect of spending her life alone even less, another consequence of allowing Del—and his little girls—into her life.

Her thoughts made her still more restless, and she opened the side door to see if it had started to snow. Just before sundown, gray clouds had drifted in from the west. By the time she'd helped carry the last of Brittany's shower gifts to her mother's car she could smell snow in the cold wind blowing down Oak Street.

Her weather prediction had been wrong. It wasn't snowing. The clouds had broken up and snatches of moonlight appeared among the tatters. Hannibal hurried up the porch steps, wrapped himself around her ankles, allowed her a quick stroking behind his ears and then paced into the kitchen with all the dignity of his kind.

She'd better feed him right away or he would have his nose out of joint all day tomorrow. Christy found her gaze riveted to the mailbox. The lid was half-open. She was certain she'd closed it that morning after looking inside. Her breath quickened and her heartbeat pounded in her temples. She reached out, hesitated, then lifted the lid the rest of the way and looked inside. A small envelope glowed white against the dark interior.

Christy was almost afraid to touch it. She couldn't get the memory of the first threatening note she'd unwittingly opened back in Atlanta out of her memory. She'd been totally unprepared for the threats of violence and raw hatred it contained. But this wasn't Atlanta and, so far, the little valentines had been unsettling but not menacing.

Still, it took a lot for her to pull the note from the mailbox. It was even harder to find the courage to open it. It was a picture of a luridly colored octopus this time, with exaggerated tentacles and the caption, *You're My Squeeze.* Again there was a message taped to the back. *I'll be with you on Valentine's Day,* it read. It was signed, *A Friend,* just as the others had been. A shiver that had nothing to do with the temperature raced down her spine.

She turned and walked into the house, went to the telephone, picked it up to dial 911 and then hesitated. What was she going to say to the dispatcher when she answered? *I'm receiv-*

ing anonymous valentines in my mailbox. They have scary sharks and monsters on them.

They would listen, of course. The dispatcher would contact Del's father or one of the other members of the small Otsego Rapids police force and they would come to check out her complaint. They'd listen to her story of what had happened in Atlanta, take the valentine and leave, promising to do what they could, and privately thinking that Christy Herter was growing just a little odd, a little eccentric like her aunt Sarah.... She put down the phone and grabbed her coat from the closet. She needed to go for a walk and think this through before she did something about it, set wheels in motion that she might wish she hadn't.

Once on the sidewalk she found herself heading toward Del's house on Maple Street and didn't try to change direction. She hurried onto the porch and knocked before she could change her mind. It probably wasn't wise to involve him any further in her problem but she couldn't seem to help herself. She needed to hear his voice to make her feel safe and secure again.

She needed him to love her again.

She almost turned around and ran as the enormity of what she'd just admitted to herself

seared its way through her brain. She was on
the verge of falling in love with Del Jensen for
the second time in her life. She took a step
backward. She would rather go back to her
aunt's silent, empty house with the unsettling
note in her pocket than face Del with her feelings still so out of control that she had no doubt
he would be able to read them on her face. The
door opened and Del stood there looking at her.
She tried to smile and hoped she'd gotten it
right. She couldn't look him in the eye, not yet,
so she settled for staring at a spot just past his
left ear.

"Christy? Come in." The warmth of his
voice drew her in despite her reluctance. He led
her into the main room of the house. It was
softly lighted by floor and table lamps. There
was a fire burning in the small brick fireplace.
She could see a narrow dining room beyond,
the oval table crowded with coloring books and
boxes of crayons and Barbie dolls. Beyond the
dining room were doorways leading to the
kitchen, and a hallway where the bedrooms and
bathroom were most likely located.

Del's gaze followed her eyes. "Sorry, it's
kind of a mess tonight."

"It's not messy. It's lived in." In her apartment in Atlanta there was never anything out of

place. Why should there be? She lived alone. She worked long, exhausting shifts at the hospital and she was seldom there except to sleep and change clothes.

"What's wrong?" he asked. "What brought you out on such a cold night?"

She took the envelope out of her pocket. "I got another one."

He took the envelope, opened it and studied the little valentine. He turned the envelope over in his hand. It was blank. He looked at the valentine and its printed message again. "I don't get it," he said. "It's a child's valentine. You can buy them anywhere. They've even got them at Bostleman's Drug Store. Dani chose this kind to exchange with her classmates." He smiled. "You know she hates—"

"Anything girly," Christy finished his sentence. This time she didn't have any trouble finding her smile. "I know. Are the girls asleep?"

Del had been smiling too, but now his smile disappeared. He nodded shortly. "I just sent them to bed a few minutes ago." His face darkened. "Their mother was supposed to call today. She didn't. Kara was pretty upset and it was hard to get her settled."

"I'm sorry."

"So am I," he said. He continued to study the valentine. "It's not exactly threatening. It's not even addressed to you."

"I know. That's what makes it so unnerving."

"Especially in light of what happened in Atlanta."

"Partially, but mostly because there's no reason for it here. I haven't even had much contact with people besides you and Hilda Westhoven. I certainly don't think Hilda's behind this."

Del stood up. "I'm going to phone my dad, then go over to your place and have a quick look around."

"Oh, Del, no. You can't leave the girls here alone."

"I'll ask Mom to come by and keep an eye on them."

She hesitated. It would be nice to have someone take care of her for a change. She had felt so isolated and alone in Atlanta when the harassment started. Her parents were in Florida and there had been no one else she could turn to. "I would appreciate you having a look around."

Del picked up the phone and punched in a number. "Dad? Can you meet me at Sarah Herter's house in ten minutes? Christy's over here at my place. She's been finding some odd notes in her mailbox and I think it's time someone looked into it.''

"Dani?"

Dani sat up in bed. She rubbed her eyes. "I'm awake."

Del leaned down and pulled Kara's covers up around her neck and then sat down on the side of Dani's bed. "You should be asleep. There's school tomorrow."

"I was thinking about the Valentine party. I was thinking I should find a box to put my heart cookies in instead of a plastic bag. I don't want them to get all crumbly." It was nice when her dad came into her room like this and they talked.

"Dani, I have to go to Christy's for a little while. She has a problem and I need to help Grandpa check out her aunt Sarah's house. Grandma's coming to stay with you."

"Grandma doesn't have to come. I'm big enough to watch Kara. It'll be just like you're working late in your office."

"I know you're a big girl but when I'm out in the office I'm only a few feet away. I'll feel better knowing Grandma's here. Okay?"

"Okay." She really didn't want to stay alone

anyway. "Why do you and Grandpa have to go check out Sarah's house? What's wrong?"

"Someone is sending Christy scary valentines and she just got another one."

Dani's heart started beating so hard she could hardly breathe. Her throat got tight. Kara made a little sighing sound and her dad looked over at her bed, giving Dani a moment to catch her breath. "You said scary valentines?" Sure the pictures had been a little scary. But her dad was a guy. He wouldn't be sending Christy secret admirer valentines that were girly.

Del held his finger in front of his mouth. "Shh, not so loud. We'll wake Kara up. Yeah, monster valentines like the ones you got for school. I'm sure it's just a prank or something."

Dani nodded. She couldn't talk. This was awful. *Christy was afraid.* What was she going to do? She couldn't put another valentine in Christy's mailbox with her dad's name on it. Then Grandpa and the other police would think he'd been trying to scare Christy all along. They didn't know anything about the heart pizza that Grandma'd promised to pick up on her way home from work on Tuesday. Or the cookies, or the rose, or anything.

"I won't be gone a minute longer than I have to."

Dani nodded. "Okay."

"'Night, Tiger. Pleasant dreams."

Dani snuggled down under the covers until Del left the room. Then she sat bolt upright again. So did Kara. Her eyes were big as saucers in the glow of the seashell night-light by her bed.

"I thought you were asleep."

"I was pretending. Christy's afraid," Kara whimpered. "They called Grandpa. You know what he always said about us getting in trouble. That we should always be good because people would expect him to be real tough on us if we weren't."

Dani nodded. Her mind was in a whirl. All her plans were going wrong. What if someone had seen her at Christy's today?

"What are we going to do?"

"I don't know. I'll try and think of something to make it all right."

"You'd better," Kara said, sniffing back tears. "I don't want to go to jail."

Chapter Seven

DEL WAITED AT THE BOTTOM of the staircase as Christy and his dad descended. The chief was in uniform. In a town as small as Otsego Rapids even the Chief of Police pulled weekend duty. "Everything okay upstairs?"

"Everything checks out upstairs and down. How about outside?"

"There's no lock on the woodshed where Sarah keeps her garden tools, but it doesn't look as if anything's been disturbed." Del handed his dad the big flashlight he'd loaned him for the search.

"Thanks for coming over, Chief," Christy said. "I'm sorry to be causing you so much trouble. I just can't imagine who's doing this."

"It's no trouble, Christy. I agree, the note seems harmless enough but let's not take any chances."

"I wish you'd come and spend the night with me and the girls," Del said.

"I didn't let Jacky Ortiz drive me out of my

apartment in Atlanta, and believe me his threats were far more explicit and detailed than these notes.'' Christy's chin came up. ''I'll be fine.''

''Then I'll be on my way,'' the chief said. ''You've got my pager number. I can be here in five minutes from any place in town.''

Christy's smile took Del's breath away even though it was meant for his dad and not for him. ''Don't worry. If I hear so much as a board squeak that I can't explain I'll be on the phone.''

''You're too sensible not to. Good night, Christy. Del, can I give you a lift back home?''

''Thanks, Dad. I'll walk.'' He wanted to make one more attempt to get Christy to spend the night at his place. He didn't want her to be alone.

Christy saw his dad to the door and then turned back to Del. ''I'd forgotten how good it is to live in a small town. In Atlanta when I got the first threatening note, the police made me feel like I was the criminal. They actually asked me what I might have done to provoke such behavior.''

''Small towns have their advantages,'' he agreed.

''Would you like a cup of coffee before you

leave? You must be cold. It's almost down to zero already."

"No, I don't want coffee unless you want me to make us a cup at my place."

Christy shook her head. "Del, I can't—"

"I don't want you spending the night alone."

He took a step forward. Christy's hand came up to toy with the gold chain she wore around her neck. In the light from the brass and crystal chandelier above their heads, her hair glowed with the same soft, golden highlights as the necklace. The style was shorter and more sophisticated than it had been when she was seventeen. It suited the strong, independent woman she'd become. "I don't want your neighbors to see me coming out of your house tomorrow morning. It would be embarrassing for Aunt Sarah."

"Then stay until lunchtime." He hadn't meant to say that, to put his longing and desire for her into words.

Christy's eyes widened. She shook her head, taking a step sideways as he closed the distance between them. Her tone was light, but the tiny quaver along the edges of the words belied her indifference. "Hilda Westhoven will be here at eight in the morning. If she finds me gone she'll be worried. She might even call your father and get him out of bed. I wouldn't want that to happen.''

She'd backed herself up against the carved pocket doors that separated the foyer from the parlor. He put his arms on both sides of her shoulders, trapping her within the circle of his arms. ''Call her now and tell her what's happened.''

''Del, please. This isn't wise.''

''I can't help myself.'' He lowered his head to kiss her. He'd wanted to do it all day. He'd wanted to do it for a decade. Her mouth was soft under his, pliable. Inside he caught fire. He bracketed her face with his hands, felt the softness of her hair at the nape of her neck, the smoothness of the skin at her throat. She made a little sound, half protest, half surrender. Her arms came around his waist. Her lips opened under the pressure of his. He leaned against her, bringing their bodies close together.

Her body molded itself to his. She fit him like a glove, like they were meant for each other. He scooped her into his arms and carried her to the antique fainting couch before the tiled fireplace in the formal parlor. The room was dark, the gas logs in the fireplace unlit. The only illumination came from the streetlight on the corner filtering through the lace curtains at the window. As a teenager he'd dreamed of sweeping Christy off her feet and making love to her. But he hadn't been strong enough or brave enough to try it then. Now it was different. He was a man who knew what he wanted and how to make the woman in his arms want it too.

He laid her against the pillows, rested his forearms on either side of her head and kept on kissing her. Her breasts were soft and full against his chest, her hair tangled like skeins of silk in his fingers. Her mouth was sweet and warm and beckoning. She wrapped her arms around his neck and kissed him back, holding him to her as though she never wanted to let go. Her tongue met his, thrust for thrust, and Del let his mind carry that mating further to a vision of their bodies joined as a man and a woman were meant to be.

Del kissed her eyelids, her cheeks, the curve of her throat. He traced the slope of her shoulders, the indentation of her waist. He slid his hands beneath the soft wool of her sweater and cupped her breasts. She moaned and arched against him. He stretched out beside her and his erection pushed against her thigh. He reached for the snap of her slacks and she stiffened.

"Del, no. We can't."

He didn't want to hear her say no. "Shh, Christy. It's all right." He kissed her again. Their tongues met and melded and time stood still, until he moved once more to get rid of their clothes.

"Del, wait. We can't make love," she said breathlessly.

"Why not?" He wasn't thinking with his head but with that hidden, unacknowledged corner of his soul that had wanted her with a fierce, hot desire for all the time they'd been apart.

"Because I don't want to be hurt again." She was watching him with eyes that were dark shadows in the pale oval of her face. Her voice was soft and a little unsteady.

"I'd never—" Del caught himself up short. He had hurt her. Hurt them both badly and was on the verge of causing them both more pain. He stood up, ran his hand through his hair. "God, Christy. I tried to tell you how sorry I was for what happened."

"I know you're sorry, Del. And I know you'd never deliberately hurt me again. But if we let this go any further we'll both end up with scars.''

"I'm not talking one-night stand here.'' He didn't know what he was offering her exactly. His heart, for sure, but he hadn't gotten any further than that.

"What more could it be?'' she asked, rising to stand beside him.

He turned on her, his fists clenched at his sides. "For God's sake, Christy. Give me some credit.''

She lifted her hand and placed her palm against his cheek, silencing his words and diluting his anger. "Forgive me, Del. I didn't mean it that way. My head's spinning. I don't know what I'm saying.''

"You're saying you don't want to make love to me.''

"No. I'm saying we can't afford to take up where we left off. My life is in Atlanta. Yours is here. It's a surefire formula for heartbreak.''

"Don't be so certain of that. It's seems we're still on the same wavelength, physically, at least.''

"I'm not denying that. But it doesn't change reality. Too much time has passed. We're two different people now.''

"We're the same two people, just older and I hope a little wiser."

"And our lives have gone in different directions."

"We could work something out."

She wrapped her arms around herself like a shield against the passion that still beat between them. "I've tried long-distance relationships, Del. They never work."

He thought back to the time he'd been in Saudi, the frustrations that arose from missed calls and mixed signals. She was right and they both knew it. She had a life and a career in Atlanta. His support system was here. He couldn't uproot the girls, no matter what his heart wanted him to do. They'd had too much upheaval in their lives already.

She was watching him closely. "You know I'm right, don't you?"

"I loved you then, Christy Herter," he said softly. "I love—"

She put her hand to his lips. "Don't say it, Del. I'm not made of stone."

Her words gave him hope. "Come home with me, Christy. Let me watch over you tonight. Let me think of some way for us to be together."

She shook her head. "No, Del. I'm staying here tonight."

"I promise you, nothing will happen."

She traced a finger down the buttons of his shirt. "I can't promise you the same thing." She smiled a little sadly. "Thanks for everything you've done for me these last few days, but Del, I don't think it's wise for us to see each other again."

He knew he could change her mind if he could hold her in his arms again, show her with his hands and his mouth and his body that he loved her even more today than he had ten years ago. As if sensing his intentions, she stepped backward and held out a warning hand. "Go home, Del. Go home to your girls."

Chapter Eight

"DADDY? IS THAT YOU?" Dani stuck her head around the bedroom door. It seemed like a long time since her dad had left, but it had really only been forty-five minutes. She'd looked at the clock.

"It's me. I thought you'd be asleep." He was standing at the end of the hallway, taking his coat off.

"Did Grandma go home?"

"She just left."

"Is everything okay? Is Christy all right?"

"Everything is okay."

"Did you figure out who's sending her the scary notes?" She held her breath.

He turned away. "Grandpa thinks it's someone trying to play a joke on her."

"A joke?" It wasn't a joke. It was a great idea. Dani was briefly indignant before she remembered how much trouble she could be in.

"A not-very-funny joke." Del hung his coat in the hall closet and came toward her. Dani felt her heart skid down to her tummy. They thought her secret admirer idea was a not funny joke. That made her heart and her tummy hurt.

"Is Christy mad at who did it?"

"Yes, I think she might be." He hunkered down in front of her.

"Is she afraid?" She didn't want Christy to be afraid. Nothing was working out like she'd hoped it would. She felt tears prick at the edges of her eyes.

"A little."

"Maybe she could come and stay with us." The words came out before she could stop them. The last note. The one with her dad's name on it was in her desk drawer. What if Christy should find it? She wouldn't understand what Dani had been trying to do. She liked Christy—a lot. She didn't want her to be afraid, especially if it was her fault.

"She doesn't want to come here, baby." Her dad must be upset. He hardly ever forgot and called her girly names like that. She squinched up her eyes to see him better in the dim light. There was a line between his eyebrows, like he was frowning and didn't even know it. It was the way he'd looked all the time before Momma left.

"Why?" This was sounding worse and worse.

"It's hard to explain."

"Because of us?" Sometimes people who didn't have kids didn't like being around them. But Christy hadn't seemed that way. She'd been nice, really nice, to her and Kara.

"No, baby. It's because of something that happened a long time ago when we were very young."

"At the Valentine Ball?" That was a long time ago, although she didn't think seventeen was all that young.

"Yeah. Sort of. But mostly it's because we have different lives. Mine's here with you and Kara and Grandma and Grandpa, and Christy's is in Atlanta with her work and her friends."

"She could get a job here." Her whole plan was going wrong. She swallowed a sob. "We could move there," she said tentatively. She hated seeing her dad look sad, and he did. He looked very, very sad.

He reached out and gathered her into his arms for a big bear hug that took her breath away. "You really like Christy, don't you?"

She nodded, not trusting her voice. "A lot."

"So do I."

She leaned back in his arms so she could see his face. "Then—"

Del shook his head. "You can't always have what you want, baby." He stood up with her in his arms. It had been a long, long time since he carried her anywhere. She laid her head on his shoulder. She liked it even if she was too grown-up for little kid stuff like getting carried to bed. "Sleep tight. I have to go out to the office for a little. I'll leave the intercom on."

"All right, Daddy." She hadn't called him "Daddy" in a long time, either. He smiled, but it was sad, too, like the look in his eyes. "Good night."

"Good night." He stopped to pull the covers up over Kara's shoulders, turned on the intercom on the dresser and left the room.

Dani lay in her bed and stared at the ceiling for a few seconds. She had to do something. She had to make this all right. Christy and her dad were good for each other. She liked Christy. They could be a family if everything worked out. But now nothing was working out. It was all going wrong. Tears rolled down the side of her face and got her hair wet.

She got up out of bed and went to her desk and took out the last valentine. It was her fa-

vorite, a big shark Ninja smiling a toothy grin.
It said, *You're Jawsome.* Jawsome. That was
cool, not scary. But Christy didn't think so.
Dani looked at Kara's box of Barbie valentines
in the drawer beside hers. She rubbed her hand
across her eyes and tried to think.

"What are you doing?" Kara asked sleepily.

"Shh, Dad will hear." Dani glanced at the
intercom, then went over and put her ear close
to the speaker. She couldn't hear anything yet,
which meant Del hadn't turned his speaker on.
"C'mon." Dani took Kara's Barbie valentines
and a pen and headed for the bathroom, Kara
on her heels.

"Why are you crying?" Kara wanted to
know as Dani shut the bathroom door as quietly
as she could.

"Christy's afraid of my valentine notes. Dad
wanted her to come and stay with us but she
said no and I think they got into a fight."

"I don't like fights," Kara said. Even though
she'd only been five when their mom left, Dani
knew she remembered the fights. Mom yelling
and Dad walking around tight-lipped and
frowning.

"It's my fault." Dani almost started crying

again but that wasn't going to help anything so she didn't.

Kara chewed her lip. "I like Christy. I want her to be our friend."

"I wanted her to be our mom," Dani confessed. "And now it won't happen unless I fix it."

Kara didn't say no to Christy being their new mom and that's when Dani knew her little sister had been thinking about it, too. "How?" Kara asked instead.

"I'm going to write another note on one of your Barbie valentines. A pretty one that doesn't look scary. And we're going to take it over there and tell her we're sorry."

"Tonight? It's late. It's too dark and cold." Kara shook her head and backed toward the door.

"Tomorrow we have to go to school. And then there's homework and everything and, by then, maybe she'll have made other plans for Valentine's Day. Maybe Mr. Pieracini or Mr. Carter will ask her out. Remember how they were all laughing and talking this morning? They like her, too, I could tell."

"I don't like Mr. Pieracini. He's too loud."

"Then we have to do something tonight.

C'mon. Get your coat and boots while I copy the note. And be quiet. We don't want Dad to know we're gone.''

Five minutes later, she was done. Her note didn't look as nice as the printed one. She didn't know how to spell some of the words, and there weren't any squiggly red lines underneath to tell her which ones were wrong, like on the computer. But it would have to do. She added another smiley face and signed her name. There. It was ready.

Kara pushed open the door. She was still wearing her Tweety and Sylvester pajamas but she had her coat and hat and gloves and snow boots on and she was carrying Dani's stuff in her arms. Dani hurried up and dressed for outdoors, stuck the new envelope in her pocket along with the old one and took Kara by the hand. They didn't turn on the kitchen light, and Kara whimpered a little in the dark, but Dani hushed her pretty smartly.

Kara started whimpering again as soon as they got outside. "It's okay," Dani said pulling her along. The wind was icy and cut through her pajama legs before they'd gotten halfway down the driveway. She wished she'd taken the time to find their snowpants and put them on, but it was too late now. "We'll have to go down the alley so no one sees us and calls Dad and tells him we're gone."

"It's too cold," Kara said, holding back as she peered down the alley that ran all the way to Oak Street. "Let's go back."

"Do you want to help me fix it so Dad and Christy aren't mad at each other, or not?"

"Okay," Kara said, but her teeth were already chattering.

Dani walked as fast as she could. A couple of dogs barked as they went past and Kara jumped at every shadow, but she didn't ask to go home again. Dani's legs were stiff with cold by the time they got to Oak Street and turned onto the sidewalk leading to Aunt Sarah's house. It was way after ten o'clock by now. What if Christy was already asleep? She looked up and down the street. No cars were coming that she could see. She tugged on Kara's hand, urging her to hurry.

The porch light was on above the side door, but the windows on either side of it were dark. Dani's heart was beating hard in her chest. What was she going to say to Christy that would make it all right? Kara stopped at the bottom of the steps. "Hurry up. Ring the doorbell. She'll let us inside even if she's mad at Daddy. I'm so cold my fingers hurt.''

"Okay.'' Dani took a deep breath but the cold air made her cough. She walked up the steps and twisted the funny, old-fashioned doorbell just as a car turned onto Oak Street. The lights inside Aunt Sarah's house came on and, at the same time, red and blue lights on top of the car started flashing.

"It's Grandpa. He's going to catch us. Hurry.'' Kara turned and started running across the backyard. Dani wanted to wait for Christy to answer the door, but Kara's fear was infectious. She reached up, shoved the envelopes inside the mailbox and turned and ran after her sister. She'd reached the heavy shadows of the woodshed when the police car screeched to a halt. Kara was shoving on the door of the woodshed, trying to get inside. "If they catch us, Grandpa will have to take us to jail. We have to hide.''

The door came open. Kara scooted inside. Dani heard her sharp intake of breath, then stifled sobs. "It's so dark in here.'' Kara was a weird little sister sometimes but Dani loved her. Now she'd gotten her into trouble because she hadn't wanted to come out at night alone. Inside, she was just as scared of the dark as Kara. But she couldn't let that stop her now. She walked into the woodshed and slammed the door.

DEL TURNED OUT THE LIGHTS in his office and headed across the driveway. He hadn't been able to work. He hadn't been able to concentrate on anything but what had happened between him and Christy. He hadn't been prepared for the intensity of his desire for her, or the depths of pain she'd caused him when she said she didn't want to see him again. It was as though he'd fallen through a hole in time and was seventeen again and faced with the worst dilemma of his life. He had convinced himself he'd stopped loving her, tried his damnedest to make his marriage to Ashley work, but all the time, he'd still loved Christy, and he'd never known how much until tonight.

Somehow he had to make it right with her, prove to her she needed to give their old love a chance to grow into a new love, a love strong enough to last a lifetime. But he'd gotten off to a lousy start. He glanced at his watch. After ten. Too late to go back to Sarah's house tonight. Christy had had enough to contend with today.

But tomorrow, first thing in the morning, he was going over there to plead his case. And if he was lucky he'd have her beside him Tuesday night for a Valentine's dinner celebration. He would take her somewhere intimate and expensive and he'd ask her to be his wife and a mother to his daughters, and they would find some way to weave their two divergent lives into one.

The storm door was standing open, although Del was certain he'd latched it securely before he went to the garage. The kitchen was dark. The house was silent. He glanced into the empty living room as he hurried through the dining room toward the girls' room, not quite certain why he felt he should check on them the moment he stepped inside. He hadn't heard a sound from the intercom while he'd been in his office. And maybe that was why. It was too quiet. No rustling of bedclothes, none of Kara's little sighs or Dani's gentle snores. He opened their bedroom door.

All thoughts of Christy and the plans he'd been formulating drained out of his mind with the speed of light. The beds were empty, the covers thrown halfway onto the floor. The girls were gone.

Chapter Nine

CHRISTY SAT in Sarah's small parlor with the curtains drawn, staring at the fire and feeling like she'd lost something precious that had been almost in her grasp. Del had told her he loved her, still loved her and she had sent him away. Why? She'd admitted to herself only that morning that she still loved him, too. What did she have to gain by denying that? A return to an empty apartment and a small circle of casual friends in Atlanta? A job she enjoyed, but that wasn't and had never been the focus of her life?

She had always dreamed of a home and a family and a loving husband to walk through life at her side. Del was offering that and she'd turned him down. She was a fool, and by acting so foolishly, she might have lost something she could never regain. She looked at the clock on the mantel. It was after ten, definitely too late to talk to Del tonight. But tomorrow, tomorrow morning, as soon as the girls had gone to school, she'd seek him out and... Her mind began to play out just what might happen if she found Del alone, and a smile curved her lips and heat coursed through her body.

The doorbell chimed. Her fantasy faded and apprehension took its place. For a moment she sat where she was, then rose and picked the portable phone out of its cradle. If whoever was at the door was a stranger, she'd dial 911, just to be on the safe side. But if it was Del... She hurried through the dining room into the little entryway, switching on the chandelier as she went. She peeked through the oval of etched glass in the door. A shadowy figure jumped off the porch. She opened the door. Flashing red and blue emergency lights danced across the snow and the side of the house as a police car drove into the yard. From the corner of her eye she saw two small figures running through the yard before they were swallowed up by the shadows of the huge oaks and maples growing there.

"Stay where you are," a policeman yelled as he jumped out of the car. He wasn't Del's father and she didn't recognize his face. "I saw two kids run off your porch. They're probably the ones who've been leaving the notes. I'll follow them on foot."

"Okay." She wasn't wearing a coat and she didn't know what else she could do to help him. She turned to go back inside and saw the corner of the envelope sticking out of the mailbox. She ought to leave it there, she supposed, wait for the policeman to come back. But something kept tugging at the back of her mind, something about those two small figures she'd glimpsed from the corner of her eye, and she picked it up.

It wasn't just one note this time. It was two, taped together. And the bottom note was addressed to her in a child's hand. She opened the envelope, read the short heartrending message inside. *I'm sorry. It's my falt you got scared. I thout the shark cards were cool. Don't be mad. Dani.*

Then she opened the second card. It was another of the monster valentines and on the back was printed an invitation to a Valentine dinner with her secret admirer. Del.

Suddenly she was as cold inside as out. Now she knew what was familiar about the figures she'd glimpsed running away from her aunt's house. Kara's penguin waddle in her down-filled coat. The two children fleeing from the policeman weren't juvenile delinquents playing pranks. They were two little girls, Del's little girls.

She ran down the steps. "Officer, wait. Don't frighten them." She could see a flashlight bobbing around in the backyard. "Please. Come here."

"What is it, Ms. Herter?"

"I know who those children are. They're Del Jensen's daughters."

"The chief's grandkids?"

"Yes. Dani's been leaving the notes. She... she was doing it to get me to go out with her father." She held out the notes she'd just opened. Her teeth were beginning to chatter. "Did you see where they went?"

"No, it's as if they just disappeared. They probably went back home."

"I hope so. It's so cold." But the fear wouldn't go away. Small children, even if they were suitably dressed, would be at risk of hypothermia if they stayed out in this cold for too long. She remembered she was carrying the portable phone. She turned toward the house. She didn't recall Del's number, then suddenly it was there in her memory. She punched in the numbers and waited impatiently as it rang three, four, five times.

"Del here." His voice was clipped, impatient but she could hear the underlying note of desperation.

"Del, it's Christy."

"Christy? I can't talk now. The girls—"

"They haven't come home to you yet?"

"How did you know they were gone?" he demanded.

"They came here, Del." She was trembling all over now, not from the cold, but with foreboding. "Del, it's Dani that's been leaving the notes. She's been leaving them for you. My secret admirer, she calls you. They've been planning a special celebration."

"What?"

"They ran away when they thought the police were coming for them."

"They ran from my dad?"

"No, another policeman's here. He saw them and chased them. He must have frightened them."

"Don't bother explaining the rest over the phone. I'll be there in two minutes."

Del was as good as his word. Christy had just come out of the house when he sprinted up the sidewalk. He was wearing a coat, but no hat or gloves, and was carrying a big flashlight in one hand. She wanted to go into his arms, to hold him and have him hold her. She caught herself up short. She couldn't do that. Not after having told him only an hour before she didn't want to see him again. "Oh Del, I'm so frightened for them."

"They weren't on the sidewalk between here and my place."

"Officer Gibson called your father." The young policeman had told her his name a few moments earlier. "The girls haven't shown up at your parents' house either. They're on their way here now." As she spoke, a second police cruiser pulled into the yard and Del's parents got out.

Del's father reached them first, but his mother was only a step behind. "What's going on? Gibson says Dani and Kara were the ones leaving the notes."

"So Christy tells me." She passed the last two notes to Del who read them and gave them to his father.

"I recognized the shark valentines. But I never put two and two together. Probably two dozen boys and half as many girls in town must have ones just like them."

"Why did she leave the notes?" Del's

mother wanted to know. Patty Jensen's face was a study in anxiety as she read the valentines over her husband's shoulder.

Christy tried to smile for her sake. "She was matchmaking."

Patty's eyes flew from Christy's face to Del's. "Matchmaking? That explains the heart-shaped pizza. And wanting me to bake extra cookies. The roses she ordered— I thought they were for Del. But they were for…both of you."

"I never had the slightest—"

Christy reached out and laid her hand on Del's arm. She could feel the tension in the muscles and corded tendons beneath her fingers. He looked at her and his eyes were as bleak and cold as the night sky. "You can't blame yourself. Why should you have picked up on any of this? I didn't. Your mother didn't. And it isn't important, anyway. What's important is finding the girls as quickly as possible."

By now the lights and commotion had attracted the attention of Aunt Sarah's neighbors. One or two of them came across the street to find out what the trouble was. Others stood on their porch steps and watched the proceedings. In just a few minutes, the word had spread. Volunteers produced flashlights and camping lanterns. Plans were made. Del's mother would walk to Del's house calling the children as she went. One of Aunt Sarah's neighbors, a friend of Patty's, would go to the chief's house in case the girls showed up there. Other neighbors, the chief and Officer Gibson would spread out across the neighborhood backyards with flashlights.

Christy stayed with Del. They searched around the house, in the tangle of winter-bare bushes in the side yard. They looked for footprints in the rose garden but the snow was glazed and frozen hard enough for little girls to walk on, so they found nothing. They even played the flashlight beam into the lower branches of one of the big maples that Del and Christy had climbed as children. All around them they heard voices calling the girls' names, but no response, no shouts of joyful discovery. They stood silently a moment longer.

"God, how did this happen?" Del asked, his face lost in the shadows of the big maple. "I had no idea Dani was hatching such a scheme."

"She wants you to be happy, Del. And she must have thought I could be the one to make you feel that way."

He took her hand. "You could, Christy. And

I could make you happy, but I'm not going to beg you for your love. I learned the hard way you can't make someone love you. You can't make them want the same things you want.''

''What do you want, Del?''

''I want someone to share my life and my home and my children with. A woman who wants that, too.''

The moon had set, but the starlight that sparkled through the tree branches above their heads gave too little light for her to read his expression. It took all the courage she could muster to speak what was in her heart. She had told him they didn't have a future together only a little while ago. She wouldn't blame him if he didn't believe she'd changed her mind. She spoke with a sudden urgency. ''I want all those things, too, Del.''

''Just an hour ago you said—''

''Del, I—'' She lifted her hand to touch his cheek. She was still carrying the portable phone. It rang, vibrating in her hand, bringing her back to the reality of the moment with a painful jolt. It was Del's mother. She had searched his house from basement to attic. The girls weren't hiding there.

A few minutes later Del's father, Officer Gibson and two or three others joined them in the pool of illumination from the side porch light. "Nothing," Del's dad reported. Christy told them about Del's mother's call. Patty's friend had also checked in to say that they hadn't shown up at the elder Jensens' home. Dani and Kara had simply disappeared.

Christy was growing more and more anxious. If the little girls weren't found soon they could be in real danger of hypothermia, of freezing to death.

"They must be hiding, too afraid to come out," Del said, pacing restlessly along the sidewalk.

"Del, they've been gone almost an hour. We need to start thinking about expanding the search," his dad said. The older man spoke quietly, but made no attempt to hide his own apprehension for his grandchildren's safety. "We need to think about calling in some more volunteers. Checking the railroad tracks and the river."

A vision of black water closing over two blond heads made Christy's heart pound with dread. *Please, God, no,* she silently prayed. The possibility was too horrible to contemplate.

"No," Del almost shouted. "They wouldn't

go to the river or the railroad tracks alone. They know better.''

Christy grabbed both his hands. "Del, they thought the police were after them.''

The pain and fear in his eyes made her want to weep. At that moment she realized she was as hopelessly in love with Del's daughters as she was with Del. He nodded. "Okay. But are you sure you've checked every building in the neighborhood? Every playhouse, every garage, every garden shed?''

"Yes,'' the others nodded in unison.

"I checked Sarah's garage and woodshed.'' Christy recognized Aunt Sarah's next-door neighbor, Arnie Sunderhart's voice. "Both locked up tighter than a tick.''

"I checked the woodshed here, first thing,'' Officer Gibson spoke up. "There aren't any windows and the door's not locked but it's wedged shut tight. There's no way two little girls could get it open.''

Del was on him in a moment, face-to-face, nose-to-nose. "What did you say?'' he demanded.

"I said the door's wedged tight shut—''

"No, it wasn't. I checked it for Christy not more than an hour ago. It opened easily. It wasn't locked or wedged shut. That's where the girls are. In the woodshed.'' He took off at a run. Christy was right on his heels. *Dear Heaven, let them be there. And, please, let them be safe.*

Chapter Ten

"DANIELLE! KARA! Are you in there?" Del held his breath. He was afraid he wouldn't hear them over the thundering beat of his heart.

"Daddy?" He didn't know if he'd actually heard the word, or only imagined it. It didn't matter. He knew his children were inside the cold, dark little building. He put his shoulder to the heavy wood door and pushed. Nothing happened. He backed away and put all his strength against the next push. The door moved about six inches, then stopped, one corner stuck in a furrow in the frozen earth floor of the woodshed.

Del gave the door one more shove, aided by his father's considerable strength. The door swung free. Flashlights played across the bare dirt floor and walls as the others crowded closer. For a moment Del was blinded by the moving beams of light, then he saw them, huddled against the back wall, Kara wrapped in her sister's arms.

Del was across the small space in a single bound. "Dani, baby. Kara. Are you all right?"

"I'm cold," Kara whispered in a tiny, faraway voice that compressed his heart with new fear. "Real cold."

"The door got stuck. We couldn't open it," Dani said. Her teeth were chattering so hard he could barely understand her.

"Let's get you out of here and someplace warm." He gathered them close, warming them with his own body.

"Is Grandpa going to arrest us?"

"Of course not," Chief Jensen said, taking Kara from Del and cuddling her close to his heart. "Whatever gave you such an idea?"

Kara laid her head on his shoulder and wrapped her arms around his neck. "You said we always had to be extra good. We weren't good. We scared Christy. We thought you'd have to put us in jail." She started to cry in hiccuping little sobs.

"God," the chief muttered under his breath. "It's okay, cupcake. You didn't do anything wrong. Grandpa loves you to pieces."

"Del." Christy was kneeling beside him. "We have to get them inside. Get them warm. Now." Her voice was soft and comforting as she reached out to touch Dani's cheek, but there was an underlying urgency in her words. "Let's go to the house where I can check them out."

He stood up with Dani in his arms. She was shivering so hard her entire body trembled. "Baby, why didn't you answer when Mr. Sunderhart and Officer Gibson tried to open the door?"

"Kara was too afraid. She wouldn't let me. Then...nobody came back. It was so dark." Dani shuddered and he cradled her tighter still. Christy held the door as he carried Dani inside, his father hard on his heels. In a matter of moments Christy and his mother had the girls' hats and coats and boots off. "My fingers hurt," Dani sniffed.

"And my toes," Kara whimpered.

"Let me see." Christy examined their fingers and toes and ears and noses, then wrapped them warmly in soft wool afghans his mother brought from Sarah's parlor. "No frostbite," Christy said, with a smile that didn't quite reach her eyes. "But I'm worried about hypothermia. They were out a long time."

"Should we call the EMS, have them checked out at the hospital?"

"No!" Both of his daughters cried at once.

"No hospital. No doctors. No shots," Dani pleaded.

"Christy? You're the expert here."

She placed her hand on Dani's chest, under her pajamas, looked at her eyes, checked her pulse, then did the same for Kara. "I don't think they're in any danger," she said at last. This time her smile was genuine and breathtakingly wonderful. "Let's get them warmed up inside and out and I think they'll be fine. A warm bath and some warm milk to take the chill off your tummies. Mrs. Jensen—"

"Patty."

Christy smiled again. "Patty. If you'll warm some milk…?"

"Don't bother telling me where everything is. I'll find it."

"Hot chocolate," Kara said, in a stronger voice. "Hot milk's yucky. And a cookie, too."

Everyone laughed, the tension broken. Del picked Dani up off the sofa in one arm and Kara in the other. Christy led the way up the stairs to the bathroom while his dad thanked everyone for coming out to search, and promised a big neighborhood party to show the Jensen family's appreciation for their help. Del was glad his dad had thought of that. If everyone hadn't been so conscientious in their searching, and tried the woodshed door, it might have been hours before they realized it was wedged shut with the girls trapped inside. It might have been too late.

Christy must have sensed the dark turn of his thoughts. She touched her hand to his arm. "They're going to be fine, Del."

He covered her hand with his. "Thank God."

"I already have." She smiled again and it nearly took his breath away.

"Why don't you go down and see if the cocoa's ready? I'll help the girls into the tub."

"We can drink cocoa in the tub?" Kara asked. Her teeth were still chattering but some of her color was coming back. Del relaxed just a little bit more.

"My toes hurt," Dani grumbled, looking down at her bare feet from her seat on the lid of the commode.

"Good," he heard Christy say as he started back down the stairs. "That means the blood's coming back into them to warm them up."

Del met his mother at the bottom of the staircase. "Here's the cocoa, and some cookies. How are they doing?"

"Fine. Kids are so resilient."

"Yes, thank God," his mother agreed. She

handed him the plate of food. "I didn't fill them too full. There's more milk on the stove."

"Okay, Mom."

"Del, do you still love Christy?" she asked suddenly. His parents had stood by him when he got Ashley pregnant. They had supported his marriage and did their best to help when they could without interfering. They'd remained as staunchly behind him during and after his divorce. They knew he was gun-shy about getting involved romantically, but he also knew his mother hoped he'd marry again.

"Yes," he said.

"Then tell her so." Patty gripped the pineapple-shaped banister finial with both hands.

"I have."

"And—"

"She told me she didn't want to see me anymore."

His mother's face fell. "Oh." She was quiet a moment. He turned to go back upstairs. "Del?"

"Yes, Mom."

"She's perfect for you. And for the girls."

"I think so, too."

"You're not taking no for an answer, are you?"

"No," he said and watched a smile curve her lips and brighten her eyes. "I'm not."

TWENTY MINUTES LATER, Christy and Del had the girls tucked up in the canopy bed in the blue bedroom. She'd decided it wouldn't be a good idea to take them out into the cold with damp hair, even for the short time it would take to get them back to Del's, and he'd agreed. Their toes and ears and fingers and noses were pink and warm. Their tummies were full of cookies and cocoa and she was convinced any danger of hypothermia was past. What they needed now was a good night's sleep.

The chief and his wife had said their goodbyes a few minutes earlier. And Dani and Kara had both promised their grandfather they would *never, ever* be afraid to tell him anything, or do anything to scare the life out of him and their grandma again.

Now Christy stood in the doorway of the big, softly lighted bedroom and watched Del with his daughters. They were talking quietly, heads bent toward each other, and though they had their mother's coloring, they looked very much like their father.

"Dani thinks she needs the day off from school tomorrow."

"Me too," Kara piped up.

Christy pretended to consider her words carefully. Actually, she thought it was a good idea. It was very late. The girls were exhausted. "Well..."

"We were awfully cold," Dani pressed.

"And scared."

"And it's really late. Almost midnight."

Christy let herself be persuaded. "Okay. I think it would be a good idea for all of us to sleep in tomorrow."

"Where are you going to sleep tonight, Daddy?" Dani's question was perfectly innocent but Christy felt a hint of color rise in her cheeks.

"In this chair right by your bed."

"That doesn't look too comfortable."

"It'll be fine. Now you two get to sleep. I want to talk to Christy."

Dani looked first at her father then at Christy. "Okay," she said. "And Christy. I'm really, really sorry. I didn't mean to scare you with my notes. I just thought..." Her voice trailed off and she traced a petal of the blue dahlia with her finger. "I thought it would help my dad ask you out. He's shy, y'know."

Christy laughed. She gave Del a mischievous look. "Really? I didn't know."

"Oh, yes, he is. That's why when I saw the show about secret admirers on Oprah and this one guy said he sent notes to this girl 'cause he was shy, I thought, so's my dad. Dad would never have sent you notes himself."

"It's true," Del said, pushing Dani down onto the pillow with a gentle hand on her head. "I'm a real shrinking violet. That's why I can't talk to you in front of these two little pitchers."

"We're not pitchers. We're girls," Kara said indignantly. "And you're not a violet, you're Del Jensen."

"My beautiful girls," Del said with a catch in his voice. "Now go to sleep. And stay put."

"Yes, Dad." He gave them both a kiss.

"Good night, girls."

"Sleep tight," Kara murmured.

"Don't let the bed bugs bite." Christy blew them a kiss as Del took her hand and led her out of the room.

He stopped in front of the fireplace in the little parlor and reached out and took her into his arms. "Did you mean what you said out there under the maple tree? That you wanted the same things in life that I want?" he asked without preamble. Whatever reticence had been between them earlier had burned away in the terror of the past couple of hours.

"Yes," she said equally candid. "I do."

"I love you, Christy. I've always loved you someplace deep in my heart. I don't want to lose you again. But my life is here."

"I know that."

"And your life is in Atlanta."

She took a deep breath. "It doesn't have to be."

"Christy, I know it's too soon to ask you to marry me. My God, we haven't spent two hours alone in each other's company in the past ten years."

"And I know it's too soon to say yes," she answered with a smile. "But we have time, Del. I'm going to be here for almost a month."

"A month to change your mind."

"A month to know I'm making all the right choices. I love my career, Del. I'll always want to be a nurse. But I want to be a wife and mother, too. In Atlanta I only have one of those three things. Here I can have them all."

"I want more kids, Christy," he said, smoothing his hands along the sides of her face.

"I want children, too. We've solved one problem already."

He picked her up and whirled her around. "I love you, Christy Herter. From now on I'm going to say it every day of our lives."

"And I'll want to hear it every day of our lives."

He kissed her again. She felt his heart accelerate, felt her own pulse increase to match the beat of his. He lowered her feet gently to the floor, letting her slide the length of him, not breaking the joining of their lips. She pressed herself as close as she could and wished the kiss could go on forever.

"Spend Valentine's Day with me the way Dani wanted us to."

"Do I have a choice?" Christy asked, letting the love she felt blossoming in her heart show in her eyes and her smile.

"No," he said, lowering his mouth to hers once more. "I intend to start a tradition. We're going to spend every minute of the 14th of February together. This Valentine's Day and every Valentine's Day for the rest of our lives."

"WHAT ARE THEY DOING?" Kara wanted to know. She looked real little sitting in Aunt Sarah's big canopy bed. Dani had never slept in such a fancy bed and she was in kind of a hurry to get back in it, but first she had to see what her dad and Christy were talking about.

Except they weren't talking.

"They're kissing," she told Kara, diving back into bed. She was glad they were sleeping together tonight. She'd been really afraid when the woodshed door wouldn't open and Kara wouldn't let her talk to anybody whose voice she didn't recognize. For a little while she was afraid her dad wouldn't find them and they would freeze to death.

But that hadn't happened and now it looked like everything was going to be all right. Maybe even better than all right.

"What do you mean kissing?" Kara wanted to know. "Kissing, like on the cheek, like Daddy kisses us? Or kissing, like on television? You know, on the lips and everything."

"On the lips and everything," Dani said with satisfaction, crawling back under the covers.

"They aren't mad at each other anymore?"

Dani giggled and put her hand over her mouth so Christy and her dad wouldn't hear.

"Nope. I don't think they're mad. I think Christy's going to be our new mom. Is that okay?"

Kara thought about it for a couple of seconds. "Yes," she said, giggling, too. "It's okay."

Dani nodded. She thought so, too. She snuggled down in Aunt Sarah's big, soft bed and closed her eyes. Her secret admirer plan had worked out after all, even if Christy hadn't liked her way-cool monster cards. Her dad was going to have Christy to love and laugh and be happy with just like they'd been way back in the old days. And she and Kara were going to be part of a whole, real family again. "Yep," she said sleepily. "Everything worked out just right."

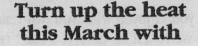

If you enjoyed what you just read,
then we've got an offer you can't resist!

Take 2 bestselling love stories FREE!
Plus get a FREE surprise gift!

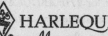